RESIDUAL

MOON

BY
KATE SWEENEY

RESIDUAL MOON
© 2008 BY KATE SWEENEY

ISBN 10: 1-933113-94-4
ISBN 13: 978-1-933113-94-4

First Printing: 2008

This Trade Paperback is published by
Intaglio Publications
Walker, La. USA
WWW.INTAGLIOPUB.COM

CREDITS
EXECUTIVE EDITOR: TARA YOUNG
COVER DESIGN BY SHERI

DEDICATION

I am dedicating this book to a quirky man I met only once and have never seen again.

Stay with me on this… While I was writing this book, I agonized over the title. I didn't like what I had chosen originally. One night, I was sitting at the bar, waiting for a table at my favorite restaurant, when I entered into a discussion with this man over the moon and its effect on human behavior. It was his experience that people reacted more unusual in the days after the full moon. As he put it: "Maybe it was the after-effects of the full moon. Like, I dunno, a residual moon."

As I said, I never saw him again. Perhaps the gods threw him in my path to trip over and come up with the perfect title.

Whatever the reason for the encounter—divine intervention or sheer dumb luck—I dedicate *Residual Moon* to that quirky man.

ACKNOWLEDGMENTS

To Denise Winthrop. I count on her good judgment more than she knows. She does so much more than beta read. Den is a constant and is consistently right; I'm not quite sure how she does that, but I no longer question it.

To my sister Maureen. She came up with the prophecy, which is an integral part in *Residual Moon*. It was perfect.

To Tara Young, my editor. Once again, proving I need to work on my adverbs. I thought I had the beast under control.

To my betas Tracey, Tena, and Maureen. They catch the things that make me cringe.

To Sheri Payton and Becky Arbogast of Intaglio, who constantly move forward and challenge their writers to be the best they can be.

And to Kat Smith, owner of SCP and director of the GCLS, another constant. As I have said before, she is tireless in her efforts to promote lesbian fiction. I wish she could find time to write that damned sequel!

Prologue

The terrified woman whimpered behind the gag, sealed in place with the tape across her mouth. She closed her eyes tight, and he knew she was praying he would end this.

"You must lie still," he said. "You're the second one. There's only one left now, then your time is done. It was a valiant effort to keep it safe, but the power will be mine once again. We've waited generations for you fools. Now hold still," he cooed and took the ornate dagger and held it to her flesh. "They'll know you on the other side now by the mark I leave."

The muffled scream lasted until she passed out from the pain. He stood over the unconscious woman and slid the dagger back into its scabbard.

"It is done. One more of you fools, and my time will be at hand once again," he hissed angrily, then took a deep calming breath. He lifted his head to the moonlit night, closed his eyes and began chanting in the ancient language of his ancestors.

He gained strength with each passing minute. The visions started again. They were more vivid since he found the second one. Visions of the ancient ways flashed through his mind.

"Soon, you will see me. So very soon," he whispered his promise into the night.

Chapter 1

Grayson fumbled in the darkness as she reached for the phone. "Yeah," she mumbled. Clearing her throat, she glanced at the clock on the nightstand—3:30. *Fuck me.*

"Grayson? It's Stan. We've got another one."

"Fuck, where?" she asked, now fully awake. She sat on the side of the bed and ran her fingers through her thick raven hair.

"Belmont Harbor. It's the same M.O."

"I'll be there in fifteen. Don't let anyone touch a thing, Stan."

"Right." The line went dead. Grayson rubbed her face and stood.

"What's going on?" the sleepy voice whispered.

Grayson nearly forgot about her. She slipped into her jeans and flipped on the light.

The blonde bed partner put a hand to her eyes. "God, you cops." She groaned.

Grayson snorted as she slipped into her running shoes and grabbed a sweatshirt. "I gotta go and so do you."

The woman sat up, pulling the sheet to her breasts. "Don't you trust me in your house?" she asked as she watched Grayson slip into her shoulder harness.

"No, I don't. I don't know you, sweetheart, so c'mon, shake a leg," she said and walked into the bathroom, stepping over the clothes that were strewn all over the floor from the previous night's escapades.

She splashed water on her face and ran her wet hands through her hair, then brushed her teeth. "C'mon, Sharon," Grayson called as she spit in the sink.

1

"It's Sheila," the woman called back.

Grayson walked back into the bedroom. "Sorry. You weren't supposed to stay the night, remember?" she said by way of an apology.

Sheila raised an eyebrow as she buttoned up and slipped into her shoes. "It's not my fault I passed out, Detective MacCarthaigh. You strapped that beast on before I knew what hit me," she said in a sultry voice. She walked up to Grayson and ran her fingers over the leather holster strap, then over the hard muscles in her arms. "You have the most intense violet eyes, like Liz Taylor," she said seductively. "When I saw you walk into the bar last night, I could see the sexual heat just radiating off your body. I knew we'd wind up in bed."

Grayson smirked and looked down into the brown eyes. Her groin throbbed incessantly. She took away the hand that had slipped under her sweatshirt. "Sexual heat? You must be a writer…gotta go."

"Will you call me?" Sheila asked as Grayson opened the front door and guided her through it.

"Probably not."

Sheila grunted and walked to her car. "You're a bit of an asshole, Grayson MacCarthaigh," she snapped as she slid in behind the wheel of her car.

"I know. You're better off. I told you that last night." Grayson stepped back quickly as the sports car peeled out of her driveway.

"Go to hell, MacCarthaigh!" Sheila yelled.

As she tore down the quiet street, dogs started barking in the distance. Grayson watched the red car pull out of sight.

"Been there," she said in a flat voice.

Stan Resnick took a long drag off his cigarette and gazed out at the starry night over Lake Michigan. He was just out there the day before having a great time on his boat. His wife and kids had a riot. It was a glorious Indian summer day until Kathy begged him again to take the job in Minneapolis. She was tired of worrying about him every time he strapped on his weapon. He was nearly forty-five, and though he'd never been injured on the job, she still worried. He couldn't blame her.

Broken from his reverie, he looked down at the covered body. They roped off the area, and the patrolmen kept any onlookers at a safe distance. He looked up when he heard the rumble of the motorcycle. The rider flashed the badge, parked, and walked over to the crime scene.

"Morning, Detective MacCarthaigh, nice ride. Where's the Mustang?" he asked absently.

Grayson smirked. "In the shop. So what have we got?"

"Well, partner…" He stopped when Grayson shot him an angry look. He smiled in spite of her intimidating glare.

"We're not partners."

"Detective MacCarthaigh," Stan began, refusing to enter into another argument with her. "We have another. Done the same way, from what forensics says. Throat cut, hogtied, and dumped here, we think. Come here and look at this," he said, and Grayson squatted next to him and the body.

Stan took his gloved hand and gingerly lifted the victim's left breast. Grayson craned her neck to see beneath it. Stan watched as his recalcitrant partner examined the area.

There was another symbol. It was about two inches in diameter just under the left breast, the same size and location as the other. This symbol was different from the other found on the first victim; however, both had been hogtied and their throats cut.

He and Grayson had been racking their brains for three weeks, trying to understand the symbol on the first victim. Now this new victim had been cut, but the symbol was different. With the first, there were three small lines in a row and a slash through the middle line.

Grayson scanned the stretch of rocks, watching the Lake Michigan waves quietly lap on the shore. She took a deep tired breath and pulled back the sheet as she methodically examined the woman.

"Same way, Gray," Stan said.

Grayson nodded but said nothing. He watched Grayson, who seemed deep in thought when he noticed the little, almost nervous habit his sullen partner had. She absently rubbed the fingers of her left hand against her palm as if trying to rub something off. He figured it was a quirky thing people do when they're thinking. His uncle used to pull at his eyebrow when he was stumped or deep in thought.

He brought his attention back to the poor woman on the beach.

The deceased was lying on her side; her arms were tied behind her back, and her ankles were tied. Several ropes bound her breasts and abdomen.

Grayson tentatively felt the rope. "It's coarse, more like heavy twine. Shit and fuck me."

"Exactly." Stan sighed tiredly. He flipped through his notes. "Of course nobody saw a thing."

"Of course." Grayson stood and walked around the other side to get a look at the redheaded woman.

"Coroner said it was duct tape across her mouth, like the other. Test results will be back in the morning." He went on flipping the pages of his notepad. Stan took a deep breath and closed it. He glanced at Grayson.

He knew Detective Sergeant Grayson MacCarthaigh was involved in a very messy situation a little over a year earlier. She had responded to a call along with other police officers—a hostage situation that went very bad. Grayson wound up with a bullet through her shoulder, and Victoria Green, the hostage negotiator, died in the foray of gunfire, saving Grayson and several other police officers.

The fact that Ms. Green and Grayson were lovers only made matters worse. Grayson went into a tailspin. The department gave her a mandatory leave of absence to get her head back together. She was a rogue now; she didn't feel comfortable with anyone. The department tried several partners, not wanting to cut her loose—Grayson MacCarthaigh was a very good cop with amazing instincts.

But now she was a brooding loner. She put in for undercover duty with vice, and Stan remembered how the lieutenant nixed the application.

"You're homicide, MacCarthaigh. It's in your blood, and with the number of homicides in my precinct alone, I can't afford to let a good detective go."

Stan watched the twitching cheek muscles of the tall dark woman as she argued. Every muscle tensed as she leaned over his desk.

The entire precinct heard them arguing. Finally, Lieutenant Keller banged his fist on his desk.

"I tell you, *Detective MacCarthaigh, not the other way around. Get the fuck out of here and do what you do best. Get over this and get back to work or you can go back and walk a beat. Goddamn it, quit arguing with me!"* he bellowed more out of frustration than anger, Stan thought.

MacCarthaigh turned on a dime and marched out of his office, then stormed out of the precinct. Stan sat there staring at the irate woman as her long legs took her out in a few healthy strides.

"What a dynamo," he whispered.

With that, Keller yelled, *"Resnick, get in here!"*

"Oh, fuck," he muttered and obediently walked into Keller's office.

Keller took a deep calming breath. Stan knew before he even said anything. *"I know. I'm her partner, right?"*

The old gray-haired man laughed tiredly. *"She's a fucking pain in my ass but the best detective in this precinct, no offense."*

"None taken. I've read up on her—graduated from the academy earlier than anyone, started out as a patrolman, like her father, and citations up the wazoo. Made detective at twenty-three and sergeant three years later…"

"She'll have my job next, and it'll be a waste, believe me. If anyone was born to be a detective in this city, it was Grayson MacCarthaigh. Her father was the same. I knew him well. He was an Irish bastard but a helluva cop," he added with a tired sigh. *"Now about this business last year with Grayson and Vicky Green,"* he started awkwardly.

"I don't care, Lieutenant. I have a cousin who's gay. It's a non-issue with me," Stan said. *"She won't like this."*

"She doesn't have to like it. I don't let my detectives go out

there alone—so that's a non-issue."

"Well, I'll go find her and tell her," Stan said, not looking forward to the meeting.

"She'll be—"

"I know. She's down at the gym. I understand she goes there to let off steam. I only hope she doesn't kick the shit out of me," he said seriously as he walked out.

Stan found her in the gym later that day at the punching bag. She wore small gloves as she battered away. She was good, very good. Stan was amazed at the well but not overly defined muscles that tensed and bulged all over her body as she beat the shit out of the bag. Her body was soaked with perspiration. She wore a black tank top and matching skin-tight shorts. Fuck, not one ounce of body fat, he thought. He then thanked God he was in shape himself.

He cautiously walked up to the bag and held it. For an instant, she stopped and her violet eyes glared.

"Go away," she muttered breathlessly as he held onto the bag. She purposely let go with two jabs and a roundhouse kick.

"Can't do that, Detective." He groaned as he held onto the swinging bag. "You know why I'm here."

Her expression softened, then she glared once again. "Fuck."

"I know you don't like this, Grayson. I know you'd rather be alone out there, but it can't happen."

Their eyes locked for a moment as they gauged each other.

"Do you spar?"

He grinned and nodded. "Just don't kick me in the balls," he said as he loosened his tie and walked to the locker room. "My wife wants two more kids."

He heard Grayson chuckle as he walked away.

Stan now remembered how he held his own that day, but Grayson did indeed kick the shit out of him. He was never so tired and sore from a workout.

He was chuckling quietly when Grayson broke him from his reverie.

"Well, let's wait and see what the coroner says. It looks the same as the other victim. She was killed somewhere else and dumped. If they did it here, there'd be blood all over."

Stan squatted next to her and agreed. "It's dried and caked. Look at the ropes, they're stained and dry."

"Trust me, Stan. She was dumped here. Did the boys make sure they got all the footprints before they trampled this beach?" she asked in frustration.

"I did like you asked. They took everything and bagged, tagged, and pictured," he assured her as they stood.

"Go home and get some sleep," she said tiredly. "I'm going back to look at that other case. One victim was bad enough, now we've got two. We've got ourselves a crazy fucker out there. Shit." She ran her fingers through her hair.

As they walked away, she glanced his way. "Um, so how are Kathy and the boys?" she asked, not looking at him.

Stan smiled. "They're good. Went out on the boat yesterday and had a blast. You should come sometime."

Grayson stopped and blinked at the unexpected gesture. She then gave a noncommittal shrug as she fished her keys out of her pocket. "Maybe that'd be okay," she said awkwardly.

Stan slapped her on the back and chuckled. "Get out of here. I'll be in at nine. You should go home, too. You look like shit." Grayson smirked as she climbed onto the black Harley. "Oh, were you busy when I called?" he asked sweetly.

Grayson offered a cocky smile and kicked the bike to life. The roar was deafening. Stan leaned in. "You're a slut!"

Grayson nodded with a grin and took off.

The precinct was quiet with only one or two detectives sitting at their desks. Grayson sat and flipped on the small light. She opened the file on the first victim: Jane Monahan, 5' 7", one hundred thirty pounds, twenty-six years old. No birthmarks. No scars. Born in Ireland. Lived in Chicago for five years.

Grayson looked at the photos. Though hard to tell, the young woman was probably very attractive. She looked at several pictures of the markings the murderer carved under her left breast.

Grayson stared at them. "Why do these look familiar?"

The markings meant something. They were put there for a reason, but why cut into the skin? Her tired mind tried to focus. For the past three weeks, she had thought of nothing else. She even attended the funeral of the victim, hoping to get some connection, some feeling. It was a small gathering. Ms. Monahan was a bit of a recluse from what Grayson could find out.

She worked at the Chicago Library in the Research Department. Had no boyfriends to speak of and did not frequent any eating or drinking establishments. When Grayson and Stan searched her loft apartment, they found nothing out of the ordinary. The woman was, however, a collector of Irish pagan artifacts. She remembered how Stan laughed at the small statue of a pagan god as he picked it up. She also had various oil paintings artfully decorating her walls. The apartment had the air of an intellectual about it, Grayson thought.

She looked at the photo now, examining how this woman was bound. The roping was very methodical. Whoever hogtied these women knew exactly what he was doing. They were bound the same way with the same type of rope.

After searching every store in Chicago, they concluded that it was basic heavy twined roping that could have been purchased from one of twenty stores in the downtown area, and one of a hundred in the Chicago metropolitan area.

It wasn't so much the rope, but how it was done. These women were not just bound and dumped. Someone methodically and professionally bound them. Instinctively, Grayson knew these poor women were not dead when this happened. They were bound helpless and alive. Someone took a knife of some sort and slashed these women with the markings. He placed duct tape across their mouths to silence them, then slit their throats.

She looked up to see a patrolman walk toward her desk holding a manila folder. He smiled slightly. "Forensics knew you'd be here, Detective. This is the prelim. They'll have more later." Grayson took the file.

She looked around to see the morning sun shining through the window. Shit, it was nearly seven, and the precinct was buzzing with the start of a new day. She had completely lost track of time.

"Thanks, Jeff," she said tiredly and took the folder.

She looked at the photos of the latest victim. "Tied the same way. Same knots," she said aloud. She was used to talking out loud to herself.

In the past year, she'd done that quite a bit. If she wasn't taking openly to herself, she was talking to Vicky's picture. This, however, usually happened after several glasses of whiskey.

After Vicky's death, visions of her haunted Grayson constantly—visions of their lovemaking and her warm smile and sarcastic grin. She remembered the time they looked for a place together. Vic needed to see the sun; Grayson needed the lake. They compromised on a nice loft apartment on the fifth floor. Vic had the sun and Grayson had everything right there in Vic's deep brown eyes.

Then the vision of Vic leaping in front of Grayson and the two other policemen, taking the spray of bullets meant for them, flashed through her mind.

Grayson had already been shot, and she lay there helpless as she watched the body of the brave woman she loved riddled with gunfire.

She closed her eyes and angrily rubbed her forehead, trying desperately to erase the visions. She should have known better; the visions would always haunt her.

Chapter 2

"Detective MacCarthaigh?"

Grayson shook herself and looked up to see Lieutenant Keller standing there offering the cup of coffee in his hand.

"Thanks."

The older detective pulled up a chair and sat down. Grayson avoided his probing eyes as she drank from the steamy cup and winced. "Did you make this?" she asked cautiously.

Keller let out a laughing grunt. "So go to Dunkin' Donuts. Now tell me what we've got."

"Another woman hogtied, cut, then the throat slit. Perhaps just in that order, I'm not sure. It's nearly an exact duplication."

"Nearly?" Keller asked as he watched her.

"Both women have some sort of markings carved into their skin just under the left breast," Grayson said, showing him the photos. "They're similar, but I have to believe very different and mean something different."

Keller examined the photos as he listened. "So what do you think, MacCarthaigh? Have we got some sick fuck into bondage and S&M?"

Grayson stared at the pictures of both women. She took another drink from the Styrofoam cup. "I don't know. My gut says it's not that simple. I'll check out the local bars that cater to that sort and go from there. Look at how they're bound."

Keller took both photos and examined them. "Seems whoever this is knows what they're doing."

"I agree. The intricacies are amazing. The knots are perfectly situated. Someone took the time to bind these women," she said in quiet frustration as she stared at the photos once again.

There was a brief moment of silence between them.

"How are you getting along with Stan?" He sat back.

Grayson pulled a face and shrugged. "He's a good cop. He's all right. I'd rather do this alone," she added, feeling her anger rising again.

"Not gonna happen, Gray," he said sternly.

She shot him an angry look. "Why not? I'm better alone. You know it."

The old man took a deep calming breath. "Such a fucking pain in my arse," he mumbled. "No, you think that. I know better. Now quit your bellyaching and get this solved. Detective Resnick is your partner—treat him like it. You're a good cop, MacCarthaigh. I know this can't be easy for you, but do you honestly think you're the first police officer to lose a friend?"

"Vicky was more than a friend, sir," Grayson said in a low voice. She felt the tears rising in her throat and cursed herself for it.

"I know, Gray, and I'm sorrier than I can say," he said in a gentle voice, "but I can't afford for you to fall apart on me now."

Grayson was overtired, overworked, and just plan tired of feeling so alone. She felt her lip quiver.

He leaned in. "You listen to me, Grayson MacCarthaigh. I knew your father for twenty years, and when you came to my precinct eleven years ago, I knew I had just struck gold. I'm sorry, but you know the media is going to play this up big, and they'll be sniffing around. I need you, Detective," he said in a sure, firm voice.

Grayson took a deep calming breath and nodded. "Yes, sir."

He stood and picked up his coffee. "By the way, how is your mother?"

Grayson looked up and grinned. "She's fine. Nuttier than ever." She chuckled.

"When was the last time you saw her?" he asked fatherly, and Grayson cringed.

"Last month."

"What?" he asked in a quiet angry voice. "The woman lives three miles away and you haven't seen her in over a month?"

Grayson frowned deeply and stood. "I've been a bit busy, sir," she said sarcastically.

"You get your ass home and shower. Then I want you to go to your mother's today, you little shit. Don't you know she worries about you?"

Grayson glanced around, seeing the smirk on several co-workers. "I'm a grown woman. I don't need a lecture," she said. "Why don't you go see her?"

The old man narrowed his eyes and breathed heavily. They were treading on dangerous ground now, and Grayson knew it. Mike Keller had known her mother, Maeve, for twenty years. When her parents moved here from Ireland, they became fast friends. He'd loved her mother ever since; Grayson knew this, as well. Her father, Dermott, died five years earlier, and Mike Keller didn't know what to do about Maeve Grayson MacCarthaigh.

"Oh, get back to work, you idiot." He turned back into the office. "What the fuck are you all gawking at? Isn't there enough crime for you great detectives?"

Immediately, heads were buried into their respective work, each of them wincing as the door slammed loudly.

Grayson grinned childishly. She just loved to see the vein pop out in his forehead.

"One of these days, you're gonna give the old man a stroke," a younger detective said.

Grayson let out a laughing snort and sat down. "He'll live to be a hundred. He's too ornery."

"What's all the commotion?" Stan called out from the doorway. He had a box of what Grayson knew was fresh from the bakery in hand and two cups of coffee. He placed them on his desk, which faced Grayson's.

All of the sudden, she was starving. Stan grinned evilly as he opened the box. The sweet aroma of cinnamon wafted to her. *Damn this guy.*

"Well, partner," he drawled as he took a healthy bite. He then looked up. "I thought I'd come in early. I had a craving for Mrs. Walinski's cinnamon rolls. Oh, would you like one? Or are you going to sulk for the duration of our partnership?"

Grayson gave him a smug look and took a pastry. "Thanks," she said and grinned slightly.

Stan's ridiculous grin covered his face. He handed her the large steamy cup. "Better than that sludge from last night. Now what do we have?" he asked with his mouth full.

For the next few hours, they agonized over the forensic preliminary report and the photos. Stan agreed with her about the professional way the victims were bound. He also agreed with Keller. "A bondage freak and sadist, I'm thinking."

Grayson was not so sure.

Grayson stood under the hot spray of the shower. Leaning her hands against the wall, she allowed the water to ease her tired body. Her mind vacillated from the murders to Vic. She tried to empty her mind for just a little while, just enough to get some peace.

The gods above would not allow it.

"Need a hand?" Vic said in a low seductive voice as she opened the shower door.

Grayson grinned and cracked open one eye, as she peered at her lover through the soap in her hair. "Your timing, as usual, is perfect." She pulled her into the warm spray.

Vic laughed as she gently washed Grayson's black curls. "I love your hair. Why don't you let it grow? I'd love to run my fingers through long hair."

Grayson leaned into the gentle massage and reveled in the feeling of the warm body behind her. "It's too much hassle. You know that."

"I don't have a problem," Vic said smugly.

Grayson laughed. "That's because you're a girl and you like girly things. Like painting your toenails..."

Vic let out a short laugh as she pushed her under the shower to rinse the shampoo out of her hair. "If I remember correctly, Detective MacCarthaigh, you love to paint my toenails."

Grayson laughed out loud and got a mouthful of water. She shook her head and pulled the woman she loved close and looked into the soft brown eyes. "You're absolutely right, and when we're done here, I'll do it again for you," she promised with a long wet kiss. She grinned as she heard the soft moan and felt the shiver.

"We've got about five minutes before this water gets cold," Vic warned breathlessly. Grayson nodded and kissed her again; her tongue easily slipped into her mouth. Both women groaned as they clung to each other. "I fall and I'll kill you," Vic murmured.

"Never," Grayson vowed as she kissed down her neck to her breast. She bathed Vic's hardened nipple with her tongue, and Vic held her wet head in place.

Suddenly, Grayson was on her knees and Vic's leg was over her shoulder. She balanced on her outstretched arms as she held on to the walls of the shower.

"Oh, God," Vic whispered, as Grayson licked up and down the length of her. She loved the taste of this woman. So sweet, so Vic...

Taking the engorged clitoris into her mouth, she gently sucked. Vic cried out, "Geezus, Gray!"

Grayson let out a deep groan; the flat of her tongue languidly slipped between her folds as she felt Vic's body begin to tremble.

"No more, sweetie. I can't..." Vic panted and Grayson quickly stood and wrapped her arms around the trim waist, kissing her deeply.

"God, I love you, MacCarthaigh," she murmured into her neck.

"I love you, too, Ms. Green." Grayson nibbled at the sensitive earlobe.

Grayson shivered as the cold water broke her from her dream. She sighed sadly, turned off the water, and grabbed a big towel. Chuckling quietly, she remembered how she and Vic rarely showered separately. They enjoyed the communal shower and intimate time together. They felt safe and protected before they joined the real world of their jobs.

"We were so close to it, Vic," Grayson said as she dried off and sat on the edge of the bed—a different bed now. After Vic died, Grayson couldn't bear sleeping in the same bed. There was just too much there. Tears formed in her eyes as she wrapped her arms around herself and rocked back and forth.

In a few moments, she took a deep angry breath and dressed. She grabbed her leather jacket and keys and slammed the door on her way out.

Grayson tiredly walked up the front porch steps and rang the bell. She grinned when her mother opened the door.

"I thought I heard the rumble of that beast," her mother said.

"Hey, Ma," she said with a crooked grin.

Maeve peered over her reading glasses and grinned, as well. "Hey, nothing, get in here. You look like hell," Maeve said and pulled her inside. "Have you eaten?" She reached up to touch her cheek. Grayson shrugged but said nothing.

"Go into the kitchen and sit. I was on the phone with Sally."

"I'm sorry. I—"

"Oh, shut up and go," she ordered and pushed Grayson down the hall. "There's coffee on the stove."

"Why don't you use that coffee maker I brought you?" Grayson grumbled.

Maeve rolled her eyes. "It doesn't taste the same. Now sit."

Grayson poured a cup of coffee, sat at the old round table in the middle of the big kitchen, and looked around. "You were always here, cooking, cleaning, and taking care of me and Dad. How you found time to become a college professor is beyond me."

Maeve cocked her head to one side. "It's not like you to be so nostalgic. I took care of you two idiots because I love you."

Grayson grinned and drank her coffee. "You're a good mother. That's why Vic and I decided…" Her voice trailed off as she stared at her coffee cup.

"I'd ask what's bothering you, but I'd need a pair of pliers to get it out of you. You must be starving." She kissed the top of Grayson's head. She pulled the leftover roast beef, horseradish, mayo, and tomatoes out of the refrigerator.

Grayson watched and grinned. "My favorite."

"I know."

"Thanks, Ma."

"You're welcome," her mother said. "So tell me what's been

going on. I haven't seen you in three weeks. That must mean you're working on something you can't talk about." She stopped as she sliced the roast and shot a worried look at Grayson. "The young woman found by Lake Michigan three weeks ago. That's your case?"

Grayson took a deep breath and nodded as she drank her coffee. She leaned on her elbows and roughly rubbed her face. "Another victim was found early this morning at Belmont Harbor, by the rocks. Both murdered the same way."

Maeve finished making the sandwich and cut it, setting it on the plate. She got an enormous glass of milk and placed it in front of Grayson.

She poured herself a cup of coffee and sat down. "So are they related?"

Grayson took a healthy bite of the sandwich and nodded. "You know I can't tell you much, but yes, I think they're related. If we don't solve this, we're gonna have a fucking serial killer in downtown fucking Chicago," she said angrily.

Her mother let out a low hiss of disbelief. "Don't swear. Drink your milk."

Grayson looked over at her mother, watching her deep in thought. She was an attractive older woman, Grayson thought. Though not nearly as tall as Grayson, Maeve MacCarthaigh had a quiet allure about her. She had black hair like Grayson, only long with a considerable amount of white in it now. She kept it pinned up and off her neck, often held there by a pen or pencil, which of course she could never find. Her blue watery eyes sparkled, and her rosy cheeks made her look as though she just finished running a race. She was a kind and considerate nut.

She taught Irish history and mythology at the University of Illinois at the downtown campus, and taught a night course of—and Grayson cringed at this—Irish Druidism at Wright Junior College every Tuesday night. *Yes, Maeve Grayson MacCarthaigh was a Druid. Oh, pardon me, a Druidess.*

"Gray?" her mother called softly.

"Sorry, I was thinking," she said. "I need to find something to go on here, Ma."

Maeve regarded her carefully. "I hear uncertainty in your voice, sweetie, and that worries me because you're not an uncertain woman."

Grayson frowned and rubbed her hands over her face again. Her mother sat back and offered an indulgent grin, which Grayson tried to ignore. She knew what was coming next. Maeve was about to...

"You know, you're a confident woman and a good detective. I've watched you grow into a self-assured person, albeit a bit arrogant at times."

Grayson chuckled but said nothing. She knew it was time to shut up and let her mother be, well, motherly.

"The day you were born in Ireland, I knew that my only daughter was destined for something great. You had that underlying heroism all your life, that sort of 'big sister' attitude," Maeve said softly and continued. "As a young girl, you were constantly coming to the aid of your friends—both boys and girls. Remember when you were ten years old?"

Grayson winced and felt the color rush to her cheeks.

"You wanted to be a sheriff in the Old West. Then being a firefighter like Uncle Jack was a better idea. Then you finally settled on your best idea..."

Grayson felt the tears sting her eyes as she looked at her mother, who was also tearing. "And became a police officer like my father."

"Exactly," Maeve said. "Now you're exhausted. You need to sleep, sweetie," she said firmly. Grayson sighed and only nodded. "I want you to come to dinner on Sunday and spend the night."

"Ma..." The word was drawn out into several syllables.

"I'll make corned beef and cabbage," she enticed with a grin.

Grayson frowned and folded her arms across her chest, instantly feeling like a five-year-old.

"Or I'll call Mike—"

"You will not call Mike Keller!" Grayson saw the challenging look on the rosy-cheeked face. She sighed as she stood. "You would. Fine, I'll be here at five on Sunday."

"And spend the night."

"And spend the night, you nag."

Maeve laughed and pulled her daughter down in a fierce hug and kissed her forehead. "Now get out of here and go solve the murders of those poor women."

Chapter 3

Grayson walked into the precinct to see Stan going over the photos on the desk. He looked up as she sat at her desk. She saw the deep frown. "Okay, what's happened?"

Stan absently scratched his forehead. "Just back from the coroner's office. They identified the second victim."

Grayson sat forward. "And?"

"Name's Nan Quigley, twenty-eight, lived in Boston, and was here on business. From the reports of her friends, who identified the body, she was supposed to be back in Boston by now. When she never showed up for work, they called her friends, who in turn, called the police and gave a description. I was going to wait for you, but I met with them a while ago. They confirmed the identity." He slid the report over to Grayson.

She glanced at the report, her eyes darting back and forth as she read. "In Chicago on business? What kind of business?"

Stan shook his head. "Her two friends didn't quite know. Ms. Quigley was staying at the Drake Hotel, and they only saw her a few times while she was here."

"Friends that don't know what she did for a living? You got their addresses?" She grabbed her jacket.

Stan nodded and stood, as well. Grayson hesitated for an instant.

"I'm going with you, Grayson. So don't even," Stan said firmly but with a smile. Grayson took a deep angry breath and just walked past him.

"C'mon then."

They drove down Lake Shore Drive, north to Foster.

"So you became a cop like your old man, huh? With me, it was my uncle. He was a cop on the West Side. He was a patrolman, not a detective. My mother wanted me to be a lawyer. My father was a plumber."

Grayson gave him a side glance and smirked but said nothing as she looked out at Lake Michigan. The sun was shining brightly in the early autumn sky.

Stan wasn't a bad guy or a bad cop, either, Grayson thought as she listened to his ramblings. She could get stuck with worse. She grunted inwardly. He could get stuck with better…

"Here's the address." He pulled across the small North Side street.

"They live on the second floor. They're, you know, l-e-s-b-i-a-n-s," he whispered in mocked awe, then laughed at Grayson's glare. "Don't lose your sense of humor, Detective," he said as they climbed the old staircase. "Do you have one?" he asked over his shoulder.

Grayson followed and shook her head. "Fine, of all the cops in the department, I get partnered with Bob Hope," she grumbled with a wisp of a smile. She heard her partner laugh as they stopped at the door and knocked.

A woman answered and noticed Stan right away. "Detective, what's wrong?" she asked a bit nervously and glanced at Grayson.

"Nothing, we just thought of a few questions if you have a minute or two. I know this isn't a good time," he said with a warm smile.

Grayson was impressed. This guy should be in public relations. She'd heard of his easygoing manner; people liked him. He was a good deal like Vic in that regard.

The woman nodded and stepped back allowing both into the small foyer. She led them into the living room and offered the couch.

"Ms. Young, this is Detective Sergeant MacCarthaigh, we're investigating the deaths of Ms. Quigley and another victim," he said by way of introduction.

"Ms. Young," Grayson started. "What type of business was

Ms. Quigley in that would take her from her home in Boston?"

"You know, I asked Carol that just the other day. We've known Nan for nearly a year. We met out in Boston on vacation and became friends. We've corresponded back and forth, you know, through phone calls and e-mails. We honestly never got into what each of us did for a living. I really don't know why she was here. We got a call from her a week ago, saying she was in town and staying at the Drake. We saw her twice for dinner, then she said she was heading back. That's when we got a call from her aunt. She found our number by Nan's phone when she never showed up at the airport in Boston. Carol and I went to the Drake and she'd checked out nearly a week before. We got a little nervous and called the police."

Grayson nodded and glanced at Stan, who was scribbling in his notebook. "Ms. Young, I have to ask you a personal question. What did you know of Ms. Quigley's lifestyle?"

The brown-eyed woman raised an eyebrow and grinned slightly. "You mean other than the fact she was a lesbian?"

Grayson smiled, as well. "Yes. I can't tell you much, but this much has been in the papers. Someone bound each woman in a very precise manner, suggesting a fondness for bondage."

Her eyes widened in surprise. "Detective MacCarthaigh, I have no idea what Nan's sex life was like. If she was into bondage, she never offered that information to either Carol or me."

"I understand. I was just hoping to get some insight or something to go on," Grayson said. "I didn't mean to offend anyone."

"No offense taken. I wish I knew more," she said, and both detectives stood. Stan offered his hand with another warm smile.

"You've been a tremendous help, thank you," he said and offered his card. Grayson did the same.

"If you think of anything, please call this number at anytime," Grayson added.

"That's how you spell McCarthy? I never would have gotten McCarthy from this," she said and looked at Grayson, who chuckled.

"It's Gaelic. Good afternoon."

21

"Well, that was a bust," Stan said as he loosened his tie. They slid into their respective seats and fastened their seat belts. "Now what?"

"Call Boston. See if the police there know anything. Then I want the aunt's name. I want to know why that woman was here in Chicago."

"You don't think she was just a random victim?"

"No. I don't think either was a random victim. I think there's a connection with this killer and both women. We need to find out," she said. "I'm going to check out the local S&M bars. There aren't too many," she said and glanced at her partner. "No, you can't come. With you looking like a clean Marine, you'll stick out like a sore thumb. Go home and kiss your wife and kids. You'll be spending a lot of time away from them till this is finished."

"Yes, Sergeant." He snapped off a salute.

Grayson rolled her eyes. "Why me?" she asked as she looked up. She heard Stan's low laughter as she walked away.

It was nearly midnight when Grayson walked into the small dark bar. She had only been in there once, when Vic wanted to know what all the fuss was about. Grayson smiled inwardly as she remembered their wild night of extremely erotic sex afterward.

She walked up and sat at the bar. "What'll it be?" a gruff woman asked.

"Jameson, neat," Grayson said. The woman came back and set the drink in front of her. Grayson pulled out a fifty, and as the woman took it, Grayson held on. "Got a minute?"

The older butch narrowed her eyes, still holding onto the fifty-dollar bill. "What'd you have in mind?"

"I need some information."

"You a cop?"

"Yes," Grayson said, keeping eye contact. "I'm investigating the murders of two women."

"The ones in the paper," the bartender added, and Grayson nodded.

"I need to know someone with experience. Someone who would know about the type of bondage that was used," she said in a low firm voice.

"Everybody in here knows bondage, lover. That's no secret." She laughed. "Hell, that's what we're here for, but that don't mean—"

Grayson held up her hand. "Look, I'm not accusing or judging anyone's lifestyle. I just need some help."

The bartender took a deep breath. "Give me a few minutes." She tugged on the fifty. Grayson pulled it out of her hand, tore it in half, and handed half of the bill to her.

The old woman laughed and took it, stuffing it in her jean pocket. "Fucking cops," she grunted. "Sit right there."

Grayson watched her as she disappeared into the back room. She took a long sip of her whiskey and toyed with the glass as she waited. In a moment, walking toward her was the sexiest woman she'd ever laid eyes on.

She was nearly as tall as Grayson with long thick blondee hair. She wore black leather pants that looked as though some lucky individual painted them on her long sinewy legs. The black silk blouse, opened to reveal ample cleavage, clung nicely to her slim body.

She stood next to Grayson, who turned slightly on her bar stool. The woman's eyes were as green as jade, and her lips were a deep ruby red. *Holy Mama*, Grayson thought as she finished her drink.

"Buy the lady another on the house, Barb," she said in a low sultry voice.

Grayson raised an eyebrow but accepted the offer. The bartender put a glass of ice water in front of the blondee.

"I understand you need some information," she said.

Grayson nodded. She took out the other half of the fifty and handed it to the grinning bartender. She explained again what she needed.

"Come with me. We'll have more privacy in my office."

Grayson glanced around the bar, trying not to notice several patrons in various stages of undress, some sporting collars and leashes, some holding the leashes in a tight grip. She took her drink and followed.

"Your name?" the blondee asked.

Grayson took her gold shield out of her back jeans pocket. "Detective Sergeant MacCarthaigh," she replied as she sat on the only available seat, a long black leather couch. The blonde woman leaned on the edge of her desk and smiled as her eyes raked over Grayson's body.

"Why should I help you?"

"Why wouldn't you?" Grayson countered logically. "Some sick fuck has killed two women, bound them in an intricate fashion, then slit their throats. I don't know why they were tied like this. Perhaps the murderer is into bondage."

"That's a bit presumptuous, Detective," the woman retorted.

Grayson heard the indignation in the voice. "I'm not saying that those who have a proclivity for bondage are potentially homicidal, but these women were bound in a certain fashion," Grayson said, looking the gorgeous woman in the eyes. "Murder tends to get me a little twitchy. I'm funny that way."

The blondee chuckled. "What does the bondage look like?"

Grayson reached into the breast pocket of her jacket and pulled out the folded pictures. The blondee walked over, sat next to Grayson, and took the photos.

Studying them, she frowned in contemplation. Grayson watched her cautiously, trying to ignore the scent of her perfume and the ache in her groin. *This is business, MacCarthaigh, business.*

"This is very intricate Detective MacCarthaigh, but honestly, it could be anything. Some like heavy bondage with many different ropes. There are Japanese types of bondage, hogtying, and the very basic slip knot actually. This, however, I've never seen. It's very…"

"What?" Grayson prodded as she turned to her. The blondee glanced at every photo taken at different angles.

"It just looks…old," she said and shook her head.

"Old? Like old ropes?" Grayson asked.

The blondee shook her head. "No, old like ancient. Wait, look," the woman said with enthusiasm. She walked over to her small bookcase and brought back a large book. "I hope this doesn't shock you," she warned with a smug grin.

Grayson gave her a cocky smile, noticing the woman staring at her lips. She then opened the book and presented it to Grayson, who raised her eyebrows as she looked at the pictures.

They depicted women in various stages of bondage, some of it painful looking. All from different time periods. Grayson noted the dates underneath each. When there were drawings instead of photos, Grayson realized she was looking at bondage from hundreds of years ago. As she looked closer, she noticed all were bound in the same way. The women in the photos and illustrations were Asian.

"It's called Nawa Shibari. It's Japanese, and it started nearly five hundred years ago. So, you see, it's not just here. Bondage is as old as time itself. I know those poor women were subjected to this kind of bondage, but honestly, I've never seen those knots before, except in these old photos. And trust me, I would know," she added in a low seductive voice and gently closed the book. "Someone is either a historian or they're over five hundred years old," she finished with a small chuckle.

Grayson took a deep disappointed breath. "Well, thanks. It was enlightening anyway." She stood and offered her hand.

The blondee smiled and took her hand, as she stood closer to her. "Are you off duty, Detective?" she asked in a sultry voice. Her free hand slid up and down Grayson's worn leather jacket.

"Thank you for the information. I'll let myself out."

The blondee held onto the leather-clad arm. "Anytime," she replied. She then snaked her hand behind Grayson's neck and pulled her into a scorching kiss, which left Grayson groaning.

Grayson pulled back, and with an audible *pop*, the kiss ended. "Geezus, woman!" she exclaimed and held her at arm's length.

The blondee slipped her card in Grayson's breast pocket and trailed her fingernails across the soft leather. "I'll be home in an hour. Call me," she said in a low firm voice.

Grayson found herself staring at the red lips. "Thanks, good night." Grayson walked out.

Chapter 4

Grayson rode the rumbling Harley down Clark Street. She'd been riding around for nearly an hour. It was two a.m. when she took the elevator up to the seventh-floor apartment; she leaned on the buzzer a couple of times.

The blondee opened the door and smiled. "Well, Detective. I'm glad to see you. Come in." She stepped back.

Grayson walked in, trying not to notice the black silk robe and tousled blonde hair.

"I'm not interrupting, am I?" she asked as she stood in the darkened foyer.

"No. I had just gotten to bed. Something to drink?" she asked as she walked in front of Grayson.

"Whiskey, neat, if you've got it," she said, watching the blondee and ignoring her libido. "I don't know your name."

"Eve," she said as she handed Grayson the small tumbler. She had one for herself. "Have a seat," she offered as she sat on the long leather couch and patted the cushion next to her.

Grayson took a healthy drink. She knew why she was here. So did Eve. *So let's quit playing games*, she thought, and slugged back the remainder of the amber liquid. It warmed her all the way to her toes—as if she needed to be any warmer.

Eve set her drink on the table and walked over to Grayson. Like two magnets, their bodies collided. Grayson let out a throaty groan as she roughly kissed Eve.

Suddenly, they were in Eve's bedroom. She stripped the leather jacket off Grayson and backed her up to the bed. Grayson had no choice but to flop back with a breathless grunt. Eve pushed Grayson's knees apart and stood between her denim-clad legs.

"Lie still and nobody gets hurt," she said in a sultry voice.

Grayson reached up and pulled her down. After a moment of dominance play, Grayson had the blondee breathless and on her back. Grayson loomed over. "Lie still and nobody gets hurt," she countered evenly.

She held Eve's hands above her head and opened her robe. Gazing at her lovely body in the darkness, Grayson ran the back of her fingers across Eve's breast, eliciting a quiet moan.

"You have a nice touch, Detective," Eve whispered and arched her back as Grayson's thumb passed over her hard nipple. Grayson lowered her head, took the aching nipple into her mouth, and roughly ran her tongue across it. As she suckled against Eve's breast, she slipped her hand down the length of her abdomen and easily parted her legs.

"Yes," Eve moaned as she lifted her hips.

Grayson slipped her fingers lower and entered her. Eve cried out as she arched into Grayson's thrusts. When she ran her thumb over Eve's swollen clit, Eve came quickly. She wrenched her hands out of Grayson's grasp and pulled Grayson down on top of her. "Don't stop," she cried out and frantically clawed at Grayson's back.

Grayson felt the inner walls tighten around her fingers and gave one more deep thrust. Eve arched one more time, then her body stilled. "Ohmygod," she whispered in a ragged voice.

Grayson kissed the top of her breast as she withdrew her fingers. She gently cupped Eve and ran her fingers through her damp curls. Eve let out a contented sigh, then rolled Grayson onto her back. "Very nice, Detective."

Grayson's heart raced as she looked up into Eve's smiling face. Visions of Vic flashed through Grayson's mind. Visions of wild nights like these when they loved long and hard all night.

When Eve started to unbutton her shirt, Grayson reached up and held her hands.

"What's wrong?" Eve asked breathlessly.

Grayson swallowed and struggled to sit up. "Nothing," she said in a coarse voice and buttoned her shirt. She felt Eve's eyes watching her intently and felt embarrassed and awkward.

"Are you involved with someone?" Eve gently ran her fingers up and down Grayson's back.

Grayson let out a small laugh. "No, I'm not involved with someone."

"But there was a someone once, am I right?"

Grayson tried to stand, and Eve gently pulled her back down. "You look like shit, Detective. Why don't you sleep for a while? I'm sure you need it."

"Look—" Grayson started awkwardly, suddenly feeling exhausted.

Eve pushed her back against the pillows. Grayson let out a deep sigh as she stretched her tall frame out on the bed.

Grayson closed her eyes and felt Eve's fingers run through her hair. As she drifted off, she whispered, "Thanks, Vic."

The cloaked figure stood in front of the roaring bonfire, arms raised to the heavens. Chanting in a low voice, he stopped and turned to the long concrete slab. A figure was bound to the altar, writhing against its bonds.

The dense fog rolled across, engulfing the figure as it disappeared into the mist. Instantly, the wolf-like creature crawled through the fog. Snarling, it leapt at the altar amidst the screams.

Grayson woke with a start and bolted up. She quickly looked around the dark room. "Shit." She ran her fingers through her hair. *What the fuck kinda dream was that?* She looked over at Eve, who was sleeping soundly. She took a moment to get her bearings and wipe the sweat from her brow. She then took a deep breath and slid out of bed.

"Are you leaving?" Eve's sleepy voice called out.

"Yes," Grayson said as she struggled into her boots. A feeling of guilt tore through her. Vic's face crowded her vision as she slipped into her jacket. "Look—"

"Don't say it," Eve said and lay on her side to face Grayson.

Grayson felt Eve watching her as she lay there. She didn't know what to say. Eve apparently did. "You've got some demon chasing you, don't you?"

Grayson stiffened and looked down at her, her body silhouetted against the filtered light from the street. She was naked under the sheet. "It's these murders," she said by way of an explanation.

"It's not the murders, Grayson MacCarthaigh," Eve whispered.

"I've got to go," Grayson said and stepped back.

"You know where I live."

"Yeah, I know. Goodbye, Eve," Grayson said and walked out.

Grayson walked into her apartment and tossed her keys on the small table. She glanced at the picture there of her and Vicky in Florida just before she died.

They were happy and content—their lives planned and their love secure. Grayson shook her head roughly as if to stop her thoughts. She stripped out of her clothes and stepped into the shower.

She dried off as she walked into the bedroom and tossed the damp towel on the chair. She slid under the sheets and let out a deep sigh. Eve now invaded her thoughts. *Good grief, MacCarthaigh, you nearly came like a teenager and she didn't even touch you.* All at once, she was extremely aroused once again.

Her breathing got shallow as her hand absently went to her breast, tweaking and tugging her nipple, the other hand went south and slid through her own wetness. Then the vision of Vic flashed through her inner sight. Their last night in this room was passionate and erotic. Grayson closed her eyes as she continued, feeling the orgasm start. Soon, she was lost in the visions of Vic as the orgasm shot through her.

"Vic!" she screamed out as she arched off the bed. "Fuck," she muttered when her breathing returned to normal. She rolled over and hugged a huge pillow. *Fine, Grayson, now you're reduced to diddling yourself.*

She faded off into an uneasy sleep. Her dreams, if she could call them that, were disjointed and unsettling. There were visions of Vic, Maeve, and someone she could not remember—someone in the shadows.

Chapter 5

The next two days found nothing new. Grayson was irritated, and Stan was the picture of understanding.

"Stan, if you say don't worry one more time, I'm gonna shoot you," Grayson said through clenched teeth as she grabbed her leather jacket.

Her impeccably dressed partner's eyes widened and he hid his grin. "Sorry, Grayson. Where are we going?" he asked as he followed her down the steps.

"Ms. Quigley's aunt is flying in to take the body back to Boston. We're picking her up at O'Hare."

Grayson was eating a hotdog as they stood by the baggage claim carousel in the United terminal.

Stan grimaced. "It's only nine in the morning. How can you eat that?"

Grayson shrugged and took another healthy bite. She glanced past Stan and noticed a tall woman in sunglasses standing by the carousel. She had long red curly hair, and for an instant, Grayson thought she looked like Nicole Kidman. A closer look showed this woman was not as thin and her features were softer. She had a familiarity about her that Grayson couldn't place.

Then the passengers started to mill around waiting for their luggage. From the description Mrs. Quigley had given Stan, Grayson recognized her right off. She was a taller woman with white hair and wore the tweed blazer as she said she would.

"There she is," Stan said.

Grayson noticed the redhead walking toward Mrs. Quigley and put a hand to his chest to stop Stan.

"What?" he asked and followed her stare.

The redhead walked up to Mrs. Quigley. They exchanged an emotional hug, and the redhead said something to the old woman, who nodded and smiled. Again, Grayson thought this woman looked familiar. It was driving her crazy.

"Who is that?" Stan asked as he watched the exchange.

"Don't know, but I'm gonna find out," Grayson said, and a small glimmer of hope and enthusiasm sparkled in her eyes for the first time in three weeks.

"Mrs. Quigley?" Grayson asked. Both women looked up and the old woman smiled and offered her hand. "I'm Detective MacCarthaigh, we spoke on the phone. This is Detective Resnick."

Stan smiled warmly as they shook hands. Grayson met the piercing green eyes of the redhead. They stared at each other for a moment until the woman blinked and looked away.

"Thank you so much for meeting me, Detectives," Mrs. Quigley said kindly.

Grayson smiled and nodded, then looked back at the redhead. "Well, it seems you already made arrangements," Grayson said evenly.

"Oh, I'm sorry. This is Neala Rourke. She was a friend of Nan's," Mrs. Quigley said. The redhead shook hands with Stan, then turned to Grayson.

"Detective," she said in a soft Irish brogue.

Grayson heard her, but she showed no emotion whatsoever as she took the offered hand.

"Well, why don't we get your luggage?" Stan suggested.

The old woman nodded in agreement and searched the luggage carousel. "There it is." She pointed and Stan retrieved the small bag.

"Ms. Rourke, will you be accompanying us?" Grayson asked.

"Yes, please, Neala," Mrs. Quigley said. "I really don't want to do this alone. It was so nice of you to meet me here."

The tall redhead smiled. "Of course, I'll come with you." She held the old woman's hand.

31

"Would you like to go to your hotel first?" Grayson asked.

The old woman smiled sadly. "Thank you, Detective, but I'd rather do this now," she said in a tired voice.

Mrs. Quigley held the handkerchief to her face as she cried. Grayson hated this part of her job.

"How could this have happened?" Mrs. Quigley whispered sadly.

Neala Rourke just stared down at the body covered in the sheet. Stan grimaced and Grayson spoke.

"We're not sure, Mrs. Quigley, but we'll find out who did this," she said confidently and led the woman out. "You said on the phone that your niece was here on business, but you had no idea what that business was."

The old woman shook her head. "Nan had a government job, I believe. She worked for the Boston City Archives, but that's all I know," she said with a helpless shrug.

Stan grinned. "That's more than we knew, thank you."

Grayson regarded the redhead curiously. "What about you, Ms. Rourke? What do you do for a living?"

Neala Rourke raised an eyebrow. "I do not work for the government, Detective MacCarthaigh." With that, her pager went off. She looked at the number. "I have to get back to work, Peg. Why don't I take you back to the hotel? If the detective is finished, that is." She gave Grayson a challenging look.

Grayson's jaw tensed and Stan stepped in. "We're through, thank you. We'll be in touch, Mrs. Quigley."

Grayson said nothing but got a quick wink from her partner. She merely nodded and watched as they walked down the steps and into Neala Rourke's car.

"Sorry, Gray, it was getting a little tense. I saw your jaw clench," he said with a grin. "So what are you thinking?"

"I'm thinking Neala Rourke knows something. And I will find out," she said in a resolute voice as the BMW pulled away from the curb.

Stan looked at his watch. "Hey, don't you have to get to your mother's?"

"Shit!" Grayson shouted and ran down the steps.

Maeve MacCarthaigh had just put the lid on the huge pot when the doorbell rang. "Why doesn't that idiot use her key?" she asked as she wiped her hands on the towel.

"This should be a regular occurrence, Grayson MacCarthaigh, every Sunday," Maeve said, and her daughter smiled.

"We'd kill each other," Grayson said as she took a big whiff. "Hmm, I love that smell."

"You have a hollow leg. I don't know how you keep in such fit shape, the way you eat."

"Vic used to say the same thing."

"She was right. Now sit."

They sat at the little kitchen table and ate their Sunday meal. Maeve noticed the distracted look. "How is the investigation going?"

Grayson sighed angrily and explained all she could. Mrs. MacCarthaigh listened as she ate and waited until her daughter had finished.

"That's a horrible way to die and a horrible thing for her aunt to go through. She's lucky to have the other woman there for her," she said and watched Grayson's brow furrow deeper. "What's wrong, kiddo?"

"I don't know, Ma. This woman, there's something about her. I can't figure it out. She looks so familiar. Damn it, I know I've seen her before," Grayson said as she picked at her food.

Maeve noticed Grayson still look exhausted. "Why don't you stop thinking about it for a while? Let it rest, then come back to it later. God knows you see a lot of people." She gave her daughter a smug grin. "Maybe you saw her at Mass on Sunday."

"Oh, very funny," Grayson countered. "Just because I..." Her voice trailed off.

Maeve saw the thoughtful pose. "What? You saw her at church?" she asked, trying to hide her incredulous tone.

Grayson frowned and shook her head. "No, but..." She stopped and took a deep breath. "I don't know. I just know I've seen her."

Maeve said nothing as Grayson's mind went to work. She sat back in her chair and looked around the room. "There's something about this woman. I…" She stopped and the grin spread across her face.

"I know that grin. Who is she?" her mother asked. "If you don't tell me…"

Grayson chuckled and sat forward. "Two weeks ago, I went to the funeral of Jane Monahan, the first victim. I sat in the back and watched everyone. And there she was, sitting a few rows back at the end of the pew, alone. Damn it, I knew it!"

"So maybe she's just a friend," her mother said logically.

Grayson snorted in disbelief. "What are the odds of her knowing both victims? No, Ma, this woman knows something. I can feel it," she said, then tiredly rubbed her face.

"What else, Gray? I can tell there's something else bothering you," her mother gently prodded.

"I don't know," Grayson grumbled. "Both victims had markings on them."

"What kind of markings?" Maeve asked with a grimace.

"I know you hate this, but I need…" She stopped abruptly. She sat back and took a deep stubborn breath.

"Grayson, you need to talk this out. I know you. So start talking. I'll be honest with you, kiddo, I don't like this dehumanizing part of your job, but it's the nature of murder, I suppose. So tell me what you're thinking." Maeve patted her hand.

Grayson leaned in. "Both women were cut, Mother, under the left breast."

Maeve blinked and swallowed her revulsion. "Wha—, um, what," she stammered. "Cut?" she asked with an incredulous squeak.

Grayson leaned back and laughed quietly. "Cut as in with a knife or scalpel," she said evenly. She reached over, took the pencil out of her mother's hair, scribbled the markings on a paper napkin, and presented it to her stunned mother.

Maeve blinked and looked at the napkin. She frowned and cocked her head to one side. "This looks familiar," she said as she studied the markings.

"That's what I said. I know I've seen these markings somewhere before, but I'll be goddamned if I can remember," she said angrily.

"Stop swearing," Maeve said absently, as she continued to look at the napkin. She then blinked and sat back.

"I know that look, Ma," Grayson said. "You have the same look when you figure out the final word in a crossword puzzle."

"Shush for a minute, let me think," Maeve said and waved her off.

Without a word, she rose and walked out of the kitchen, leaving Grayson sitting there confused and impatient.

After a minute of grunting and groaning, Maeve walked back into the kitchen. Grayson groaned as she noticed the huge book. "Mother, not the 'How to Be a Druid in Three Easy Lessons.' Please," she begged in earnest.

Her mother ignored the sarcasm as she sat and opened the leather-bound book. "Let me see. I know I've seen these before."

Grayson moaned helplessly as she looked at the book.

"I see that look. Now stop scowling," Maeve said as she leafed through the heavy book.

"It's the bible to the Druid world. I know," Grayson moaned. "Druids, bards, and ovates alike all had this book or something similar. It's the history of Druidism from the beginning with the Tuatha Dé Danann and the gods and goddesses, to Brigid to St. Patrick, who took all the Druid beliefs and made them 'acceptable' in the eyes of Rome," she continued.

"Don't sass the Church," Maeve said as she turned the old pages. "But I agree about St. Patrick."

"And they say that St. Brigid herself was a triple goddess," Grayson said with a shake of her head.

"Yes, they were all over the place back then," Maeve said dryly as she looked through the book.

"All my life, Druidism surrounded me. If it wasn't you, it was Sally or even Grandma," Grayson said and laughed. "I remember Grandma Grayson and you. You'd sit for hours at a time reliving and retelling Ireland's history and mythology. As a kid, I was enthralled and felt a connection, but…"

"But as you got older, it waned until it became a flight of fancy, nothing more than an old story one tells at Halloween to scare the daylights out of all the little kids," Maeve said as she concentrated on the book. She looked up to see her daughter grinning evilly. "You're thinking of Steve O'Brien, aren't you?"

Grayson laughed out loud. "I scared Steve O'Brien so bad he wet his pants. He deserved it being the bully he was."

Maeve continued leafing through the book in silence. Grayson still felt that inner pull in her gut whenever she thought about being a Druid.

"You can't deny it, sweetie," her mother said softly. "It's in your spirit, like it is mine and your grandmother and God knows how many other ancestors."

"It's ancient folklore—mythology, Ma," Grayson said logically. "Nothing has been proven that the Tuatha Dé Danann even existed. The Milesians were the first recognized inhabitants of Ireland…"

Her mother waved her off. "I wish I knew where you got this annoying logical side. It had to be from your father."

"Yes, being logical is a curse."

Maeve smiled and looked up. "It is when you deny your heritage."

"Mother," Grayson insisted. "I am not a Druid."

"No, you're not," her mother agreed. "You're a Druidess."

"I give up." Grayson sighed and rubbed her temples.

"I knew it!" her mother said triumphantly.

Grayson jumped at the exclamation. "What?"

Her mother turned the big book, so both of them could see. Grayson peered at the symbols and markings. It was then she realized what it was. "Ogham, damn, I knew I saw these before."

Maeve nodded. "Each is a letter in the ancient Irish Ogham alphabet. Some mean whole words, some have a special meaning," she said with such enthusiasm that Grayson had to smile as she watched the green eyes sparkle.

"I'll get the photos tomorrow and bring them over. I'll look at them then. It has to be. This could be a big breakthrough if this is what I think," she said in a hopeful voice. She ran her hand across her eyes.

"What are you doing tomorrow night?" her mother asked.

Grayson stopped in mid-rub and peered through her fingers when she heard the eager tone. "Why?"

Maeve laughed at the terrified pose of her tough detective daughter. "There's a benefit at the Field Museum. The Irish government has some historical artifacts on display. Chicago is their last stop. They're here for a month, and this is their last week. Good grief, Grayson, don't you read the papers? My God, you're a detective."

Grayson narrowed her eyes at her mother's grinning face but said nothing.

"So I want you to go with me. I can bring a date," she said, and Grayson cringed. "I know what you're thinking. You love your mother, but the thought of spending the entire evening with Sally, Marge, Rose, and any other Druids was not on your list of top ten things to do.

It's not a Druid convention, though you'd do well to pay attention. It's in your blood, as well, young lady. I've been invited because I teach Irish history and mythology, and for your information, I am very well respected in academic circles," she said firmly.

Grayson had the grace to blush. "Sorry, Ma. Let me think about it." She yawned wildly.

"Good grief, we've been sitting here for five hours. It's nearly ten o'clock. It's time for bed," she said.

Grayson looked at her watch. "Holy shit, I had no idea it was this late. I'd better be going." She stretched as she stood.

"You are not riding that rumbling beast home at this hour. You're tired and you'll run off the road. You're staying and that's final," Maeve said in a firm voice as they cleared the dinner dishes.

"Go on, your room is all ready for you. I'll make breakfast in the morning and you'll eat every bite. Now go take a hot bath and get to bed," she ordered as she pushed Grayson out of the kitchen.

The hot bath did the trick. Grayson nearly fell asleep in the tub. She took a pair of boxers and a T-shirt out of her old dresser drawer. As she slipped into the makeshift PJs, she chuckled as she noticed that her mother hadn't changed much in her room.

Her old basketball trophies were still standing on the dresser with the ribbons attached, along with a picture of the three of them in Ireland when she was fifteen. She smiled fondly at the picture of her and Vicky and her parents, which also hung on the wall.

They were at some dinner for one of her mother's Irish friends from school. Vic sat between Grayson's mother and father; Grayson stood behind them with her arm around her parents and her cheek touching Vic's. They looked like a family—they were a family. Grayson laughed as she remembered all the nutty people her mother knew. They all wanted to meet her and Vic.

God, Vic looked so gorgeous with her blonde hair and soft brown eyes. Her smile was always captivating. "I miss you so much, Vic," she whispered as she took the photo off the wall and studied it.

She blinked several times and frowned as she noticed a few people in the background. Her heart beat wildly as she concentrated, making sure she was seeing this correctly. She then ran across the hall and banged on her mother's bedroom door. She didn't wait for an answer as she barged into the bedroom.

"Good heavens! What's wrong?" her mother exclaimed as the book she was reading flew out of her hands.

Grayson quickly stood at her bedside and presented the framed photo. "Do you know who this is?"

Maeve replaced her reading glasses that had fallen off her face. "It's a picture of your father, you, Vicky, and me, sweetie," she said cautiously.

Grayson rolled her eyes impatiently. "No, mother, the woman behind us," she said, tapping her finger on the glass.

Maeve adjusted her glasses and looked at the tall redhead. "Oh, that's Neala Rourke, dear."

Grayson nearly collapsed on the edge of the bed as she sat down. "How do you know her?"

Her mother raised an eyebrow. "I'll tell you, Detective

Sergeant MacCarthaigh, if you get that tone out of your voice," she said severely.

Grayson took a deep breath and shook her head. "Mother..."

"Okay, she's the curator of the National Museum in Ireland. She was at that dinner at our personal invitation. I've met with her several times, and I've known her for a few years. Why?"

Grayson stood and paced back and forth. "You invited the curator of a famous museum to your witch's convention?" she asked absently. Then she froze as she realized what she had said. She cautiously turned to her mother, who was quietly seething. She had the look of certain death etched in her rosy cheeks. "Ma, I'm sorry. I didn't mean that."

Maeve continued to glare. "We do not sit around the cauldron all the time, you know. Why is Neala so important?"

"She's the woman at the victim's funeral. She was at the airport this morning helping Mrs. Quigley."

Her mother's jaw dropped as she blinked several times. "Grayson..." she said.

The serious low voice made the hair on the back of Grayson's neck stand on end. "What? I'm so afraid to ask."

"The benefit tomorrow night at the Field Museum," she started slowly.

"What about it?"

"The National Museum is sponsoring the display. Neala Rourke is a guest speaker."

Grayson grinned and nodded. "And I'll bet she's been in town for the entire month, right?"

"I know what you're thinking. You can't be serious. Neala Rourke is a respected woman. She's, well, she's—"

"A suspect," Grayson said. "What time is this clambake tomorrow, and is it black tie?"

"Seven o'clock, and yes, it is. You don't own a black tie."

Grayson shrugged and kissed her forehead. "I can rent a monkey suit as well as the next person. G'night, Ma."

"Good night, sweetie. Oh, and we're taking my car. I am not going to an elegant dinner on the back of that disgusting bike," she said as she continued reading.

"Gray, you have to tread lightly here," Keller reminded her as she and Stan sat in his office. She had just finished telling him about the latest information.

She grumbled and fidgeted in her chair. "Look, this woman knows something, I can taste it."

Stan grimaced playfully. "Yuck," he mumbled. Grayson glared at him.

"Knock it off, you two. I'm serious. The Irish government has a soft spot for Chicago. The mayor's office courted them for a year to get them to agree to make Chicago their last stop. Do you have any idea how much money was involved in this?"

"I don't care, Lieutenant. I'm a detective, not a politician. We have two women brutally murdered within three weeks of each other and not much to go on. This woman knows something, Mike, I can feel it."

"Well, I have to care, Detective. Now you'll behave this evening and you'll take your partner with you."

"Shit! That's just what we need. Damn it, Lieutenant, I'm trying to get information out of her. If she sees both of us tonight, she won't open up," Grayson said and ran her fingers through her thick raven hair.

"Stan is going."

"It's a bad idea."

"Stop fucking arguing with me, goddamn it!" he bellowed helplessly.

"Um, excuse me," Stan interjected quietly. Both of them shot him a look. "I have an idea."

Grayson rolled her eyes and leaned back.

"Go ahead," Keller said as his red face returned to normal.

"I could go with my wife and not with Grayson at all. That way, we just look like a couple of patrons of the arts who donated money. Ms. Rourke will surely notice us. She seems to be a very intelligent woman, but at least we won't be joined at the hip."

Grayson grumbled and Keller nodded. "Good idea. It's done. Now get the hell out of my office," he said and dared Grayson to say another word.

Her partner quickly rose and gave Grayson a pleading look; Grayson growled lowly and stormed out.

They sat at their desks, not saying much. As Grayson cooled off, she realized that it was indeed a good idea. If Stan had to be there, this was the only way. She glanced up to see Stan studying the files.

"So what did you find out about the symbols on the victims?" she asked as she cleared her throat. Stan did not look up.

"Nothing yet. I'm waiting to hear back from our guy in research. He's got the photos, and he's trying to make some kind of match, cross-referencing them with other similar murders."

"That's a good idea," she said awkwardly as she glanced at him. Still, he did not look up.

"I have my moments. More than you realize, Gray." He looked up and sported a goofy grin.

Grayson shifted in her seat. "I-I'm sorry, Stan. I'm not used to relying on anybody else. You're a good cop," she mumbled and blushed furiously.

Stan continued to grin. "Thanks. Now what time is this benefit tonight?"

"Seven and it's formal of sorts, I guess."

Stan watched her and hid his grin. "I take it you don't own a formal?"

Grayson chuckled and tossed down her pen. "I can't wear my prom dress. No place for my weapon."

"Guess we'll both be renting tuxes," he said, trying not to laugh.

Grayson met the smiling eyes. "Let's not show up dressed the same, all right?"

Stan laughed heartily and agreed.

Grayson chuckled along, hoping the evening would find them one step closer to the murderer. Neala Rourke had a bit of explaining to do.

Chapter 6

"My God, Grayson Fianna MacCarthaigh, you are beautiful," Maeve exclaimed as her daughter blushed furiously.

She wore simple black belted pleated slacks with a crisply ironed white shirt tucked in and opened at the collar. Maeve was proud to see her only daughter wore the Celtic cross around her neck on a delicate chain of stunning white gold. *Good Lord, she's wearing earrings.* She nearly staggered at the sight. Two small diamond studs that she knew Vicky had bought for their anniversary adorned Grayson's shapely earlobes. A black tailored blazer rounded out her evening attire until she looked down at her feet—cowboy boots. At least they were black.

Grayson followed her look and laughed. "It's better than my biker boots," she said, and her mother heard the serious tone in her voice. "You look damned gorgeous yourself, Mrs. MacCarthaigh. Is that the shawl and the Tara brooch Dad bought when you were in Ireland?"

Her mother smiled happily. "It sure is. Goes with the gray silk dress, don't you think?" She adjusted the gold Tara brooch that held her shawl in place. "Thank you, kiddo," she said affectionately and hugged her daughter. She immediately pulled back and opened Grayson's blazer stunned to see the shoulder harness and weapon tucked under her arm.

"Grayson, is-is that necess…" she stammered.

Grayson buttoned the blazer and led her out the door. "Yes, it's necess. Now let's get going. I'm starving. We will be fed at this thing, won't we?"

Grayson told her mother about Stan as they drove to the

museum.

"So he's your new partner, huh?" she asked and stole a glance.

"I guess." Grayson sighed.

"Good, you need a partner. You can't do this alone," she said softly, both knowing she meant more than her job.

"I know, Ma. I just don't want anybody. It's too soon." She stopped as her voice caught in her throat.

Maeve reached over and touched her arm. "Someday. You'll be ready someday," she assured her and sat back. "But sleeping around isn't the way," she scolded severely.

"Ma…" Grayson groaned helplessly.

"All I'm saying is that you're a good woman and Vicky wouldn't approve of your choices lately. She'd want you to find a good woman to build a life with, that's all I'm saying. I won't say anything more." She adjusted her hair.

Grayson rolled her eyes at the hopeful yet impossible idea. Mercifully, they pulled up in front of the Field Museum with no further discussion of Grayson's tawdry sex life.

Grayson grabbed a glass of champagne for her mother and a bottle of Pellegrino for herself. The exhibit was filled to capacity, and Grayson noticed the mayor and his wife along with several other aldermen and women.

"Swanky," a voice whispered behind her. She turned to see Stan grinning standing next to a shorter woman who smiled warmly.

"Hey," Grayson said.

"Hey," he chimed in. "This is my wife. Kathy, this is Grayson MacCarthaigh. You two finally get to meet. What'll it be, honey?" he asked, looking at his wife.

"Are you nuts? Champagne," she said seriously. Stan kissed her and walked away.

Grayson felt awkward standing there. Kathy offered her hand. "It's nice to finally meet you, Grayson."

Grayson took her hand. "Nice to meet you, as well, Kathy. Stan's talked about you," Grayson said, not knowing what else to say.

Kathy's blue eyes smiled and her dimples deepened. "I doubt that. He's not one to talk. It's a cop thing, I believe, but it was nice of you to say so," she said with a wink.

Grayson instantly liked her. She let out a nervous chuckle as she drank her water.

"Stan does, however, talk about you," Kathy said kindly.

Grayson looked down into the sparkling blue eyes. "Well, don't believe everything," she said with a shrug.

Kathy smiled as Grayson fought the uncomfortable feeling of a compliment about to happen. "Stan was right, you're drop dead gorgeous. Good damned thing you're a lesbian."

For a moment, Grayson was flummoxed. She then laughed but said nothing.

"He also said you have great instincts, and he's lucky to have you as a partner. Would you do me a favor?"

Grayson looked up and nodded.

"Take care of him for me," she said seriously.

Grayson smiled and nodded again. "Will do," she assured.

For the first time since Vic, Grayson felt like she had a partner—to watch someone's back and to trust him to watch hers.

"Thanks, he can be a little hard to take. He's always joking."

Grayson laughed then. "Yes, he is, but I think I'm lucky to have him as well, Kathy," she said, then leaned in. "But if you tell him that, I'll deny it."

Kathy let out a hearty laugh and Grayson joined in.

"Okay, this is not good. I know you're laughing about me," Stan grumbled and handed his wife the fluted glass.

"Not entirely," his wife lied.

"Well, I thought I lost you," Maeve called out, and Grayson whirled around. "Where did you go off to? I wanted to show you off to the girls."

"Please, Ma," Grayson begged, feeling very much like a teenager.

"What? I'm proud of you," her mother continued.

"Ma…" she warned and glanced around.

Stan and Kathy exchanged glances. "This is the tough sexy

detective?" Kathy whispered to him. Stan glared playfully.

"Mrs. MacCarthaigh, I'm Kathy Resnick," Kathy offered the introductions.

"I'm sorry, Ma. This is Stan, my partner, and his wife, Kathy," Grayson said. She was out of practice here. Maeve smiled at both as she shook hands.

"I'm Maeve MacCarthaigh, this goof's mother. It's nice to meet you both."

As Grayson suffered the accolades from her mother, she looked around and saw her. Neala Rourke was standing in a small gathering. Grayson noticed a tall man, impeccably dressed, listening to her. His long jet black hair was pulled back in a small ponytail. Grayson chuckled. *Got enough gel in that hair, pal?* She watched Neala as she listened intently to what her companion was saying when all of the sudden Neala's head shot up, and she looked right at Grayson, as if she called her.

Grayson blinked as their eyes met from across the room. Her heart pounded in her chest, and she heard nothing of what her mother was saying. Their eyes locked, then Neala Rourke quickly looked at the woman who was talking and offered an apology.

Grayson drank her water, finding her mouth suddenly dry. The intense feeling now gone, she looked over to see the tall man looking at her with the same intensity. From where she stood, she felt the dark eyes boring into her. Grayson gave him an unwavering look back. He smiled so slightly it might have been a smirk as he took a drink of his champagne, then concentrated on the conversation. Grayson glanced down at her mother, who was still rambling.

Kathy was fascinated. "Druids? Like in witches and magic?" Grayson rolled her eyes and Maeve nodded with glee.

"Well, not witches, dear, but close. You see, Druidism goes back thousands of years from Europe and the Roman times, to Ireland to Scandinavia. With the Irish, there were three types: a Druid, a bard, or an ovate. Now the Druid was a priest, for lack of a better word…he or she would be responsible for relating the mores or lore of their people. They possessed great wisdom and were very revered. Wars started or ended on their opinion. Even the most barbaric savage would yield to the wisdom of the Druid or Druidess, so they say. Now, a bard is the poet, which pretty much speaks for itself. Finally, the ovate—the healer or seer—these could be men or women. They were the doctors. So you see, they had all the bases covered. Now…"

"Um, Ma, look at their eyes. They're glazed over. Give them a break," Grayson pleaded in earnest.

Maeve blushed horribly and sneered at her. "Party poop," Maeve grumbled and grabbed another glass of champagne.

Kathy chuckled and leaned in. "We'll talk more about this later, okay? It's very interesting," she whispered. Maeve grinned and nodded.

Grayson looked back at Neala Rourke. "Introduce me, Mother," she said and grabbed her under the elbow, then looked at her partner.

"You go, we'll mingle." Stan pulled his wife along with him.

As Grayson and Maeve made their way up to the tall redhead, she looked up and glanced back and forth between them.

"Maeve! I didn't see you come in. I'm glad you could make it," Neala said warmly and kissed Maeve's cheek.

"I wouldn't miss this. I understand they found another tomb?" she asked excitedly.

Neala grinned wildly and Grayson found herself staring. The smile transformed the redhead's face completely. She looked almost childlike in her enthusiasm.

"That they did. Ireland can certainly hold her own with the rest of the archaeological world, that's for sure," she said with her soft Irish brogue.

"Oh, I'm sorry. I know you've met my daughter, Grayson MacCarthaigh," Maeve said dryly.

Neala was astonished. "Detective MacCarthaigh, I didn't put the two together. This is a surprise. Are you interested in Irish history?"

Grayson shrugged. "As much as the next, I suppose."

"I had an extra ticket," her mother chimed in, and the tall redhead laughed.

"I see. Well, whatever the reason, we appreciate the support."

She looked into Grayson's eyes. "Well, how about I give you the ten-cent tour?"

Maeve's eyes lit up. "I was waiting for you to say that. Lead on," she said happily and grabbed Grayson's arm.

They walked by the elaborate exhibit. Grayson noticed many artifacts, all Celtic in design. There were the typical ancient pieces of pottery, a Tara brooch, and handmade ancient weapons used in battle. She was barely listening to Dr. Rourke as she spoke. Maeve examined the artifacts with pride.

"This is one of the prized pieces we found," Neala said with a wide grin as she looked at the exhibit table.

Grayson looked, as well. "Looks like a rock," Grayson said as she watched Neala Rourke.

"Yes, I suppose it does," Neala said. "To someone who is ignorant of Irish history."

Maeve cleared her throat. "My daughter may be ignorant, Neala," she glared at Grayson, "but not of Irish history."

Grayson grunted and avoided her mother's scolding as they stood behind the red velvet rope that separated the exhibit from the guests. As they leaned in to get a better look, Grayson noticed it was triangular in shape and about twelve inches in diameter. The edges of the triangle looked rough and somewhat jagged, as though it had been broken. There were markings on the face of the smooth rock.

Grayson examined it as best she could; she was dying to pick it up. It was then it struck her. She glanced at her mother, who was looking at the etchings, as well; her eyes widened in recognition and she looked at Grayson, who nodded. "Ogham," Grayson whispered.

Neala looked from Grayson and Maeve. "Exactly so. Perhaps you do know your ancient history, Detective."

Grayson heard the challenge and took the bait with a smug grin. "It's an ancient Irish alphabet. Certain lines mean certain words or names. Notches usually are vowels. Ogham dates back as far as the third century, perhaps further."

Neala nodded, showing her approval. Grayson offered a wry grin and bowed slightly in a sarcastic gesture before continuing.

"What does the inscription on that stone say?"

"That's something we've yet to determine."

The three women whirled around when they heard the deep baritone voice behind them; it was the man Neala had been talking to a few minutes before. Once again, he and Grayson locked eyes.

"Phelan," Neala said. "These are friends of mine. Maeve MacCarthaigh, who is a professor of Irish mythology, and her daughter, Detective Grayson MacCarthaigh. This is Phelan Tynan."

Maeve smiled. "Nice to meet you, Mr. Tynan," she said and shook his hand.

"Phelan was instrumental in assisting the archaeologists and their work," Neala continued.

"Really? How so?" Grayson asked.

Phelan grinned slightly. "Funding, Detective."

"You must have a boatload," Grayson said as he offered his hand. Grayson shook his hand and got immediate goose bumps. While his handshake was firm and steady, his hand was cold and clammy.

Phelan smiled thinly. "More like a fleet."

"Well, I for one, am glad you could offer your assistance," Neala interjected. "This was the most interesting and historical find in decades."

"Where was all this dug up?" Grayson asked.

Neala glared at Grayson. "We *dug* it up near St. Brigid's Monastery in Kildare. Mythology tells us that before Brigid became a saint, she was a pagan."

"Some say Brigid was not human at all, but a goddess, a triple goddess," Phelan said.

"The pagan goddess who would be a saint," Grayson said. This guy gave her the creeps.

"As pagan as they come," Maeve said. "Though the Church will tell you differently. Catholic historians believe her only connection to paganism was her father, who was a pagan and a chieftain in Leinster. Brigid was loved by everyone."

"Yes," Phelan agreed. "She was chosen."

Grayson gave him a curious look. "Chosen?"

Phelan blinked and looked at Grayson. Grayson thought he was looking at her; he seemed to be looking through her. He then smiled thinly. "Yes, the people of Ireland loved her dearly. The Church had no choice but to make her a saint."

"This isn't about Christianity," Neala said as they looked at the stone.

"No, Neala, it's not," Phelan concurred.

Everyone watched as he gazed at the stone. Grayson raised an eyebrow in curiosity. "Care to elaborate, Mr. Tynan?"

"Over a thousand years ago," he started, "gods, goddesses, Druids, sorcerers—they ruled ancient Ireland. They held the power, ruled the clans, decided wars." He stopped and smiled slightly. "What a time they had."

They stood in silence for a moment until Maeve chuckled. "You sound like you have firsthand knowledge."

It was then Phelan blinked and looked at her. He laughed quietly. "Now that would have been a grand time."

"I wholeheartedly agree, Mr. Tynan," Maeve said wistfully. "I think I would have made a wonderful goddess."

Grayson shook her head as everyone laughed. All but Phelan; he smiled slightly. "Yes, Mrs. MacCarthaigh, I believe you would have. You were born in Ireland?"

"Yes, County Roscommon, as was Grayson," Maeve said with a wide grin.

Stan's voice called out from behind them as they approached. "You're not an American?"

Grayson laughed. "Dual citizenship, partner."

Kathy nudged her husband. "What did we miss?" She turned to Neala and Phelan Tynan. "What happened to the gods and goddesses and the rest of them?"

"They, well, they died, Kathy," Grayson said in a grave voice. Stan laughed and Maeve glared at her.

"Gods and goddesses do not die, Detective MacCarthaigh," Neala said.

Grayson heard the serious tenor in her voice and raised an eyebrow. As if her mother knew she was about to say something sarcastic, Maeve reached over and pinched her triceps very hard. Grayson grimaced and glared at her mother.

Neala offered her theory. "According to Irish mythology, the Tuatha Dé Danann—"

"Too-ahha de whatann?" Stan interjected.

"Tuatha Dé Danann," Neala repeated slowly. "Its literal translation is—the people of the goddess Danu—she started the race of Irish gods and goddess. It is said they lived on the islands in the west and perfected the art of magic. They came to Ireland on a cloud of fog and settled there. They were the rulers of Ireland until the Milesians, the people of the Spanish king Milesius, drove them to the underworld. The Milesians are considered the ancestors of modern Ireland. It is said that the Tuatha Dé Danann still live in the underworld as invisible beings. In a just battle, they will fight beside mortals. When they fight, they are armed with lances of blue flame and shields of pure white." She stopped and looked at Maeve.

Grayson watched the exchange between her mother and Neala. A shiver ran through her.

Stan interjected, "Is that where you get the idea of leprechauns and fairies?"

Phelan glanced at Stan and smiled. "Ireland is full of mystery, full of magic."

Neala glanced at Grayson, who was staring at the stone. "Detective MacCarthaigh? How is your knowledge of Irish mythology?"

Grayson glanced at the stone, then looked at Neala and smiled slightly. "Who says the Tuatha Dé Danann is a myth?"

"Exactly so, Detective," Phelan said as he watched her.

Chapter 7

"I agree with Mr. Tynan. Most people say the Tuatha is a myth," Maeve said.

Grayson watched Phelan Tynan. For some reason, this guy bugged her. Maybe it was his slick-backed hairdo. Couldn't have been his scary dark, nearly black eyes.

"Well, there's Sally," Maeve interjected. "I have to talk with that woman. I'll be right back. Grayson, behave," she said over her shoulder, and Grayson frowned deeply as she watched her mother weave in and out of the crowd.

Phelan cleared his throat. "I'll take my leave, as well. I just spotted the mayor. I need to speak with him. It was nice to meet you, Detective MacCarthaigh."

Grayson nodded and watched his tall figure filter through the crowd. She turned back to the smirking Irishwoman.

"I have a feeling, Detective, that you're not only here for the exhibit," Neala challenged.

With that, Stan pulled his wife away. "Let's go grab some food, honey."

Grayson waited until Stan and Kathy had walked over to the buffet table until she spoke. "No, *Dr.* Rourke, I'm not."

"You've done your homework, I see," she said, stiffening a bit.

"A little," Grayson agreed with a nod.

"And what did you find out?" the redhead asked in a clipped voice.

Grayson shrugged in a bored fashion. "Oh, not much. Born in Dublin, graduate of Trinity College, master's and doctorate in Irish history. Curator of the National Museum in Dublin for six years. Not bad for a young woman," Grayson said with a cocky grin.

"Would you like to check my teeth?" she asked in a terse voice.

Grayson continued smiling. "No, that won't be necessary, but I would like to know how you were acquainted with Nan Quigley."

Neala took a deep breath as Grayson snatched another bottle of Pellegrino and a glass of champagne from the wandering waiter. She handed the glass to the doctor, who took it but said nothing.

"Look, Dr. Rourke, two women have been brutally murdered. I need something to go on. First, I see you at Jane Monahan's funeral. Then I see you at the airport meeting the next victim's aunt. I may not be the best detective in Chicago, but that does smack of a coincidence and—"

"Are you accusing me, Detective MacCarthaigh?" she asked, her anger surfacing. "Am I a suspect?"

"No. I would just like to know how you knew the victims. When did you get into Chicago, if I may ask?"

"Ya may not! I have a very important job, and it doesn't entail suffering the inane accusations from the Chicago Police Department."

Grayson narrowed her eyes. "I'm not accusing you, Dr. Rourke—"

"It certainly has all the ear markings, Detective," she interrupted. "I'm very busy. If you would like to talk to me, make an appointment." She turned and marched away.

"Arrogant jackass," she muttered, just loud enough for Grayson to hear.

"Snooty bitch," Grayson said under her breath. She turned to see Maeve standing behind her. As she opened her mouth, a tall blonde man walked up to her.

"Detective MacCarthaigh, I'm Jason Lattner from the mayor's office. Am I wrong or did I just hear you arguing with the curator of the National Museum in Ireland about these murders?"

Grayson rubbed her temples. She looked at this young pup. *Little toady prick.* "No, Mr. Lattner, I was not arguing—"

"Good. Because it took me over six months to get the Irish government to agree to have Chicago and not Boston as their final sendoff. Do you know how many Irish asses I had to kiss? You'd better get back over there and apologize. If the press gets wind of this—"

"Look, junior. I have bigger worries. Like two women brutally killed right here on the mayor's lakefront. So don't go preaching to—"

"Hey, Gray. The food is awesome," Stan's voice called out.

Grayson and Jason turned to see him standing there, grinning. Kathy was wild eyed as she listened. Maeve was just shaking her head.

Jason Lattner pasted on a political grin. "I'm glad you're enjoying it. Have a good evening." He smiled and nodded. As he walked away, he glared at Grayson, who waved bye-bye.

She looked over at her smirking mother. "In exactly ten minutes, you've managed to thoroughly set the mayor's plan back six months," she said, and Grayson sighed deeply.

"Nice work, partner," Stan added with a toothy grin, then his face paled considerably. "Oh, fuck."

Grayson turned, following his gaze. It was Captain Jenkins, red faced and marching toward them.

"Fuck me," Grayson grumbled.

"Come with me, both of you," he said angrily and walked past them.

Stan kissed his wife and winked. Grayson was already marching right alongside her captain. He stopped at a small office and opened the door. Both detectives followed.

"Detective MacCarthaigh, Mr. Lattner just informed me of something I couldn't believe. Tell me it's not true that a detective in one of my precincts is accusing a prominent visiting figure of being a suspect in a murder case. Okay. Let's have it."

Grayson took a deep breath and told him all they knew. When she finished, she leaned against the desk.

The captain rubbed his face. "I'm too old for this. Do you honestly think Dr. Rourke is a suspect?" He looked at both detectives.

"I agree with Grayson, sir. I think she knows something. It's just too coincidental. She may not be directly involved, but we can't overlook the possibility," Stan said firmly. Grayson felt the pride swell deep within her as she listened. Stan could have easily hung her out to dry.

"Look, I understand there's a great deal of pressure on you to get this solved, but I cannot stress enough the importance of discretion. Do I make myself clear?"

"Yes, sir," they said in unison, then glanced at each other.

The old man narrowed his eyes at them. "I suggest you go and unruffle a few feathers, Detective MacCarthaigh. And do it tonight." He walked out of the room.

"What's she like?" Stan asked.

Grayson snorted. "She's a cold bitch."

"With a killer body," Stan said absently.

Grayson had to agree completely. She hoped killer was not the right word.

"Want me to talk to her?" Stan asked as they made their way back through the crowd.

"No, I'd better. I started it. Damn it."

"How'd it go? Do we still have your pension?" Kathy asked half seriously.

Stan laughed and pulled her into her arms. "Yes. Grayson is fired, though," he said, and Grayson laughed openly as did Maeve.

She looked around to see Dr. Rourke escorting several people around the exhibit.

"Ma, the markings on that stone..." Grayson said as she watched Dr. Rourke.

"I know what you're thinking," Maeve said. "You think there's a connection with those women."

Grayson nodded absently. "What do you know about the area where they found that triangular stone?"

Maeve took a deep breath and let it out slowly. "It was nearly under the monastery in Kildare. You know where that is, Gray, you've been there many times."

Grayson nodded as she remembered her youth in Ireland.

Though they lived in Roscommon, they traveled to the monastery often. Grayson's mother knew the abbess who lived there; her mother had friends, Catholic and Druid, who she would visit, taking Grayson with her.

As Grayson matured, it occurred to her that the women who still practiced Druidism would sit at the same table with the abbess of St. Brigid's Monastery. She remembered sitting alongside her mother who joined in the discussion; her mind drifted back to when she was a small girl.

Grayson sat between her mother and the abbess, Sister Daniel, a short old woman who smelled like the peat fire that was constantly going no matter what the weather. She looked up at the abbess, who was smiling at her.

Sister Daniel placed her cold wrinkled hand on Grayson's cheek. "You are bored to death, aren't you, my child?"

Before answering, Grayson glanced back at her mother, who was talking with the other nuns and women. She looked back at the nun and nodded.

Sister Daniel laughed and patted her cheek. "Off with you then." She motioned to the door. "Tell Liam I said you can help him with the rose bushes."

The old nun then looked at Maeve. "It's all right, Maeve, the girl is bored with all this talk. We'll have more time when she's older."

Grayson looked up at her mother who grinned. "Okay, sweetie. Go play with Liam but leave the cows alone." She winked and ruffled Grayson's dark hair.

"Okay, Mama," she said and looked at the old abbess. "Thank you, Sister."

"You're welcome, child."

Why would she remember that right now?

"Grayson?" Her mother's soft voice broke her from her reverie. She stopped and scratched her cheek. "What are you thinking?"

"There's a connection here," Grayson said.

Stan put his hand on Grayson's arm. "With the murders?"

Grayson nodded. "The markings on that stone are the same

markings on the victims. I'm sure of it."

"Well," Maeve said. "That stone is certainly something they will be studying for quite a while…" Her voice trailed off as she stared at the stone.

"What is it, Ma?"

Maeve blinked and avoided Grayson's look of concern. "Oh, nothing, sweetie, nothing."

Grayson gave her a doubtful look. "Ma, what's going on?"

"Nothing, nothing. Good grief, don't be such a worrywart… Now you have to go and talk to Neala."

"Yes, I do," Grayson said. "Stan, please take the ladies and get something to eat." She started to walk away.

"Aren't you hungry, Gray?" her mother asked.

Grayson shook her head. "No, I've got a little crow to eat, so I'm sure I'll have my fill. You enjoy, though," she said over her shoulder as her partner burst into laughter, turning more than a few heads.

Chapter 8

Neala Rourke turned around to see Grayson standing there with two glasses of champagne. She tried to ignore the light fluttering in her chest. Detective MacCarthaigh was a handsome figure of a woman; there was no doubt. Her outfit was tailored to fit every line from her slightly broad shoulders to her narrow waist. Her curly raven hair hung nicely right at the collar of her starched white evening shirt. *Those dark blue eyes, saints above…* Neala took a deep calming breath. *Arrogant jackass.*

"Detective MacCarthaigh, I really don't have time to get into another row with you," she started, and Grayson offered the glass of champagne.

"Dr. Rourke, I came over here to apologize, not to argue," she said seriously.

Neala took the offering and said nothing as she sipped the bubbling wine. She watched Grayson as she took a very long drink from the fluted glass. She decided to let the poor stoic woman down easily.

"Detective MacCarthaigh, I realize you're only doing your job, but I had nothing to do with the death of those poor girls," she said, looking Grayson in the eye.

"You know something, Dr. Rourke. I know you know something. So please, if you'd just tell me," she said in almost a pleading voice. She stopped and ran her fingers through her hair in a gesture of pure frustration and exhaustion. "Look, I'm sorry if I offended you. I'm not the best at delicate situations. If you would please call me when you're ready to fill me in on whatever you know," she said, her voice starting to rise once again. She stopped and closed her eyes as if counting to ten.

"Please call me or Detective Resnick, if you feel more comfortable." She looked into Neala's eyes before continuing. "There's a sick person out there, Dr. Rourke. I need to find him and stop him before he brutalizes another woman. Please think about it. Good night." She set her glass down and walked away before Neala could say a word.

It was just as well; she couldn't speak if she wanted to. The deep blue eyes filled with so much emotion tugged at her heart. *Damn*, she thought, and gulped down her champagne.

"Detective MacCarthaigh," she called after her. Grayson stopped and turned around. "I can't talk to you here. Can I call you in the morning? Or perhaps after the exhibit is over tonight?" she asked in a hesitant voice.

"Doctor, I don't care if I have to camp out on your doorstep until this thing is over. Thank you," she said, sounding relieved.

Neala offered a smile. "Well, I don't think it'll take that long, perhaps another hour or so." Grayson smiled and offered her hand.

As Neala took it, she looked once again into the violet eyes. The detective's hand felt warm and sure in hers. For a moment, neither woman moved. Then Grayson slipped her hand away.

"I'll just hang around. I'll find you," she said in a low voice, then walked away.

Neala watched her retreating figure before heading back to the exhibit.

"Stan, can you take my mother home? Dr. Rourke agreed to talk to me, and I don't want to give her a chance to change her mind. I just have to wait until the exhibit is over." She turned to her mother. "Sorry, Ma."

"Don't be. You've got work to do. Just get home at a decent hour and get some rest, sweetie. Bring my car around in the morning," she said and pulled the tall frame down for a kiss. "Be careful."

Grayson pulled away and gave her mother a curious look. "Don't worry, Ma."

"Grayson, I'm serious."

Grayson raised an eyebrow. "One of your feelings?" Her mother nodded. Grayson smiled. "Okay then, I'll be extra careful," she promised and saw the relief on her mother's face.

She watched Stan escorting both women out and did not turn until they were out the door.

"Detective MacCarthaigh?"

Grayson turned to see a young man regarding her with a smile. "Dr. Rourke asked me to have you wait in her office. If you don't mind."

As she followed the young man, she felt eyes on her once again. Glancing around the crowded room, she saw him—Phelan Tynan—just watching her.

"Detective?" the young man said.

Grayson tore her eyes away from the intense scrutiny and nodded. She followed him down the hall and stopped as he opened the door and stood back.

"Can I get you anything?" he asked, and Grayson shook her head. The young man then quietly closed the door.

She sat at the end of the small leather couch and let out a sigh. It felt good to lie down. Now if she could just get out of this jacket and itchy shirt. She turned slightly and stretched one leg out on the couch. Putting her head back, she thought about Dr. Rourke.

Shit, she was gorgeous. She looked so sexy in her midnight blue evening dress; her milky white skin a stark contrast with her freckles all over. Grayson shivered as she caught the sensual curves of her body. *Okay, enough drooling, MacCarthaigh.*

Grayson didn't want to believe she was involved somehow, but there was just too much there. Why was she at Jane Monahan's funeral? Why meet Mrs. Quigley at the airport? *What are you into, Dr. Rourke?* She closed her eyes for just a moment.

Neala Rourke finally finished with the remaining guests and personally made sure the security system was working. The artifacts were locked down for the night and she nearly forgot about the detective.

"Mother of God," she said and ran down the hall.

As she opened the door, she stopped dead and smiled slightly.

There on the couch was a sleeping Grayson. Her frame much too tall for the small couch, she half sat, half laid in an uncomfortable position. Her black jacket was opened, and Neala swallowed as she noticed the swell of her firm breast and the holstered gun under her arm. She walked up quietly, hearing the deep breathing. It was then Grayson twitched in her sleep. Neala stopped and watched in silence as the detective's brow furrowed and her left arm twitched. Then she rubbed her fingers along the palm of her left hand in a nervous gesture, as if the detective was trying to rub some foreign substance off her palm.

"Detective MacCarthaigh?" she whispered, and the woman instantly woke and bolted up. "Easy, easy. I'm sorry," she said in a soft voice.

Grayson blinked and chuckled quietly. "No, I apologize. I fell asleep," she said awkwardly and stood. She ran her fingers through her hair and rubbed her face. "So everything locked up?"

"Well, yes, but would you mind if I double check? I know I'm being overprotective, but the closer we get to Ireland, the more nervous I become," she finished with a nervous chuckle.

Grayson nodded and adjusted her jacket. "I understand. I'll go with you."

Grayson followed her out of her office and waited as she locked her door. "This way." She motioned down the darkened hall, illuminated only by the exit signs above the entranceways.

In what Neala thought was a protective gesture, Grayson put her hand under her elbow. However, she said nothing as she listened to the sound of her heels clicking against the tiled floor that echoed through the lonely hall.

As they walked into the exhibit room, everything looked in order. The light dimly lit the exhibit table and around the room. Neala walked from table to table as Grayson followed closely behind.

"All in order?" Grayson asked in a low voice.

Neala nodded. "Can we just check the doors?"

Grayson nodded and followed her out of the exhibit room and down an adjacent hall. A security guard was standing nearby, making his rounds. He flashed the beam of his flashlight on them as they approached.

"I'm Dr. Rourke," Neala said. "Just checking to make sure everything is locked down."

The guard nodded and glanced at Grayson, who flashed her badge. "Okay, Detective."

After making sure the doors were locked, they made their way back through the exhibit room. "I know I'm bein' silly, Detective, but…" She stopped dead in her tracks.

Grayson bumped into her, then followed her gaze. Standing by the exhibit table was Phelan Tynan. He was staring at the table and didn't notice them come into the room.

Grayson put her hand on Neala's arm as she started forward. She looked at Grayson, who was watching Phelan. For a moment, they stood still and just watched.

Phelan reached over and caressed the stone. Neala thought she heard him talking in his low baritone voice. It was then he looked up and noticed them.

"Dr. Rourke," he said with a small smile. "I thought everyone had left."

Neala and Grayson slowly walked up to the table. In the spotlight was the stone. Neala was very grateful it was still there.

"So did we," Grayson said evenly. "What are you still doing here, Mr. Tynan?"

He continued to smile. "I'm fascinated by this exhibit, and like you, I wanted to make sure it was still safe and sound. It is."

Neala ran her fingers through her hair. "Well then, I think we can all sleep tonight. You scared the life out me, Phelan."

He laughed. "I am sorry." He glanced at Grayson. "However, you had Chicago's finest with you. I'm sure you were quite safe."

They stood for a moment in silence. Neala looked at Grayson, who looked decidedly perturbed as she watched Phelan.

"Well, I will say good night then." He smiled and walked out of the exhibit room.

"He gives me the creeps," Grayson said in a low voice.

Neala raised an eyebrow. "Is that a professional term, Detective MacCarthaigh?"

Grayson scowled and led her out of the exhibit without another word.

"How about some coffee?" Neala asked as she slipped into her jacket. "I have nothing in my hotel room."

"That sounds like heaven. I know of a nice little place."

They walked into a bistro on State Street. "Hey, Gray. Long time," a man's voice called out.

Grayson grinned and took the offered hand. "Hey, Tommy. We need a little table—"

"Out of the way. I get you," he said and winked at both women. Grayson winced apologetically, and Neala blushed to her roots.

"Here you go, nice and roman—"

"Thanks, Tommy. Just some coffee," Grayson said quickly and urged the confused owner along.

Neala slid into the plush leather booth opposite Grayson. "This is a nice place," she said, looking at the menu. "You must come here quite a bit."

"I used to," Grayson said in a quiet but dismissive voice. Neala looked up and let it go, seeing the dark look that flashed across the handsome features.

Tommy came back with a pot of coffee and two cups. "Have a feeling you're gonna have more than one cup," he said, grinning, and looked at both women. Grayson glared at him.

"Thanks, Tommy, we'll let you know if we're going to eat."

"Oh, right, right," he said and looked at Neala. Grayson took a deep patient breath.

"Tommy, this is Dr. Rourke. Tommy is an old friend and a pain in my arse," Grayson said, trying her hand at an Irish brogue. Neala laughed openly as did Tommy as they shook hands. He then looked at Grayson.

"It's high time you showed that Irish mug of yours around here. We missed you and—"

Grayson looked up and Tommy stopped and gave her an apologetic look. Neala watched the exchange as she poured the coffee. The dark-haired man reached down and kissed the top of Grayson's head.

"Beat it, will you?" she grumbled. Tommy smiled and walked away. She looked across the table. "Okay, can we get down to this?"

Dr. Rourke raised an eyebrow. "Certainly. What would you like to know?"

Grayson leaned in. "What would you like to tell me?" she countered sarcastically.

Neala glared, then took a deep calming breath. "Detective MacCarthaigh, there are things in this world that…" She stopped and Grayson just listened. *How in God's name do I start this?* Neala thought. She looked across at the circles under the detective's eyes and the lines of exhaustion etched in her brow.

"Do you know anything of Irish mythology, Detective MacCarthaigh?"

Grayson's frown deepened, if that were possible. "My mother, as you know, teaches Irish history and mythology, Dr. Rourke. So yes, I have a working knowledge of all gods and goddesses. Please tell me this is leading somewhere," she begged as she drank her coffee.

"I wish your mother were here."

In the next instant, Grayson started laughing. Neala glared at her, thinking the laughter was at her expense.

Grayson held up her hand. "I'm not laughing at you, Doctor. It just struck me that I'm sitting across from a beautiful woman who wishes my mother were with us. It's just too…" She stopped abruptly when she realized what she said. Neala blushed once again and drank her coffee.

"What about my mother?" Grayson asked, trying to get back some semblance of control and professionalism.

"She is very well versed on the subject. Actually, they were going to contact her when this tragedy happened here, as well."

Grayson looked completely confused. "Who was going to contact my mother, and what do you mean it happened here, as well? Dr. Rourke, I'm overtired and at my wit's end. Please stop talking in this cryptic bullshit and give me a straight answer."

"You wouldn't believe me if I told you," she said angrily.

Grayson nearly growled as she leaned forward. "Try me."

"The Dark Lord, Detective MacCarthaigh. The Dark Lord is killing your women," she said evenly.

Grayson just sat there and blinked. Neala thought she looked like a deer caught in the headlights. Finally, Grayson leaned back and sported a smug grin.

"Two women cut, bound, and throats slit. Of course, the Dark Lord," she said. "Why didn't you say so?"

Chapter 9

"I know you don't believe me." Neala shook her head.

"I'm very tired. Would you just tell me how you know these women? I saw you at the funeral. Neala, tell me what you know because you're sounding a little crazy right now," Grayson said in a dead serious, logical voice.

Neala frowned and took a deep breath. "I'm not crazy, Detective MacCarthaigh." It did not go unnoticed that the detective used her first name. For an instant, she liked the way it sounded coming from the confident yet arrogant woman.

"I'm sorry, that was insensitive of me. You're not crazy. Please, continue."

"Jane Monahan and Nan Quigley were associates of mine. We had done work together back in Ireland nearly eight years ago. At that time, we were all at Trinity together studying ancient Irish history and folklore. Nan was a..." She stopped and gave Grayson a wary glance.

Grayson in turn scratched her brow impatiently. "A what, Doctor?" she prodded and gulped her coffee.

"You drink too much coffee, Detective MacCarthaigh. I..."

Grayson gave her a warning glance. Neala said no more on the topic. "Nan was a novitiate of sorts," she said, trying to pick her words correctly.

"A nun?" Grayson suggested patiently.

"Of sorts," Neala said with a tentative smile.

"A sort of nun. Okay. Nan Quigley was studying to be a nun, right?"

"Well, yes, in a manner of speakin'..."

Grayson let her head drop to the table with a thud. Neala

winced at the sound and put her hand out. Her fingers nearly touched the soft black waves before she pulled her hand back.

"Was she studying to be a nun or not?" the muffled voice asked.

"Not a nun but she did work at a monastery in Ireland, in Kildare. You see, this is not a simple thing to explain."

Grayson lifted her head. "Really?" she asked dryly. "Let's skip Sister Nan for a minute. What about Jane Monahan?"

"Well, now. Jane was not a novitiate."

"Fine, now we're getting someplace." Grayson sat up.

"She was a bard," Neala said quickly.

Grayson closed her eyes and put her head back. "A bard?" she asked with her eyes closed. "As in a poet or storyteller? Like a Druid, a bard, or an ovate?"

"Exactly!" Neala said in a triumphant voice. "You do understand."

Grayson gave her a disturbed look. "Understand what? You haven't told me a thing." Grayson heard the squeak in her voice. She cleared her throat. "Dr. Rourke, there is a sick individual out there butchering these women. You knew these women. Now you tell me some Dark Lord is killing them. I don't suppose you know who this guy is."

Dr. Rourke grimaced and shook her head.

"What he looks like?"

She shook her head once again.

"A name, besides the Dark Lord, 'cause I gotta tell you, Doc, I can't go to my superiors and tell them the Dark Lord is killing these women and to put the net out around the city and catch him. They'll just throw the net over *me* and be done with it," Grayson said seriously. "And one other thing—and this is not meant to scare you—but if this Dark Lord killed two women you know, who were associates of yours, did it occur to you that he knows where you are?"

Neala instinctively put her hand to her neck and turned stark white.

"I'm sorry, I keep saying insensitive things. Whoever this guy is, he won't get close to you," Grayson promised.

"How can you be so sure?" Neala asked in a quiet voice.

Grayson took a deep breath. "Because I'm not letting you out of my sight. You wanted my mother, well, you've got her," she said and enjoyed the stupefied look on the redhead. She took out her cell phone.

"Ma? Sorry. Yes, yes, I'm fine," she said, then rolled her eyes. "Okay. I swear on Grandma's grave that I'm telling you the truth. Now how would you like to have a guest for a few days?"

Neala shook her head and Grayson ignored her. "Yes, Dr. Rourke. I'll fill you in. We'll be there in an hour. Thanks, Ma, love you." She flipped the phone and hailed Tommy for the check.

"Detective, I will not inconvenience your mother. This is silly. I can take care of myself."

"I'm sure you can take of yourself and anyone else, but this story is too bizarre not to have some merit, and as long as you're in my city with a nutbag running around, you'll do as I say. I'll take you back to your hotel and you check out. Tell no one where you're going, not even at the museum," she said as she pulled her out of the restaurant.

"This is kidnapping!"

"Protective custody," she corrected her rudely and pushed her into the passenger seat.

Maeve stood at the stove and saw the headlights in the driveway. She glanced at the clock; it was nearly midnight. *Grayson better have a good reason for making Neala stay here.*

She ran to the door and Grayson smiled. "Hey, Ma," she said and pulled the angry redhead along.

Maeve noticed the tension between the two women. How could she not? Grayson practically dragged her into the kitchen.

"Hello, Maeve, your daughter has the manners of a goat," she said angrily, and Maeve nodded sadly in agreement.

"Gets it from her father, Neala. I tried to beat it out of her." She sighed.

Grayson laughed. She stripped off her black jacket and placed it on the back of the chair. She then slipped out of her holster and stretched.

"Now tell me, what's happened?" Maeve asked.

"Dr. Rourke knows both victims, and she could be in danger. I want her to stay here with you until she leaves in two days. No one knows where she is. I need to get a handle on all this," Grayson said as Neala sat down at the kitchen table and looked at Maeve. Grayson poured two cups of coffee and set one in front of Neala.

"Neala?" Maeve gently prodded. There was an agonizing moment of silence. It was so quiet in the kitchen Maeve could hear the clock on the wall.

"The Dark Lord, Maeve," Neala finally said in a low voice.

Maeve's back stiffened as she leaned back. She felt her daughter's eyes upon her.

"Ma?" Grayson sat down. She groaned and closed her eyes. "Why do I have the feeling that you know exactly what Dr. Rourke is talking about?"

Maeve still watched Neala. "It's true then?"

"What's true?" Grayson asked quickly.

"I-I think it tis, Maeve. They were going to contact you when they found out about these two women."

Grayson shot a look from her mother to Neala and back again. "They who?"

Maeve let out a long tired breath. "I cannot believe it."

"Believe what?" Grayson demanded and rapped her knuckles on the table several times.

Maeve gave her a weak smile. "Grayson, I want you to remember back, long, long ago when you had an open mind."

Grayson glared at her, and Maeve chuckled quietly, as did Neala. "Why?" she asked cautiously. "And I have an open mind."

"Not like you used to, sweetie." Maeve patted her hand. "Remember Sister Daniel, the abbess at St. Brigid's Monastery. Remember our conversations."

"What about them?" Grayson asked confused.

Maeve groaned helplessly. "It's your father's doing. Him and his logic. You can't have forgotten."

Grayson sported a helpless look and shook her head.

"Forgotten what, Ma?"

It was then Maeve noticed Grayson was scratching the palm of her hand, the nervous gesture she had since she was a little girl. She glanced at Neala, who was watching Grayson with interest but said nothing.

Maeve saw the look of exhaustion on her face and decided to forgo anything further for the time being. "Never mind, sweetie. It's late and you need some sleep."

Grayson nodded. "I will agree with you there, Ma. I'll take the couch. Dr. Rourke can have my old room."

"That old couch isn't long enough for you," Maeve said.

"I'm so tired I could sleep on a bed of nails. Tomorrow we talk, Dr. Rourke. Right now my brain is mush," she said through her yawns.

She walked out, locked up the house, and mumbled a good night as she grabbed her holster and jacket and left the kitchen once again.

Both women watched the retreating detective. Maeve then looked at Neala Rourke.

"Tell me what's happening, Neala."

"It's happening, Maeve. What we've protected all these centuries is in great danger. I don't know why Nan and Jane were killed in such a horrible fashion, and I don't know why here in Chicago. I don't know."

All at once, she was exhausted. Maeve stood.

"Why were they going to contact me?"

Neala ran her fingers through her red hair and shook her head. "I don't know. I didn't have a chance to talk to anyone. Between the exhibit and Nan and Jane dying, I haven't been able to keep a clear thought."

"What were they doing that got them killed?"

"I don't know, but I'm sure it has to do with the new findings in Ireland."

"Well, tomorrow, when you and Grayson have clear heads and aren't at each other's throats, we can talk about this," Maeve said, and Neala snorted sarcastically.

"Your daughter is—"

"I know, a goat or whatever you said earlier," Maeve said and struck a thoughtful pose. "I never saw her as a goat. An ass perhaps, but not a goat," she said seriously, and Neala laughed.

Maeve turned to her then. "Neala, don't be too hard on her. I know she hasn't said anything to you, but she's been through a great deal in the past two years. It nearly killed her. I don't know what brought her back, but I thank the gods above for their intervention. Someday, I hope she'll tell you. She needs to heal. And you being an ovate, the healer, perhaps you can help her."

"How did you know I was an ovate?" Neala asked as she put a hand on her arm.

Maeve smiled affectionately and patted her hand. "The same way you knew I was a Druidess when you first met me. Like speaks to like. We're all connected, sweetie," she said. "So is Grayson, if she'll get out of the 'cop' mode for a while. Now off to bed. It's late."

They walked out of the kitchen and Maeve shook her head. There lay Grayson on her stomach, looking like she threw herself at the old couch. One leg hung off and her left arm flopped on the floor. "Didn't even take her boots off, the silly ass," her mother said. "See, she is more of an ass than a goat."

Neala snorted and tried desperately not to laugh and wake Grayson. Between them, they got Grayson's boots off and lifted her leg onto the couch, causing a small snore from the tall detective. Neala took the afghan off the back of the couch and covered her with it.

Maeve stood back and watched as the redhead tucked it around her daughter, then lightly ran her fingers through the thick hair.

Whatever was happening, Maeve knew her daughter would find out. It was her way; she was the loyal warrior. Whether she believed it or not, Grayson was destined for this. Maeve hoped she was right all those years before when she let the memories fade for Grayson. She wanted a normal life for her only child. They warned her there would be a time, a time when Grayson would be called upon to fulfill her destiny. Part of Maeve hoped they were wrong—silly Irish mythology.

"Come, let's get you to bed," Maeve said and led Neala to

Grayson's room. "The three of us will figure this out."

The three of us. Threes, Maeve thought. Everything happens in threes. It was the Druid way of teaching all things. It was a good way—learning from nature, respecting it and the world around you. Now some force was toying with the ways of the old Druids.

It's happened, Neala had said. Maeve hoped that Neala was wrong.

She prayed to God and to the gods of old that she did the right thing with Grayson; she prayed Neala was wrong.

She prayed for her only daughter.

Chapter 10

As Neala set her suitcase on the chair, she readied herself for bed and glanced around the bedroom. *This is where Grayson MacCarthaigh lived as a child*, she thought with a smirk. She stood in front of the dresser and read the engravings on the trophies. *First Place, Most Valuable Player, Player of the Year, Team Captain*. For some reason, those fit the arrogant dark-haired woman downstairs.

Neala then looked at the picture of Maeve, her husband, and Grayson. She saw the green mountains in the background and knew the picture was of Ireland. Next to it was another picture of the three of them; only in the middle was a gorgeous blonde woman. Grayson had her cheek pressed against hers. She was smiling in a way that Neala had not yet seen. It was peaceful, that serene smile that only comes from total bliss. The detective looked entirely different in this picture.

Grayson needs to heal, Maeve had said. Perhaps she could help, she thought as she crawled into the old bed and snuggled the quilt around her. *If the arrogant fathead would let me*.

The image of Grayson sleeping in this bed flashed through her mind. What in the world made her think of that? She shook her head, pulled a pillow close, and faded off into a deep peaceful sleep.

Downstairs, Grayson woke with a start. She jumped up, completely disoriented. The couch? Then she remembered where she was. She walked upstairs and looked in on her mother who was sound asleep. Across the hall, she quietly opened the bedroom door. Dr. Rourke was fast asleep. She took a pair of shorts and slipped out of the bedroom.

Still in her slacks and shirt, she peeled them off, slipping back onto the couch in her sports bra and shorts. A lump in the middle cushion kept her tossing and turning for the remainder of the night. As she drifted off, she thought of Dr. Rourke in her bed upstairs.

What in the hell made you think of that, MacCarthaigh? God, get some sleep, she thought, and punched the pillow under her head and faded off into another fitful sleep.

Neala walked downstairs early the next morning and noticed the missing detective. She walked into the kitchen to find Grayson standing by the stove; she was wearing a pair of shorts and white sports bra. Neala swallowed convulsively as she noticed the strong back muscles and defined triceps. Looking closer, she noticed she wasn't moving.

"Detective MacCarthaigh?" she whispered and walked toward her. She peeked around the tall woman and bit her lip not to laugh. She was sound asleep leaning against the refrigerator.

She watched Grayson for a moment, remembering Maeve's words the night before. She asked Grayson to remember long, long ago when she had an open mind. At the time, Neala thought it was very amusing seeing the befuddled, embarrassed look on the detective. Now she wondered if all the stories she had heard from the abbess at St. Brigid's Monastery were true. Were Nan and Jane's deaths connected with her and the exhibit? With that, the coffee on the stove hissed loudly as it perked and boiled over. Grayson was instantly awake.

"I'm up, I'm up," she said quickly and looked around. She noticed Neala and chuckled.

"You were asleep standing up. That's amazing," Neala said, trying to avoid looking at the firm breasts and the nipples straining against the cotton fabric. Grayson smiled sleepily, which Neala thought extremely sexy. She turned her attention to the coffee.

"I tend to sleep when I can. I actually slept for nearly thirty minutes once standing at the airport. It was a record," she said proudly.

Neala laughed. "You still look tired. I'm sure that couch was horrid. Why don't you go back to your room and sleep for a while longer? I don't have to be at the museum until ten."

Grayson closed her eyes and leaned against the counter. "Go on, Detective. Go back to bed." She guided her out of the kitchen and upstairs to her bedroom.

"Maybe just for a few minutes. I gotta call Stan. Don't let me sleep too long. There's too much to do." She groaned happily as she saw her old bed. She sighed as she stretched out, her legs a bit too long. "Just a few minutes, 'kay?"

"All right, I'll wake you," Neala said in a soft voice.

Grayson smiled as she faded off. "You have such a soft voice, Vic."

Neala could barely hear her as Grayson fell sound asleep. It was then she noticed the jagged scar by her collarbone and quelled the urge to run her fingers along the scarred tissue. For a moment or two, she watched her as she slept. Grayson looked younger. No worry lines etched on her brow, which she touched lightly, brushing back the thick lock of hair.

"Sleep well, Detective," she whispered, then slipped out of the room.

When Grayson woke, the sunlight streamed into the bedroom and the aroma of coffee and bacon filled her senses. Grayson tried to ignore the subtle fragrance of the doctor's perfume that lingered. Stretching, she looked at her watch.

"Fuck!" she cursed and jumped out of bed. She grabbed the phone and called the precinct.

"Good morning, Detective MacCarthaigh," Stan's voice called out. "Late night?"

"Yes, but not much fun. I had an odd and confusing talk with Dr. Rourke and my mother. I'll be there in thirty minutes."

"Don't rush. You sound pooped. I told Lieutenant that you were questioning the doctor this morning. Besides, I'm waiting on the FBI. I'm checking as you said, trying to match any murders with ours. I agree with you, Gray, so I went international. I should have something back this morning. Why don't you see what you can get out of the leggy redhead and I'll just sit here behind the desk? You have all the fun, you realize that?"

Grayson snorted. "Right, some fun. I have to drop her off at the museum, then I'll be in. Call my cell if anything comes up. Thanks, Stan."

"Will do."

In ten minutes, Grayson had showered and slipped into a pair of very faded blue jeans and a white T-shirt. She ran her fingers through her damp hair as she jogged downstairs.

She barged into the kitchen to see Dr. Rourke at the stove and her mother sitting at the table drinking tea. Both women jumped.

"It's nearly nine o'clock!" Grayson exclaimed angrily.

"When I told you I wanted a grandfather clock with chimes, this is not what I meant, kiddo. Good morning," her mother said with a grin.

"Why did you let me sleep so late? Dr. Rourke, I told you to wake me in a few minutes," she continued blustering.

The doctor whirled around with a spatula in her hand. "You were dead on your feet, Detective MacCarthaigh. You needed to sleep. You're welcome."

Maeve drank her tea and watched. "There's enough spark between you to light up Chicago."

Grayson glanced down at her mother, who gave her a scathing, motherly look, which immediately reduced Grayson to feeling like a five-year-old.

"Thanks," she mumbled and walked over to the refrigerator and took out the container of orange juice.

"In a glass," her mother warned.

The urge to drink right out of the container was so great—she reached for a glass. "You don't have to make me breakfast."

"Your mother is hungry, sit down."

Maeve gave her daughter an innocent smile and batted her eyes. Grayson sat.

"You still look tired, sweetie," her mother said.

"I'm fine, Ma, please don't worry." Grayson drank her juice and ate ravenously. She hadn't eaten dinner the night before or lunch for that matter.

"That was great, thanks," she said. As she finished, her cell phone went off, and she flipped it open. "MacCarthaigh."

"Gray? Now no yelling," Stan said quietly. "But the FBI is taking over the case. Seems they found a couple of murders in Ireland, back in nineteen fifty-two and ninety-eight. It's the same. Two women bound, marked, and throats slit. Lieutenant Keller wants you here right away."

Grayson stood and paced as she listened. "Goddamn it!" She slammed her fist on the refrigerator. "Fuck, Stan. Right. I'll be right there."

"This sucks, Gray, but the feds are involved now."

Grayson snapped her phone shut.

"What is it, Gray?" her mother asked.

Grayson walked up to both of them. "The FBI is taking over the case. And do you know why they're taking over?" She looked down at the doctor, who frowned deeply. "It seems that two other women were murdered the same way. Both bound the same, cut the same, then their throats slit—in Ireland. And do you know when it happened?" She didn't wait for an answer. "Nineteen fifty-two and nineteen ninety-eight. Obviously, they never found the murderer."

Neala and Maeve sat there in stunned silence. Grayson still watched Dr. Rourke. "I don't suppose you know anything about this, Dr. Rourke."

The doctor shot her an angry look. "Do you think I would know something like that and not tell you? God, you're…" She stood and Grayson roughly grabbed her.

"Yes, Doctor, I do. I think you know what's going on, but I can't go to Lieutenant Keller or now the FBI, with some insane story of a Dark Lord…"

"Grayson, you and I need to talk, sweetie," her mother said. "And you're right. You can't tell them about the Dark Lord."

Grayson angrily took a deep breath. "Mother, I love you, but if you don't level with me—"

"I will. It will all make sense," she promised.

Grayson took another deep breath and let it out slowly. "I highly doubt that, Ma," she said and kissed her head. "But we'll give it a shot."

She drained the contents of her coffee cup. "I have to go downtown. Dr. Rourke, please get ready. I'll drive you to the museum."

"I'll—"

"Dr. Rourke Please, will you just for once do as I ask?"

Neala glared at the angry face and stormed out of the kitchen. Grayson sank into the kitchen chair. "Shit."

"Gray, what's going to happen?"

"The Chicago Bureau is already handling it. Stan had to hand over all our work, which I guess wasn't much. I have to go talk to Lieutenant Keller. He wants to see me right away. Damn it, Ma. This thing that Neala is talking about, it is true?"

Maeve looked her in the eye, which scared the shit out of Grayson. "There's something big going on and Neala is in the middle of it. You don't honestly believe she would know about those poor women and not tell you or the police, do you?"

"I don't know, Mother. I just don't know anymore." Grayson sat back.

Neala walked into the kitchen. Grayson's heart ached at the dejected look on her face. "Thanks, Maeve, for the bed. It was nice to see you again."

"Hold on. Nothing has changed, Dr. Rourke. You're still staying here until you leave in two days. I may not be on this case anymore, but you're still in my city and there's still a murderer running around. I'll pick you up this afternoon at three. You're coming back here."

"God, you're insufferable," Neala said.

Maeve grinned and avoided the angry look. "Yes, but not a goat," she said into her teacup. Neala laughed and now avoided Grayson.

Grayson ignored the exchange and slipped into her leather jacket. She kissed her mother on the head. "I want you to stay in contact with me all day."

"Why?"

"I don't know. It's just a feeling. Just call me throughout the day. I mean it, Mother."

"When you call me Mother, I know you mean it. All right, I'll check in, Detective MacCarthaigh." She kissed her cheek. "You two get going and no arguing while you're driving. You're in my car."

Grayson dropped Dr. Rourke off at the museum. Neither woman spoke during the ride.

"I'll pick you up at three," Grayson said firmly.

"Fine."

She winced as the car door slammed.

Grayson walked into the precinct and saw Sergeant Cooper, who rolled his eyes. "This is bullshit, Detective," he said. Grayson nodded and patted his shoulder but said nothing.

Stan was in Keller's office with several other suits. *Fucking FBI*, she thought angrily.

"Detective MacCarthaigh, my office please," Keller said. Grayson walked with a purposeful gait as she watched the old man. He looked her right in the eyes, and Grayson saw the resigned anger in his watery blue eyes. "Temper," he whispered as she passed. She took a deep calming breath.

Captain Jenkins was also in the room. She looked around at the five faces, settling on Stan, who smiled slightly and winked.

"Gentlemen, we're a fire hazard," she said as she squeezed around one chair. One agent smirked and stood, offering his chair. Grayson graciously declined and leaned against the wall.

Jenkins spoke first. "Detective MacCarthaigh, in light of what Detective Resnick found, the FBI now has jurisdiction. The two women in Ireland are definitely connected with these two recent murders. You will give them your cooperation completely," he added as he watched her.

"Yes, sir."

The old captain regarded Grayson warily. "Did you find anything from Dr. Rourke?"

All eyes were on her. She shrugged and looked around the room. The three agents seemed bored. One was looking at his tie. The taller older agent with short brown hair watched her intently.

"Dr. Rourke knew both women. They went to college together back in Ireland. They had similar interests in ancient Irish history. Other than that, I don't know."

"Why didn't you tell us this before?" the agent asked.

Grayson smiled slightly. "I just found it out last night."

"After you left with her?"

Grayson tried not to show her surprise. "Yes, she told me over coffee. I called Stan this morning to tell him. That's when I got the wonderful news that you guys were gonna save us, Agent...?"

"Morrison," the older man said, his face void of any emotion. "We usually get the call when you locals can't handle it."

Grayson took an angry step toward the smirking agent.

"Detective MacCarthaigh, that's enough," Jenkins said firmly. "We're on the same side here, people. Let's leave everything else outside. Now do you have everything you need?" he asked Morrison, who nodded. He was still smirking at Grayson, who stared him down while she breathed deeply through her nose.

"I would like to talk with this Dr. Rourke. Just in case you missed something, Detective MacCarthaigh."

Grayson wanted to bury her fist in his ugly face as she clenched it by her sides. "She's at the Field Museum for the next two days," Grayson said in a steady voice. She flipped out her phone and dialed the number.

Grayson's heart skipped a beat when she heard her voice. "Dr. Rourke."

"It's Detective MacCarthaigh, Doctor. Would it be possible if I stopped by later today? An FBI agent would like to speak with you. They'll be handling the case and they just have a few questions."

There was silence for a moment. "Grayson, I'm worried."

"Don't be, Doctor. I'll be there, as well." Grayson thought she heard a sigh of relief.

"I should do this?"

"Yes. How about two o'clock?"

"That'll be fine, I'll see you then."

Grayson flipped the phone shut. Morrison never took his eyes off her. "Well, I think we have all we need. I'll meet you at the museum, Detective MacCarthaigh."

"As you wish, Special Agent Morrison," Grayson said with more than a hint of sarcasm. *Fuckin' feds.*

Chapter 11

When the two agents left with files in tow, Grayson sat in the vacated seat. Stan loosened his tie.

"Well, that's that," the captain said. "I don't like handing any case over to the feds, you both know that. However, in light of the previous murders, it's now a federal issue. Let's make the best of it." Jenkins said this mostly to Grayson, who was scowling deeply. "Detective MacCarthaigh, do you agree?"

"No, sir, I don't. Stan and I have worked our asses off for nearly a month. It's been kept out of the papers and now with these other murders, we just needed a little more time... Shit!"

"Detective, I understand your passion, but it's out of my hands and your temper is not helping. I'm sure there's enough crime to go around," he said and walked out of the small office.

The three of them sat there in silence. Stan was the first to speak. "Well, let's not make a federal case out of this."

Grayson hid her grin and glanced at the lieutenant, who took a deep breath but said nothing.

"What is it about the FBI that I just don't trust?" Stan continued.

Keller chuckled quietly.

"Well," Stan said. "I got an anonymous tip on the case Detective Spaulding was working on before she had her meltdown."

Grayson had forgotten about their other case. Young punks were dying off like flies. Misguided youth following some cult hero, they thought. When Detective Spaulding showed up in a mental hospital, a couple of weeks earlier, the case was given to Grayson and Stan.

Grayson knew Carey Spaulding; she almost knew her too

well. One night not long ago, she and Carey were out with other officers after work. They went to their favorite watering hole to unwind. Grayson tried to drown the images of Vic in a whiskey glass, and Carey, being the opportunistic woman she was, naturally saw the chance in Grayson's vulnerability. As they left the bar that night, things almost got out of hand as they stood by Grayson's motorcycle.

"I can't believe you ride one of these," Carey said absently and ran her fingers over the leather seat. "I don't think it's a good idea for you to ride this home, Grayson."

"Neither do I," Grayson admitted. She knew she drank far too much. "I'll get a cab."

As she pulled out her cell phone, she swayed momentarily, long enough for Carey to reach out and grab her around the waist. "Easy there. Why don't you let me take you home?"

Grayson looked into her dark eyes, and for a moment, she saw Vic. Carey reached up and brushed the lock of hair off her forehead. She then leaned in and kissed Grayson. For an instant, Grayson responded to the kiss, then just as quickly, she pulled back.

Carey sported a challenging look but said nothing.

"I don't think your girlfriend would like this," Grayson said and stepped back. She stood on the curb and looked for a taxi. Carey walked up behind her and ran her hand up and down her leather jacket.

"We're not getting along. Alex is, well, she's naïve."

Grayson hailed the cab and turned to Carey. "Naïve?" she repeated and laughed. "I saw the doctor. She didn't look naïve to me."

"It's this case, I guess. I don't know who these kids are following. I just need to blow off some steam."

The cab pulled up to the curb. Carey frowned and stepped back. "Blow it off with your girlfriend. Talk to her, Detective," Grayson said and opened the car door. "You got two choices. Go to your redhead, or I'll drop you off at home. You're not driving, either."

Grayson remembered now Detective Spaulding didn't go to

her girlfriend's. She was dropped off, and it wasn't at her home. It was then that Grayson realized Carey Spaulding was an asshole. She was an egomaniac, and her detective skills left little to be desired. Even now, no one knew how she wound up in that mental hospital. However, Stan was right—the unlikable Detective Spaulding did indeed have a meltdown.

"Somebody called in this morning. Said he had information but didn't want to come in. He sounded petrified. So I thought I'd go out there since we haven't anything else to do today," he added sarcastically and angrily. Grayson grinned. It was the first time he showed any anger.

"Where are you meeting him?" Keller asked.

"In an abandoned warehouse on the North Side," Stan said and flipped through his notes. "If I'm not mistaken, it's where those victims were found."

"Both of you go and don't do anything stupid without backup," the lieutenant ordered.

"So you're really pissed, aren't you?" Stan asked as he drove out of the downtown area toward the North Side.

Grayson let out a deep breath. "Yes. I'm really pissed. Damn it, I know Dr. Rourke knows something. She was on the verge of telling me and now, shit."

"It sucks, but maybe with the murders in Ireland, they'll have something to go on and catch this sick fuck."

"Maybe. Hey, thanks for taking my mother home last night."

"No problem. She's a nice lady. Kathy and she talked all the way home. I didn't know your mother was into all the magic and Druid stuff. Hell, I didn't think that Druid shit was around anymore. Can she really do spells?"

Grayson cringed at the idea. She remembered when she was a kid she was constantly tormented by the kids at school. Maeve MacCarthaigh was not a witch, but Sally Edwards had a big mouth. Once it was out that she taught a class on Druidism at a junior college, it was all over. Grayson got many a bloody nose defending her mother. However, she caused more bloody noses than she received.

"No, Stan. She doesn't practice Wicca…anymore."

"What's Wicca?" he asked seriously. "Anymore?"

"White magic. It's a religion. You know a spell for good weather, good crops. They worship nature." She rubbed her temples. "Can we talk about something else?'

Stan laughed. "Sure, how about them Cubbies?"

"I'd rather talk about Druids."

They pulled into the parking lot of the abandoned building. "This figures. Couldn't your anonymous source have us meet at Starbucks?" Grayson asked as they got out.

"He said he would be right outside," Stan said and glanced at his watch. "Right on time."

They looked around the old building with its broken windows and tall weeds that took over the front entrance. "I don't like this, Stan. Something's not right."

They slowly walked up to the front entrance and Grayson drew her weapon. Stan did the same. "Okay, we check this out quickly," she said, and Stan nodded.

Walking inside the dark entryway, the pungent odor of stale urine filled the air.

"Shit!"

"That too," Grayson whispered in agreement as she looked in all directions. Stan swallowed as they walked over broken glass and empty beer cans. It was too quiet for her liking.

Suddenly, something moved overhead. Both jumped when a dozen pigeons flew out of the rafters. "Geezus!" Stan exclaimed and held onto his heart.

Grayson laughed as she straightened. "Done in by a pigeon, that would be fitting after all this," she said and looked around. "Stan, let's get out of here. I don't like this."

With that, they heard the movement behind them. Both whirled around with weapons drawn. A young man, looking decidedly petrified walked out of the dark hallway. Grayson studied the young man, quickly committing everything to memory: baggy jeans, baggy leather jacket; ears, lip, eyebrow pierced. Hair—white blonde, dark circles under his eyes. Panic splashed all over his face.

"You cops?" he asked as he rubbed his arms in a nervous gesture.

"Us cops," Stan replied. "Who you?"

Grayson cautiously watched him. "What's your name?"

The young man shook his head. "You can't stop him."

"Who?" Stan asked.

Grayson glanced around the building. She really didn't like the feel of this.

"He's not human," the young man tried to explain. "It's gotta be him." He ran his fingers through his hair.

Grayson shot the youth a curious look. "You need to tell us what you know so we can stop him."

The young man laughed. "You can't stop him. I told you."

"Why don't you tell us who he is and let us decide?" Stan said in a steady voice. "What do you know about the kids who were killed? Who were they following? What kind of hold does he have on you?"

He stared at nothing in particular, then pulled up his sleeve to the elbow and presented the inside of his arm.

Grayson leaned in, fully expecting to see needle marks. She frowned deeply at the two puncture wounds on his wrist. They looked swollen and raw and decidedly deep.

Stan raised an eyebrow. "That's an unusual wound, pal. What happened? Was you bit by a vampire?" he asked with sarcasm and looked up.

The young punk swallowed convulsively. Stan chuckled quietly; Grayson glared at him.

As he tried to pull his arm away, Grayson held it. "What's that?"

Farther up his arm, she saw it—the same markings that were cut into both victims. It looked like a tattoo. "Where did you get this?" She pointed to the markings.

The young man roughly tried to pull his arm away. "Look, lemme go. This was a mistake. I—" He yanked his arm free of Grayson's grasp and pulled the sleeve down while he frantically looked down the darkened hallway.

Stan did the same; Grayson continued to watch the petrified

young man. "What's got you so scared?" she asked in a low almost reassuring voice.

That's when she heard it—an animal howling.

Stan heard it, too. "What the fuck is that?"

"Sounds like a wolf," Grayson said in a quiet voice. It's exactly what it sounded like—a wolf, somewhere off in the distance.

"In the middle of Chicago?" Stan asked.

She glanced at the young man who looked as though he might vomit. She grabbed his upper arm and pulled him around to her. "Okay, what the fuck is going on? Vampires and werewolves? Don't fuck with me right now, pal. I am so not in the mood."

He backed up and shook his head. "You have no idea what he can do. I saw him. He killed her—"

"Who? The others? Is he the one they're following?" Stan asked quickly.

"No! But he knows about us now," the young man said frantically.

"Us?" Grayson prodded. "What do you mean us?" She looked down at the two small holes in his wrist. "You need to come with us. We can get to the bottom of this, but not here—" She stopped when they heard the low howling.

"Okay, never mind. I was wrong," he said quickly and backed up.

Grayson grabbed his arm.

"Lemme go! I was wrong," he cried and pushed past them and dashed toward the door.

"Hey!" Stan called.

As they turned to chase down the terrified punk, Grayson saw it near the entrance behind a small crate—the small detonation device with the wires attached.

"Fuck, Stan, run!" she yelled and grabbed him by the arm.

The explosion was horrific. As they ran through the door and into the parking lot, the force from the blast sent them flying through the air along with the shards of glass and concrete.

Through the din, Grayson heard Stan scream. The side of Grayson's head exploded in pain as her body hit the ground. With a painful groan, she looked through the smoke to see Stan lying there motionless. Wiping the blood off her face, she crawled to him.

"Stan!" she cried and cautiously turned him over. A long shard of glass stuck out of his abdomen. His eyes fluttered open. "Lay still, Stan."

She scrambled to the car and called for an ambulance. It was then she saw the young punk, lying in a pool of blood and debris, his leg bent underneath him at an odd angle. Grayson saw his lifeless eyes staring at the sky.

Within moments, she heard the sirens. "You hold on, goddamn it, Stan. Don't you dare leave me," she said as she gently took his hands away.

The long thick piece of glass protruded from his left side. He wasn't losing much blood with the glass firmly imbedded.

"Stay with me, Stan," she said firmly.

He nodded and opened his eyes. "Gray, listen…"

"Fuck you. Save your strength," she said, not wanting to hear the inevitable.

Stan smiled and grimaced. He reached a blood-soaked hand up and grabbed her shirt. "Gray, please."

Grayson glared down at him. "No, I'm not taking care of Kathy or the kids. That's your job and you're not weaseling out of it. Just lay still. The ambulance is here," she finished in a softer voice.

"Thanks."

The paramedics stabilized Stan, and in a matter of minutes, he was in the ambulance.

"Detective, you need to sit down before you pass out," a paramedic said, leading her to the back of another ambulance. She pulled away from him.

"Gray!" Keller called as he shot out of his car. "What the fuck happened?"

The paramedic was trying to stop the bleeding from the jagged slash over her left eyebrow and cheek. "You need stitches, ma'am."

Grayson glared at the young paramedic. She explained to Mike what had happened.

"Sonofabitch, let's get you to the hospital, as well. Don't even think about arguing," he added and turned away barking his orders.

Stan was in surgery as Grayson lay in the emergency room.

"Well, I'm not going to lie to you, Detective. That wound over your eye and cheek is extensive. You've got a severely bruised right shoulder, lucky it's not dislocated, and various contusions on your back and neck. You're lucky you were wearing that leather," the doctor said as he picked up said jacket; the back of it was peppered with small holes and rips.

Grayson sighed and put her head back. "How's Stan?" The side of her head was pounding.

With that, Keller poked his head in. "C'mon in, she's not going anywhere," the doctor said.

He walked up to Gray and stood by the bedside.

"How's Stan?" she asked again.

Keller nodded. "Still in surgery, but they think he'll be fine. We won't know for a while."

"Did you call…?"

Keller put his hand on her shoulder. "I called Kathy. She's up in the waiting room. I called your mother. Just relax and do as the nice doctor says." He winced and looked away as the nurse administered several shots of lidocaine.

Grayson laughed quietly. "Go wait outside, Lieutenant, before you faint."

"I'll be outside. I'll wait for Maeve," he promised, and Grayson gave him a grateful albeit painful smile.

Maeve and Neala rushed into the ER as Mike Keller walked out of the cubicle.

"Maeve," he called.

Suddenly, she was standing right in front of the big man, his strong hands on her shoulders. "She's fine, just a few bumps and bruises. She needs a few stitches. You know Grayson."

Maeve put her hands to her face and let out a sob of relief. All the way over, she wouldn't allow herself to think of her daughter seriously hurt again as she was two years before.

"Thank you, Mike."

Mike smiled and kissed her forehead. "She's a tough one. Like her old man," he said and pulled back. He looked at the redhead.

"Oh, I'm sorry. Mike, this is Dr. Neala Rourke," Maeve said. Mike shook her hand.

"Is she really...?" Neala started to ask when they heard Grayson's voice.

"I'm not staying. Just stitch it up and let me get the fuck out of here!"

Maeve shook her head. "She's all right," she assured Neala.

Chapter 12

Nearly an hour later, Neala was curious and worried as she peeked into the cubicle just in time to see the doctor stripping off the latex gloves and tossing them in the wastebasket. Neala saw the blood and shivered. Since she got the call from Maeve, her heart had been in her stomach. The thought of this woman hurt made her heart ache in a way Neala had never thought possible. She shivered uncontrollably now.

"Who claims the detective?" the doctor asked as he walked out of the cubicle.

Maeve raised her hand. "Guilty. She's my daughter."

The doctor chuckled and held out his hand. "She'll be fine. She took thirty sutures above her left eye, twenty on her cheek. It was a jagged cut, I'm afraid there'll be scarring. She's lucky. The glass missed her eye by inches. Her right shoulder will be sore as hell for about a week. Keep it iced and immobile as much as possible. As I told her, she was lucky to be wearing a leather jacket. It may have saved her life. She's got a few lacerations on her neck and upper back. Nothing serious, they needed no suturing. She wouldn't let me give her a shot of painkiller. I honestly thought she was going to hit me," he said seriously. "I'd like to keep her overnight, but I can't force her. She'll be fine in a few minutes. Just make sure she rests for a few days."

"I will, Doctor, thank you."

"I noticed a scar near her left clavicle and back. It looks recent," he added and looked at Keller. "Gunshot?"

Mike Keller nodded. "She was shot two years ago. Bullet went through, shattered her collarbone, and exited out her back."

He and Maeve exchanged a sad smile. Neala listened wild

eyed and wondered what else happened to Detective Sergeant Grayson MacCarthaigh two years earlier.

"Hmm," the doctor grunted. "Well, it was good work. Take care of her. I have a feeling that won't be an easy job."

"Thank you again, Doctor," Maeve said.

They walked into the cubicle to see Grayson sitting on the side of the examination table. Tears formed in Neala's green eyes as she saw the jagged stitching on Grayson's brow and cheek. The bruise was already forming. Small cuts dotted the back of her neck. Dried blood smeared her once white T-shirt. She took a deep controlling breath.

Grayson looked up and smiled. "Hey, Ma. Sorry. I didn't mean to scare you," she said, sounding like a wayward schoolgirl. Maeve walked up to her and pulled her into her arms.

"There's no reason for you to be sorry, kiddo. Are you all right?"

Grayson nodded and pulled back. "I'm fine. Let's get out of here," she said firmly, then noticed Neala. "Dr. Rourke, thanks for taking care of her."

"It was my pleasure, Detective MacCarthaigh. Are you sure you shouldn't be staying tonight?"

Grayson looked into her eyes for a moment. Neala felt the blood surging through her veins as she gazed into the confused blue pools. "N-no, I'm fine," Grayson finally said and stood. She swayed for a moment. "I need to go see Kathy. I don't want her to be alone."

"Gray..." Keller started, and Grayson gave him an incredulous look.

"He's my partner," she said logically and grabbed her jacket.

Kathy sat in the small waiting room with another woman.

Grayson smiled and walked up to her. "Any word?" she asked, easing onto the cushion next to her. Kathy shook her head. Grayson saw the trembling lips and put her good arm around her. That did it. Kathy started to cry and buried her head in Grayson's shoulder.

"He'll be all right, Kathy. I was with him, he was awake and alert the entire time. He'll be fine," Grayson whispered as she rocked her.

Maeve and Neala pulled up two chairs. Kathy pulled away from Grayson's comforting embrace and sniffed.

"I promised myself I wouldn't cry. I want to be strong. Nothing has ever happened to Stan in fifteen years on the force. If anything happens to him…"

"Nothing is going to happen. Stan has a good strong heart," Grayson said firmly.

Kathy smiled and wiped her tears. She then got a good look at Grayson. She reached up and gingerly touched her cheek. "Good God, Grayson. Are you all right?" She winced at the sight. "I'm sorry. This is my sister, Melanie."

Grayson smiled and offered her hand as did her mother and Neala. "Where are the boys?"

"They're with my mother," Kathy said and took a deep breath. Her sister put an arm around her and gave her a reassuring hug.

Neala saw the exhaustion on her face. "Well, how about some coffee?" she asked. Melanie stood and ran her fingers through her short blonde hair.

"I'll go with you," she said.

"Thank you, Dr. Rourke," Kathy said.

"Neala and you're welcome," she said and walked away.

"She's a nice woman," Kathy said as they watched her walk down the hall with her sister.

Grayson nodded. "Yes, she is." She watched the redhead walk down the hall to the elevator.

After two more hours, the doctor finally walked into the waiting room. Grayson stood and stifled a groan; she put an arm around Kathy, giving her a quick reassuring hug.

"Mrs. Resnick? I'm Dr. Curtin. Your husband is doing fine," he said, and Kathy put her hands to her face and sobbed. Grayson tightened her arm around her. Kathy quickly recovered and wiped her tears.

"The shard of glass was deeper than we thought. It lacerated one kidney, which we repaired. However, we had to remove his spleen. He can certainly live without it. He'll have to be careful of infections from now on, but he'll recover completely. He'll be in for a couple of weeks, then home for at least six. You can see him in a few minutes, they're just getting him into a room."

As Kathy and Grayson stood at Stan's bedside, Grayson noticed he looked too pale for her liking. Kathy held onto his hand, gently stroking up and down. His eyelids fluttered as he focused on Kathy. He smiled slightly.

"Hello, wife," he whispered, and Kathy swallowed her tears and smiled.

"Hello, husband. Don't think this is going to get you out of taking me shopping," she said, desperately trying not to cry. Stan grinned and closed his eyes.

"Take Gray. I'm sure she loves to shop."

Grayson laughed quietly. "Not on your life, partner. You took a vow."

Instantly, she remembered Vicky and all those years ago. Her heart ached and her head pounded in pain. She took a deep calming breath and smiled.

"God, Gray, your face. Are you okay?" he asked.

"I'm fine. You get some rest. I'll see to Kathy and the boys."

Stan nodded. "Thanks. That means the world to me."

Grayson winked, and as she started to walk away, Stan grabbed her forearm. Grayson stopped and gave him a curious look. "What?" she asked and grinned. "No, I will not bring you a beer."

"In that building, Gray. What was that kid talking about? What were those marks on his arm? And that wound? I was joking when I made that crack about a vampire."

"I should hope so," Grayson said seriously.

"But we both heard it."

Kathy interrupted them. "Heard what?"

Grayson was watching Stan—he was fading fast. "We heard a wolf howling," he said, still looking at Grayson.

"Stan—"

"A wolf?" Kathy asked and gave both a skeptical glance. "In

Chicago?"

"Let's skip the Sci-Fi Channel for now." Grayson gently pulled his hand off her arm. "Here," she motioned to Kathy, "you hold this. It belongs to you."

Kathy laughed and held onto her husband's hand.

"Whatever that kid knew, he took with him," Grayson said. "Whatever Detective Spaulding knows, we won't know until she comes back. Now you get some rest and let Kathy baby you. I'll check in later."

She walked out of the room, leaving the couple to their intimate moment. She remembered her own intimate moment with Vicky just before she died. She leaned against the wall and closed her eyes.

"You live, damn you, Grayson MacCarthaigh," Vic whispered through her pain. "You live and love and be happy, or I'll come back and haunt you for eternity."

Tears streamed down Grayson's face as she held onto her cold hand. "Haunt me then, Vic. Just don't leave me alone in this world," she begged helplessly.

Vicky smiled as the tears pooled in Grayson's blue eyes. "You'll never be alone, Gray. Please promise me," she said, her voice failing her. Grayson shook her head furiously.

"No! I won't promise. You're not going to die. You fucking hold on, goddamn it!" she cursed angrily and pulled her into her arms. Blood soaked her hands as she held on.

"I love you."

Grayson heard the whisper as the woman she loved simply died in her arms. Grayson MacCarthaigh looked to the heavens and let out a loud mournful wail.

"No!" she cried and rocked the blonde woman back and forth. The paramedic placed a hand on her shoulder.

"Detective…"

Grayson pushed them away. "No! You fucking can't have her. You can't have her." She sobbed and buried her head in her cold neck.

"Detective, please…"

"Detective?"

Grayson quickly opened her eyes to see Neala standing in front of her. "I think you need to get some rest."

Grayson took a deep breath and nodded. She then noticed her mother standing beside her. Maeve smiled fondly and nodded in understanding. Grayson's lip quivered slightly as she looked down in the blue watery eyes.

Maeve reached up and gently touched her battered face. "I know, sweetie. I know. Let's go home now," she said, and Grayson shook her head.

"I want to make sure Kathy gets home," she said in a tired voice.

"Her sister is here. You need to get off your feet, Grayson. Come now," her mother said.

Neala listened to the tender exchange and wiped the tears from her eyes. With that, Kathy Resnick walked out and closed the door.

"How is he?" Maeve asked, and Kathy nodded with a smile.

"He'll be fine." She looked up at Grayson. Her face was bruised and the sutures looked like a rugged road map along her brow and cheek. "He told me you pulled him out of that building, Grayson. You saved his life." She hugged her fiercely.

Grayson winced but held on to the shaking woman. "He's my partner, Kathy. He'd do the same for me," she assured her. "Your sister is in the waiting room. Would you like me to take you home? You haven't eaten and I'm sure the boys are hungry."

Kathy cocked her head to one side and shook her head in amazement. "What force of nature brought you into our lives, Detective MacCarthaigh, I will never know, but I will forever thank them. No, you get home and rest. Melanie will take me home. She's going to stay with us for a week or so."

Grayson barely remembered the ride home. She vaguely remembered getting into bed. She recalled Dr. Rourke's concerned look and her mother's soft voice pleading with her not to argue.

She must have dozed off, for when she opened her eyes, she saw Dr. Rourke sitting in a chair pulled up by her bedside. Her head was resting on the back of the chair, her eyes closed. Grayson blinked, sending the searing pain through her temple. Gingerly, she reached up and felt the heavy sutures on her brow and cheek. *Fuck*, she thought, as she tried to move. Wincing, she realized her right arm was immobile and freezing. Then she remembered the day.

Whatever that young punk knew, he took with him to his grave. And who planted that explosive device? If Grayson hadn't seen it when she did, they both would surely be dead. Once again, she tried to move, and her body rebelled as she let out a deep groan, which woke the slumbering doctor.

Neala immediately shot forward and put a hand on her arm. "Lay still, Detective, please." She sat on the edge of the bed.

Grayson let out a dejected sigh. "What time is it?"

"It's nearly ten o'clock. You've been out for several hours. Can I get you anything?"

Grayson let out a small chortle. "For instance?"

Neala laughed quietly. "I see your point. How about a drink of water?" She didn't wait for a reply. She reached for the glass as Grayson reached for it. "Lay still. I don't want you spilling it all over you." She put her hand on the back of the detective's neck, mindful of the small cuts.

Grayson allowed the doctor to put the glass to her lips as she gulped the cool water. "Easy now," Neala cooed, and Grayson nodded, then lay back against the pillows.

"Thanks. I'm all trussed up here," she said impatiently.

"The doctor said to keep your shoulder iced," she said, "but I think it's nothing but water now." She grinned and removed the ice pack.

"Thanks," she said, looking into the green eyes.

"You're welcome," she said kindly. "Now are you hungry? I know it's late, but Maeve's been cooking since we got you to bed."

Grayson laughed. "She has a tendency to do that when she's upset."

"Well, she's doin' wondrous things with a beef roast. Why don't you get a little more rest? I'll bring you something in a bit."

Grayson moved uncomfortably under the blanket. "I'm fine. I don't need any rest. I just need to get out of bed."

Neala raised an eyebrow. "You're not used to bein' taken care of, are you?" she asked, though it was not a question. Grayson glared at her and struggled to sit up. Neala watched as Grayson finally sat on the edge of the bed.

Grayson realized she was wearing an unfamiliar pair of flannel pajama bottoms and a tank top. Neala noticed the confused look.

"They're mine. I hope you don't mind, but your clothes were a bit bloodied."

Grayson offered a curious grin. "Who changed me?"

Neala blushed horribly. "Why don't you lie back and I'll bring you a tray?" she asked, avoiding the question completely and in doing so, answered it. Grayson grinned at the crimson face.

"Nope, I'm getting up." She stood too quickly and swayed slightly. Neala was at her side, her arm encircling the trim muscular waist. Grayson looked into the green eyes that gazed into hers. After a moment, she grinned wildly. "You can let me go now. I think I can make it."

Neala immediately dropped her hand and stepped back. She then glared at the cocky grin on the detective. "You're an arrogant one, Grayson MacCarthaigh," she said and marched out of the room. "I hope you don't fall flat on your face!" She yelled and slammed the door on the chuckling detective.

"Is she up?" Maeve asked. She then saw the angry doctor and sighed. "She's up."

"Your daughter is an arrogant—"

"I know—a goat or whatever we decided. I take it she won't stay in bed and she's coming down for something to eat."

"She's a stubborn bull, that one," Neala said as she sat at the kitchen table.

"First she's a goat, now she's a bull. Heavens, Neala, make up your mind," Maeve said with a grin. Neala chuckled along.

Both women looked up to see Grayson walk slowly into the kitchen. She eased herself into a kitchen chair with a minimal amount of groaning. Inwardly, Neala Rourke wanted to strangle the stubborn woman. However, she admired her tenacity.

"Hungry, Gray?" her mother asked over her shoulder. "The roast is done, and I made roasted potatoes and gravy."

Looking extremely exhausted, Gray laughed openly. "A full meal at ten o'clock at night. You must really be upset. Thanks."

Both women noticed the pained tone in the raspy voice and exchanged glances. Maeve put a glass of milk in front of her. Grayson reached for it with her right hand and winced, then let out an impatient breath and picked it up with her left hand. She mumbled something under her breath.

"No swearing," her mother called from the stove. Neala bit off a laugh and Grayson glanced her way and blushed deeply.

After the wonderful dinner, Grayson looked as though she could fall asleep in her coffee. Her mother was about to suggest bed.

"Now tell me about the Dark Lord," Grayson said to both women. "Dr. Rourke, you told me that some fellow that goes by the name of the Dark Lord is responsible for killing Jane Monahan and Nan Quigley. Ma, since you're a Druidess, I think you'll understand more than I would."

"You'd understand if you kept up with it," her mother said. "I suppose that was my fault."

Neala looked back and forth between mother and daughter. "Kept up with it?"

Grayson shook her head. "Let's not derail whatever train we're on right now, however psychotic the ride may seem," Grayson said firmly. "Now earlier you said 'they' were going to ask my mother for help when this tragedy happened 'here,' as well. Let's go from there."

"I-I lied to you, Detective," Neala said in a small voice.

Grayson watched her, still skeptical of this woman. "I know. Why?"

"Those murders in Ireland were never solved. It was almost fifty years ago. I…" She stopped. "It can't be the same person."

"Why not?" Maeve asked and leaned forward.

All the while, Grayson was watching the doctor. "Because that would make our murderer very, very old. And this Dark Lord?

Who is he, Dr. Rourke?"

"I don't know, Detective," she countered angrily.

Gray sat forward and winced. "You know a great deal. You'd better start talking because the feds will start putting this together and you will be a suspect," she said seriously. "Now start from the beginning."

Maeve reached over and patted Neala's hand, then took Grayson's hand in her own. "I'll start from the beginning."

Chapter 13

Grayson's eyes never left her mother. Maeve took a deep breath and let it out slowly. "I want you to try to remember when you were a little girl in Ireland, Gray," she said.

Grayson frowned deeply. "Ma, I don't have to try, I remember my childhood. We were a normal family," she insisted, then chuckled. "Well, as normal as a family can be when the mother is a Druidess as was her mother and…" Her voice trailed off and she searched her mother's face. "Sister Daniel, the abbess of St. Brigid's Monastery in Kildare. She was always around, or we were always around her."

Maeve nodded. "Yes, that's exactly right. She's a wonderful woman." Maeve looked at Neala, who nodded in agreement.

Grayson watched both of them. "You know Sister Daniel?"

Neala nodded. "I do, though I haven't seen her since we found the stone. That woman is a wealth of Irish history and mythology and a wonderful storyteller."

Grayson smiled. "I do remember that. She told some wild stories of gods and goddesses, battles with giants, magical nights of Beltane and bonfires and spirits from the otherworld." Grayson stopped and laughed. "She scared the shit out of me, actually."

Neala and Maeve laughed along as Neala watched Grayson. "Tell me what you remember about her," her mother said.

Grayson sat back and struck a thoughtful pose. "Sitting at that long table with her and you and other women. Sister Daniel would talk of St. Brigid, Patrick and Columba, and Christianity. You and the ladies would talk about Brigid, the gods and goddesses, and paganism." Grayson looked at her mother. "The conversations were so opposite—Christianity, paganism—but you never argued who was right or who was wrong."

Maeve shrugged. "That's because there is no right or wrong. We believe there was a time when both co-existed, sweetie."

Neala agreed. "Before St. Patrick, before Brigid became a saint, the people of Ireland had the gods and the goddesses and Druids who taught them the ancient ways."

Grayson listened to both women. "And you think all of this has to do with the death of those two women?" she asked pointedly and leaned in. "I want to know how." She looked at her mother. "Now would be a good time, Ma."

Maeve leaned in and held her teacup with both hands. "There are those who believe when the gods and goddesses freely roamed Ireland, the Druids were responsible for the teachings of the pagan ways. The Tuatha Dé Danann ruled for centuries until the Milesians defeated them and sent them underground. On the eve of their defeat, the Druid hierarchy decided to protect their world, to divide the power so that no one individual had all the power, all the magic that the Tuatha Dé Danann possessed."

Grayson shook her head. "Whoa, I never heard of this. What power?"

"Do you recall the Stone of Destiny, Grayson?" her mother asked.

Grayson raised an eyebrow. "The stone that's at Tara, the seat of all the kings of Ireland? Sitting on top of the King's Seat is Ireland's ancient coronation stone—the Lia Fail, or Stone of Destiny. It's said that the Tuatha Dé Danann brought it to Tara, according to mythology. The stone that was said to roar when touched by the rightful king of Tara? The stone that the English believe they have at Westminster Abbey?" She stopped and gave both women a smug grin. "That Stone of Destiny?"

Maeve returned the grin and nodded. "That would be the one."

Neala toyed with her coffee cup. "But it's not the only stone."

Grayson looked from her mother to Neala. There was an agonizing moment of silence. It then dawned on her. "The stone that was dug up by your archaeologists, the stone at the exhibit."

Neala looked into Grayson's eyes and smiled slightly. "That would be the one."

"So this stone you dug up has powers?" Grayson asked, trying to keep up with these two women.

"Yes. Maeve, I think you know more about it than I do," Neala said.

"I've read all the legends, but it's been decades since I've thought about it. Not since we left Ireland when you were a young girl, Gray."

Grayson remembered the day they left. She was twelve. Her grandmother had passed away the year before, and her father was to join the Chicago Police Department. She remembered her mother crying and hugging Sister Daniel.

"I'll write to you often," her mother said through her tears.

Sister Daniel cupped her cheek. "This is God's will, Maeve. There is a reason for you to go to America. He has a plan for Grayson, believe that."

Maeve sniffed and nodded. She looked down at Grayson, who was crying, as well, and pulled her into a hug. "I believe it, Sister."

Sister Daniel put her hand out to Grayson. "Let me say goodbye to Grayson. We'll be right back."

Maeve nodded and wiped away the tears.

Grayson looked up at the abbess, who was smiling and looking at the green rolling hills as they walked down the dirt path away from the monastery.

"You will love America," she whispered.

Grayson nodded. "Yes, Sister. Da says we have relatives in Chicago." She stopped and felt the tears stinging her eyes. "I'll miss you."

The abbess looked down and smoothed the raven hair off the young child's forehead. "We will meet again, Grayson. Perhaps not soon, perhaps not in this world." She lifted Grayson's face. "We all have our destiny. When you realize it, embrace it. When the time comes, you may not believe it or understand, but listen to your mother. She is wise and she loves you. You may be frightened, my child, but always remember—the will of God would never lead where the grace of God could never keep you. Do you understand what I'm saying, my child?"

"I-I think so, Sister. Trust Him?"

Sister Daniel smiled and nodded. "Trust Him. Trust your mother. It's all connected, Grayson—all of it, from the beginning of time. Be prepared to believe in that which will not come easy to you." She looked into Grayson's eyes, then took her left hand and turned her palm up. She ran her fingers over the large crescent-shaped scar on Grayson's palm. "You are destined, my child. I pray you will never be called upon to fulfill that destiny. I shall pray with all my heart."

"What are you thinking, sweetie?" Maeve asked quietly.

Grayson shook her head. "I'm not sure," she said and winced as she moved her shoulder. "This is all connected and I need to get a handle on it. I will get a handle on it." She glanced at Neala, who had been silent.

"You're too quiet, Dr. Rourke," Grayson said. "What's on your mind?"

"The council at the abbey believes because of our finding at the monastery, Nan was murdered. They're not sure of Jane Monahan's death. That's why they want your help, Maeve. For some reason, your name and only your name was mentioned by the council."

Maeve was silent. Grayson watched her mother intently. "Mother, why would they want you? What do you know, and what is this legend?" Grayson watched her mother. "Ma, tell me what you know. I-I remember…" Her voice trailed off as she gingerly touched the stitches on her brow.

"Detective…" Neala started softly.

Grayson looked up with a tired smile. "After all this, I think you can call me Grayson, Dr. Rourke."

Neala smiled in kind. "All right, it's Neala then."

"Grayson, there is much you don't remember," her mother said. Grayson looked away from Neala when she heard the sad tone; she reached over and took her mother's hand. Maeve looked up with tears in her eyes.

"Ma, please, what's going on?" Grayson asked. "What about

this stone, the council, and these murders?"

"I'm not sure about the murders. I honestly have no idea what they have to do with this. However..." She stopped and took a deep breath. "I hoped you would remember on your own. Your father, well, when we moved here, we didn't talk much of what happened in Ireland. We wanted a normal life for you..." Her voice trailed off.

Grayson frowned in confusion. "As compared to what, Ma?"

Maeve looked directly into her eyes. She reached across, took Grayson's left hand, and turned the palm upward. She ran her thumb across the scar that nearly covered the entire palm.

Neala looked at Grayson's palm. "That's an interesting scar. How did you get it?"

Grayson was still watching her mother as she spoke. "I-I don't remember. I think I fell on some glass when I was eight or so..." she whispered.

Her mother smiled sadly but said nothing. Grayson felt a pulling sensation in the pit of her stomach as her mother caressed her palm. Her skin broke out in goose flesh and she shivered uncontrollably. There was a buzzing in her ears now as she shook her head. "Ma..."

Neala watched, transfixed and said nothing. She looked at Maeve, who took her hand away and took a deep quivering breath. Grayson instantly scratched the palm of her hand, then rubbed her palms together. Neala looked from Grayson's hands to Maeve. Grayson saw the incredulous look on the redheaded doctor. "What?" she asked as she continued to rub her hands.

"Maeve? Tell me I'm crazy for what I'm thinking." Neala ran her hand through her hair.

"What?" Grayson asked again. "Crazy for what?"

"No, Neala, you're not crazy," Maeve said slowly.

"Mother of God," Neala whispered and sat back. "It's true then."

"What's true?" Grayson tried again. She may as well have been invisible. She felt like she was having a stroke; she was confused and tried to get a handle on this. "Okay, I've nearly been blown to pieces. I have two murders in Chicago that I can't solve. My partner is lying in the hospital. You're talking about a Dark Lord, gods, goddesses, and Christianity all together, and some powerful stone from the Tuatha Dé Danann. What the hell is going on?" Grayson asked with a definite edge to her voice.

"I don't blame you, Grayson," Neala said. "I'd have a hard time believing it myself if I were you."

Grayson closed her eyes and took a deep calming breath. Every muscle in her body ached and her head was pounding. "Believing what?" she asked through clenched teeth.

Maeve reached over and took Grayson's hand once again. "It's nearly midnight and you need to get to bed, Gray. We'll talk of this in the morning. I'll fix up the couch for Neala. You get to bed and get some sleep. Grayson, you will figure this out, though you won't like it."

"What won't I like?" she asked as her eyelids felt like lead. "You two are driving me nuts."

"You've been out of the Druidess loop for quite some time," Maeve said. She then shook her head. "Logic. You get it from your father, that's for sure. I tell you it's a damned nuisance."

Grayson smiled slightly. "Well, in my world, Ma, logic comes in pretty handy."

Once again, Grayson locked eyes with her mother as she reached across and took her hand once more. When Neala's hand rested on her forearm, she was aware of the warmth that spread through her at the touch.

"Grayson," her mother started. "Get some rest. You're going to need it because we aren't going to be dealing with your world any longer."

Chapter 14

"I'm taking the couch, and that's final, Grayson," Neala said and pushed Grayson out of the living room. "Good night."

Grayson relented. "G'night," she mumbled and headed upstairs.

After a hot bath, she toweled her aching body and stood in front of the sink and wiped the foggy mirror; she got a good look at herself.

The rugged stitches started across the top of her brow and down, ending across her cheek and under her eye. "You look like ten miles of bad road, MacCarthaigh." She gingerly touched her cheek. It had turned a deep purple and looked decidedly swollen. She flexed her shoulder and winced. She was grateful nothing was broken and no separation—just sore as hell.

She stood there for a moment leaning on the sink and staring at her reflection in the mirror. Suddenly, she saw a face superimposed over her own. Her heart beat like a drum, as she stood there transfixed. The face, or more accurately a ghostly figure, was definitely female. Grayson tried to remain calm as she took a deep breath and reached her hand up toward the mirror. She was breathing heavily as she saw another hand rise up. It was then that Grayson saw the scar on the palm of the white, ghostly hand; it seemed to reach out to her.

Not thinking, which was a first for Grayson, she rested her palm against the steamy mirror as the hand from the other side did the same. She instantly felt a warm, tingling sensation spread up her arm. She stared at the face in the mirror. Was it her face? She shivered violently.

"Garda," the voice whispered.

Grayson was shivering, even though her body was sweating and warm. In the next instant, the mirror shattered and Grayson blinked and jumped back. "Fuck!"

She looked at the mirror—it had not broken.

"What the fuck is goin' on?" She took deep calming breaths. "Okay, Gray, you need a good night's sleep, that's what you need. You're seeing things now."

Feeling every bit like Ebenezer after seeing Marley's ghost, she slipped into bed and pulled the covers over her. "Enough with mythology." She yawned. "Ma, you've got a lot of s'plainin to do."

Maeve sat at the desk in her library. She looked at Neala, who anxiously bit at her bottom lip. "Don't look so guilty, Neala," Maeve said over her reading glasses as she dialed the phone.

"Perhaps we're wrong, Maeve—"

"We are not wrong and don't look at me like that. If I told Grayson everything right now, she'd have me locked up and you along with me. No, I know my daughter." She then dialed the overseas number she hoped she would never have to call. "Her logical mind has been her savior as a detective. However, now… it may be her ruin."

"St. Brigid's Convent, Sister Daniel."

Maeve paused when she heard the old nun's voice once again. She took a deep breath. "Hello, Sister. It's—"

"Yes, Maeve, hello. We've been expecting your call," she said. Maeve heard the soft kind voice she remembered and nearly broke down. "I know this is not what you would want. It's not what any of us want. However, the time is at hand."

"Then it's true?"

"Yes, we must only assume that the two other parts of the stone are in their possession. They must not be allowed the final piece. Have you spoken with Grayson? Does she know? Does she remember?"

"She remembers little, Sister, but I think it's coming back to her slowly…"

"Not too slowly. Time is of the essence, but for now, she must guard the stone. You must bring it back safely to Ireland."

Maeve heard the quiet urgency in her voice. She glanced at Neala, who was watching. "Yes, I have Dr. Rourke here. The exhibit leaves tomorrow, and we'll leave with it. I just need to get things in order."

"Good. I truly wish we were speaking under better circumstances. I miss you and Grayson."

"I miss you, as well, my old friend."

"I will pray for your safe trip home," Sister Daniel said and hesitated. "I will even pray to the gods and goddesses."

Maeve heard the smile in her voice and chuckled quietly. "Don't go too far. I don't want to put you in the hot seat with the man upstairs."

The old nun laughed quietly. "I miss that sense of humor. And do not worry. We're all connected, don't forget—the strength of womankind is stronger by far than any force in this world. Although, mankind may blow it up before we get a chance to save it."

Maeve laughed and agreed. "Truer words were never spoken, Sister. If it were left entirely to *man*kind, God knows—"

"Is that with a capital G?"

Again, Maeve laughed. "We're all connected, remember." She heard the old nun laugh heartily. "We'll see you in a few days, Sister, with Grayson kicking and screaming."

She hung up the phone and sat back. Neala sat on the edge of the desk. "What do we do next?"

Maeve shook her head. "We're accompanying you back to Ireland."

Neala gave her a curious look. "We? As in you and Grayson?"

Maeve nodded gravely. Neala winced. "I don't know your daughter very well, but I don't think she'll go for it."

"Well, let's sleep on it and see how she is in the morning."

As they walked out of the library, Neala turned to Maeve. "I wish I knew more about the stone and what power it supposedly has."

"I know someone who does. He's a bit eccentric, but he's the best authority on Irish mythology. Maybe you've heard of him—Tim Kerrigan."

Neala's eyes bugged out of her head. Maeve backed up in surprise. "Good heavens. What's the matter?"

"Corky Kerrigan?" Neala asked.

"You do know him," Maeve said happily.

"He's daft!" Neala said loudly, then whispered, "He's a nut."

Maeve laughed as she put the blanket on the couch. "Oh, he's not that bad."

"Maeve, he was thrown out of Trinity College. He actually ripped pages out of a history book in front of a very well-known professor," she said, as if trying to make Maeve understand. "And they had to restrain him when this exhibit left Ireland. He looked ridiculous lying on the floor with that security guard kneeling on him."

"In light of what's been happening, Neala, he's our key to understanding what's going on. So he can be as nutty as he wants." She kissed her cheek. "Get a good night's sleep. We're all going to need it."

Maeve crept into Grayson's room and stood by her bedside. She reached down and brushed the black lock of hair off her forehead. Tears stung her eyes when she looked at the heavy stitches on her brow and cheek.

"She's a fighter, that one," Sister Daniel said with an amused laugh.

Maeve nodded as they watched Grayson playing soccer. She was the only girl on the team, and the coach, Father Peter, was not fond of the idea of a girl playing with the rough boys. He and Sister Daniel had a nice chat; the next day, Grayson proudly wore her uniform. Now she was the best player on the field.

"Yes, she is," Maeve agreed. "Dermott was as thrilled about her playing as Father Peter."

Both women exchanged side glances and burst into laughter. "Men," Sister Daniel said. "When will they learn you can't keep a woman with spirit down for long?"

"The Church has done it for centuries," Maeve reminded her.

Sister Daniel nodded as she watched Grayson rush up and down the field. "Yes, it has, but times are changing. I can't see anyone holding Grayson down... not even the Catholic Church."

"Laws made by men for men," Maeve added with disdain. "Lately, I have such a hard time being a Catholic."

Sister Daniel looked up into the blue Irish sky. "I understand. But you must always remember," she said and turned to her. "There's the Catholic 'religion' and the Catholic 'faith,' and you'd do well to know the difference. Your faith is strong. Don't lose that."

"I won't, Sister," Maeve promised.

As they continued to watch the soccer game, Sister Daniel glanced at Maeve. "Now say three Hail Marys and two Our Fathers... Ya heathen."

Maeve smiled as she remembered that summer day so long ago. Grayson was indeed a fighter. She'd survived bullies while growing up; she survived her father's disappointment when she proudly told him she was gay; and she survived Vicky dying in her arms.

"Too much for a young woman," she whispered and kissed her forehead. "I'm sorry for this, sweetie. I wish with all my heart I was the one to go into battle and not you." She quietly walked out and closed the door.

As she lay in bed, Maeve's mind wandered back to Ireland and Dermott MacCarthaigh, the man she loved and married. He was a handsome man and Grayson mirrored his coloring, as well as Maeve's: deep blue eyes and coal black hair. Father and daughter also carried that one annoying gene: logic.

She remembered when Grayson first told her father she wanted to join the police force. Maeve thought Dermott's buttons on his vest would burst with pride. He hid it well.

"Well now, is that what you want, Grayson?" he asked roughly as he wiped his finger under his nose. Maeve saw the tears misting in his eyes.

"Yes, Da, it is. I've been thinking about this logically," Grayson started.

Maeve rolled her eyes and smiled but said nothing.

Grayson eagerly leaned forward. "You see, I want to make a difference. I can't sit behind a desk, and I don't want to teach. I need to do something."

Dermott nodded and rocked in his chair. "I understand what you mean, darlin'. But you have to be disciplined. Being a policeman is not an easy job." He looked at Grayson and smiled. Maeve saw the love that was hard for this man to show. "For you to become a police officer... It would please me."

Grayson grinned and jumped up and wrapped her arms around him. "I'm glad you think so 'cause I already applied and I've been accepted at the police academy. I start next Monday."

Maeve let out a hearty laugh, which her husband ignored as he pushed Grayson away. "You've done what? You did this without telling me? Damn it, woman, you're like your mother. Why didn't you say something? I would have called—"

"That's why I didn't say anything, Da. I have to do this on my own, for myself and without any favors. Don't you see? I have to stand on my own."

Dermott MacCarthaigh grumbled under his breath. "Like your mother and her mother before." He looked up at Grayson. "I suppose it's not enough for you to be married and have a family."

Maeve rolled her eyes again but kept still. Grayson laughed and kissed his forehead. "Sure it is. Just not with a man."

Dermott closed his eyes and took a deep calming breath. Grayson and Maeve exchanged glances. "We've had this discussion, Da," she reminded him.

He opened his eyes then. "It was not a discussion. I don't remember you askin' if I agreed with it or not."

Grayson cocked her head to one side and put her hands on her hips. She grinned wildly. "As if I could change."

He shifted uncomfortably in his rocker and glared at Maeve. "I suppose you go along with this."

Maeve smiled and took off her reading glasses. "It's not my life, Dermott. For some reason, God saw fit to—"

Dermott stood then. "Don't bring God into this!"

Grayson sighed and rubbed her temples and sat back down

111

on the couch.

"Dermott MacCarthaigh," Maeve started, "we sit at Mass every Sunday. We believe that we are created in the image and likeness of God. Why? Because we're good Irish Catholics? Let's not start with the sanctimonious rhetoric that the Church spews out!" Maeve tossed her book on the table. "We are all His children. Even your daughter!"

"There are rules and laws. What would we be without rules?" He tossed down the newspaper.

"Free-thinking individuals?" Grayson chimed in.

Maeve hid her grin. Dermott closed his eyes and mumbled once again. Both mother and daughter stood on either side of the pouting Irishman. "I love you, Dermott MacCarthaigh," Maeve whispered and kissed his temple.

"Me too." Grayson kissed the top of his head. "Now I'm late. I've got a hot date." She dashed out of the living room and bounded up the stairs.

Dermott turned to Maeve. "It's a sin, Maeve."

Maeve put her hand to his weathered cheek. "And do you think it's a sin that I believe in Wicca? Because if you do, then you're the only MacCarthaigh that's going to heaven."

Dermott shook his head. "You and your cronies will be the death of me. Thank God, Grayson at least doesn't buy into all that Druid talk."

Maeve glared at her husband. "That she doesn't remember does not mean she doesn't buy into it. She had my world when we lived in Ireland. She's had your world as a young adult. Now she'll live her life the way she sees fit, darlin'. It's all connected whether your logical stubborn Irish brain believes it or not."

Maeve closed her eyes and prayed to God and to the gods and goddesses of old; she prayed she was right—it's all connected.

Chapter 15

"You'll call me?" Maeve asked. Grayson heard the urgency in her voice as she slipped into her leather jacket. "Why must you wear that? It's full of holes."

Grayson winced and zipped the jacket. "Ma…" she warned.

Maeve turned to Neala and gave her a hug. "Be careful," she said quietly. Neala returned the hug, then pulled away.

"We'll be back after we go to the museum and talk to the feds, Ma," Grayson said and gingerly put on her sunglasses. Her head was pounding that morning, and her eye was swollen and discolored.

Maeve took the car keys and handed them to Neala. Grayson's mouth dropped as she stood there with her hand out. "Neala will drive. Your shoulder must be sore."

"I can drive," Grayson said in a clipped voice.

"Grayson," both women said in unison, then looked at each other. Maeve kissed Grayson on her uninjured check. "Don't be so stubborn."

With that, Grayson's cell phone went off, and she checked the number. "It's the precinct." She flipped the phone open. "MacCarthaigh."

"Grayson?" It was Keller and he sounded as if he'd been up all night. "Come down to the precinct, Detective MacCarthaigh."

"I have Dr. Rourke. We're supposed to meet with that fathead agent."

"Bring Dr. Rourke with you," he said, then lowered his voice. "This place is crawling with feds, Gray. Get down here right away."

"I'll be there in fifteen." She snapped the phone shut. She

looked at Neala and her mother. "That was Mike. He wants us to come down to the precinct first."

"Gray, what's going on?" Maeve asked.

"I don't know, Ma. I'll call you, though. Don't worry." Grayson kissed her forehead.

They drove in silence for a moment or two until Grayson spoke. "I have a bad feeling here, Neala. I don't like the tone in Lieutenant Keller's voice."

Neala gave her a quick glance, then watched the road. "What is it, Grayson?"

"I don't know, but for now, I think it best we go back to doctor and detective." She then saw the worried look. "Just hang in there and answer any question honestly."

Neala nodded and gripped the steering wheel.

When Grayson and Neala walked into the precinct, the tension in the room was unmistakable. Grayson saw Lieutenant Keller, Captain Jenkins, Agent Morrison, and another older man standing in Keller's office. When he saw Grayson, he motioned to her.

"I'm frightened, Gray," Neala whispered.

Grayson took off her sunglasses and smiled. "I'm right here. No worries."

"Good morning, Dr. Rourke," Keller said with a small smile and offered his hand. "You met Captain Jenkins. This is Agent Morrison and Inspector Garrett of the Chicago Bureau."

After introductions and requests for coffee were made, Keller offered Neala a chair. Grayson winced as she sat on the edge of the desk.

"How are you, Detective MacCarthaigh?" Jenkins asked.

"I'll live, sir."

"Well, let's get down to it," Garrett started.

"Detective Resnick is in stable condition," Grayson said with a hint of sarcasm.

"That's good to hear. Now," Garrett continued. "Dr. Rourke, we won't take up much of your time. I'd like to know how well you knew the victims."

Neala didn't hesitate in the least, which Grayson was glad to see. "I went to Trinity College in Dublin with both women, years ago. We kept in contact, but like many colleagues, we drifted apart."

Garrett nodded. "And what did you study?"

"Irish history and mythology mostly. I have a doctorate in history and archaeology. Nan and Jane studied the same."

"Curious they both died within three weeks of each other, right when your exhibit is in Chicago."

"What are you suggesting, Inspector?" Neala asked before Grayson could.

"I'm not suggesting anything, Doctor. Just trying to get a common thread." He glanced at Grayson and continued. "How well do you know Maeve MacCarthaigh?"

Grayson shot him an incredulous look. "What's my mother got to do with this?"

"Detective MacCarthaigh, we know Dr. Rourke knows your mother. How well do you know Dr. Rourke, Detective?"

Grayson leaned off the edge of the desk and faced both agents. "I met Dr. Rourke at the airport when she was there to meet Mrs. Quigley. Dr. Rourke assisted the victim's aunt in identifying the victim."

Agent Morrison spoke for the first time. "So you're trying to tell us you never met Dr. Rourke before? Your mother knew her for three years and you never met?"

Grayson felt the hair on the back of her neck bristle. "Not trying to tell you. I am telling you."

"Detective MacCarthaigh," Garrett interrupted, "it seems your mother is into mythology and…" He stopped and looked at his notes. "Druidism?" He looked directly at Grayson. "Care to elaborate?"

Grayson took a calming breath before she corrected him. "My mother is a professor of Irish history and mythology. She is an expert on pre-Christian civilization."

"How 'bout you, Detective MacCarthaigh?" Agent Morrison chimed in.

Grayson smiled sweetly. "I'm not a professor." She watched

as the agent scribbled in his notepad. "That's spelled with a double S."

Agent Morrison quickly looked up from his notepad.

"That's enough," Jenkins said. "Inspector Garrett, do you have any more questions for Dr. Rourke?"

"No, thank you, Doctor. I appreciate your coming down here," he said with a smile and turned his attention to Grayson. "Detective MacCarthaigh, I'd like to talk to you if you don't mind. Dr. Rourke, would you be so kind as to wait outside?"

Neala smiled and nodded her assent. Keller waved the desk sergeant in. "Please take Dr. Rourke to Detective MacCarthaigh's desk."

Neala walked out of the office with just a glance at Grayson, who smiled as she passed by.

"Now, Detective," Garrett started. "You took Dr. Rourke out on the night of the exhibit. Is that correct?"

Before she could reply, Agent Morrison said, "Don't bother denying it. I followed you. You two seemed very cozy."

Grayson ignored the agent as if he were not there. "No," Grayson said to the inspector. "I took Dr. Rourke to a get a cup of coffee in the hopes that she would tell me anything she knew." Grayson didn't like the feel of this conversation. She glanced at Keller, who was concentrating on his shoes.

Agent Morrison snorted sarcastically, which Grayson also ignored. "What is your point, Inspector?"

"My point, Detective," he said and leaned on the desk, "is that your mother knew Dr. Rourke and you didn't bother to tell us that—"

"I had no idea my mother knew Dr. Rourke until the night before the exhibit," Grayson argued and leaned forward on the desk, as well. "And my mother has nothing to do with this."

"I don't believe you," Garrett said.

"I don't give a shit," Grayson countered angrily.

"Detective MacCarthaigh," Jenkins snapped.

Grayson looked at both her superiors. "Okay, what gives here? Am I being accused of something?" Suddenly, she felt a pulling sensation in the pit of her stomach. She glanced into the precinct to see Neala staring at her coffee cup. She looked lonely and dejected.

Keller said quickly, "No one is accusing—"

"Now how well do you know Dr. Rourke, Detective? She suddenly checks out of her hotel, leaves no forwarding address, and we know for a fact she's been staying at your mother's house. I think you're compromising this investigation." Garrett tossed down his pen. "And I understand there is no love lost between you and the federal agents that were here the other day."

Grayson gave Agent Morrison a smug look. "Didn't your mother ever tell you no one likes a tattletale?" She turned back to Garrett. "I've done nothing to compromise this investigation. I believed Dr. Rourke might be in danger, that's why I had her check out of her hotel…"

"And not bother to tell us," Agent Morrison said.

"I thought you followed us." Grayson countered. "Couldn't you figure it out? I suppose I could have drawn you a map."

"That's enough," Garrett said.

"Detective MacCarthaigh," Jenkins started and cleared his throat. "In light of your present injuries, I think it would be a good idea for you to take a vacation for two weeks. You haven't been away from this precinct since—" He stopped short and Grayson knew what he was about to say—since Vic died.

"I don't need a vacation, Captain," Grayson said evenly and avoided both agents.

"I'm not asking you," he said firmly.

Grayson looked from him to Keller, who gave her a warning look. She unclipped her gold shield from her belt and took her weapon from her holster.

"Gray…" Keller nearly pleaded.

"In all my life, I never thought these words would come out of my mouth," she said and took a deep confident breath. "I quit." She tossed her shield and gun on his desk.

As she walked out, Agent Morrison was standing in her way with his hands in his pockets, sporting a smug grin. Without a word, she forearmed him in the throat and sent him sprawling into the cabinet.

"Goddamn it!" she heard her former captain bellow as she walked out.

Neala was as white as a ghost. Grayson was sure she saw everything. "I'll take you to the museum."

Garrett marched out of the office. "Detective MacCarthaigh, Agent Morrison will take Dr. Rourke—"

Neala whirled around. "Inspector, I am a visitor to your city, here by invitation from the mayor himself. Unless you're going to arrest me, I can come and go as I please, with whomever I please. And leaving with this oaf," she said, pointing to Agent Morrison, "does not please me. Good day to you, sir."

She turned on her heel and marched out of the precinct. She stopped and looked back at Grayson, who was standing there with her mouth open. "Are you coming, Detective MacCarthaigh, or do I have to call the mayor?"

Grayson hid her grin as she put on her sunglasses. Garrett's face was beet red with anger and embarrassment. She said nothing as she followed the feisty redhead out of the precinct.

Neala was fuming as they walked down the steps. Grayson let her go on and gently took the keys from her. "Of all the nerve! Tellin' me what to do and who to do it with! Who does he think he is? I have a good mind to call the mayor myself. Of all the nerve."

She went on as Grayson unlocked the car and opened the door for her. "And to accuse you!" she exclaimed and got into the car. "And don't be tellin' me he didn't accuse you."

Grayson just nodded and walked around the front of the car. She had a colossal headache as she slipped behind the wheel.

"And to bring your mother into this." Neala went on. "That is utter nonsense." She stopped and looked at Grayson. "Aren't you at least angry?"

Grayson glanced at her, then concentrated on the road. "You're doing just fine for both of us, but could you lower the decibel level?"

Neala chuckled grudgingly. "I'm sorry. Your head must be splittin'."

"Only horribly."

They were silent for a few minutes as Grayson drove to the Field Museum. She could feel Neala watching her. "You gave them your gun and your badge," she said.

Grayson nodded but said nothing as she stared straight ahead. Gratefully, Neala did not pursue the conversation.

Chapter 16

"Once we check on the stone, we need to get back to my mother's," Grayson said as they entered the exhibit room.

Neala nodded and examined the stone. "Seems to be intact. I worry more with each day."

"Don't worry. I'll see to it that you and that stone get safely on the plane back to Ireland," Grayson assured her as she glanced around the large room. "It sure is quiet in here."

"The last day of the exhibit is today. They open the doors at eleven. We've got about an hour."

From behind them, they heard Phelan's voice. "It should be a good turnout for the last day. So I'm told."

Grayson and Neala turned around. "I'm hoping it is," Neala said with a smile. "But I don't mind sayin', I can't wait to get home."

Grayson watched Phelan as he smiled and nodded in agreement. "I, too, long to be back in Ireland, Neala. I've been away far too long." Grayson heard the pensive tone in his baritone voice.

"Miss the Ole Sod, Mr. Tynan?" Grayson asked.

Phelan raised a dark eyebrow. "When was the last time you've been to Ireland, Detective?"

Grayson shrugged. "Quite some time." Suddenly, the disjointed and meaningless images flashed through her mind. She shook her head and looked at Phelan, who was watching her intently.

Neala glanced at Grayson, who was frowning as she put a hand to her temple. Her fingers lightly traced the heavy stitches on her brow.

"Did you have an accident, Detective MacCarthaigh?" Phelan asked.

"Yes, police business," Grayson said with a tone of dismissal. "Will you be here for the final day?"

"I would love to, but my business needs some attention, which has been lacking of late."

"You're not staying?" Neala asked. "I would think that you would want to stay to the end, especially since you've done so much."

Phelan bowed slightly. "I am but a servant of Ireland."

Grayson thought he sounded sarcastic but said nothing.

"Well, Ireland certainly appreciates your service," Neala assured him. "I honestly don't know how we would have done all this without you."

"And now we need to get this exhibit back to its home. So much needs to be done and the time is—" He stopped abruptly.

Grayson raised an eyebrow. "The time is…?"

Seemingly collecting himself, Phelan grinned. "The time is now for Ireland, Detective MacCarthaigh."

For a moment, Grayson regarded Phelan Tynan; it seemed he was doing the same to her. There was something about this man that Grayson just did not trust, and she didn't know why. She looked into his dark eyes and wondered…. "Mr. Tynan, what business are you in that you can afford to give away so much?"

His eyes narrowed for a split second before he answered. "I own Cian Enterprises. I buy and I sell and I invest, then buy and sell all over again."

"You must do it well."

"It's a gift," he said lightly, took out his card, and handed it to Grayson.

Taking the card, Grayson noticed the information was in Gaelic. "Kinda hard for the average person to read," she said and looked up.

"Ah, but you're not the average person, Detective. Perhaps your delightful mother knows Gaelic."

"Yes, she does," Grayson said absently as she looked at the card.

"The name of the company is pronounced *kee-an*," Neala said with a smug grin.

Grayson raised an eyebrow. "I read Gaelic, as well, Dr. Rourke." She put the card in her breast pocket.

"Well, I have a few phone calls to make. I'm leaving later this afternoon," Phelan said. He reached out his hand to Grayson. "It was a pleasure meeting you, Detective MacCarthaigh."

Grayson took the offering; his hand was still cold and clammy. "Same here."

He then turned to Neala and kissed her cheek. "Neala, I'll see you in Dublin in a few days. If you need anything, you know where to find me."

"I do, Phelan. Thanks again for all your help," she said with a smile.

They both watched as the tall Irishman walked out of the exhibit room and out of sight.

"He gives me the creeps," Grayson said.

Neala chuckled. "That's because you're a detective."

Grayson let out a sarcastic grunt as she took out her cell. "Not at the moment." She dialed the precinct and waited. "Detective MacCarthaigh."

"Well, well, the elusive detective."

Grayson smiled slightly when she heard Diane's voice. "Hello, Diane. How's the information business doing?"

The voice on the other end laughed quietly. "Fine, I'm just sitting here waiting for you."

Grayson glanced at Neala, who raised an eyebrow. Grayson cleared her throat. "Good, 'cause I need you. I need all the info you can get on Cian Enterprises out of Dublin, Ireland," she said and spelled the name. "I want everything, from day one. How soon?" She waited and glanced at Neala, who was frowning deeply as she listened.

"Give me a couple of hours. I'll have all you need. Who owns it?" Diane asked.

Grayson heard her typing on the keyboard already. "Phelan Tynan." She spelled that, as well. "He's Irish. After that, you're on your own."

"Hmm, not giving me much to go on, Grayson, but then you never did." Grayson heard the sarcasm and chuckled.

"You're better off. Call my cell when you have something."

"Sure, Gray. You sound serious. I'll get this right away."

"Thanks, Diane." Grayson closed the phone with a confident snap. She then saw the confused and irritated look on Neala.

"What are you doin'?" Neala folded her arms across her chest.

Grayson was getting familiar with this woman's gestures. It didn't take a rocket scientist to see her ire right now. "I may have handed in my badge, but I still follow my instincts, Neala. And my instincts tell me I need to know more about your philanthropist, Mr. Tynan."

"Grayson, Phelan is very well respected. He's worth millions," Neala argued. Grayson grunted.

"Even millionaires can commit murder, Dr. Rourke."

"You can't be serious!" Neala said quickly, then stopped. "But then you suspected me."

"Yes, and look where we are now. You're involved in this more deeply than you may know or than you're telling. My own mother is involved in it, and God help me, so am I," Grayson reminded her. "And now the FBI is involved. So, yes, I'm serious."

They both fell silent. Neala was clearly. "I have to see to the exhibit," she said calmly. "It's the last day, and I have to give a speech at the end of it, but we should be done by four this afternoon. What will you do?"

Grayson looked into the green eyes. "I'll be around," she said. "I'll meet you in your office. You have my cell if anything, and I mean anything, happens. Do you understand?"

"Nothing is going to happen, Grayson," she insisted and started to walk away.

Grayson grabbed her elbow. "Call my cell if anything happens," she repeated in a low voice.

Neala let out an exasperated sigh. "Yes, Detective MacCarthaigh." She then walked out of the exhibit room, leaving Grayson standing there wondering what indeed could happen.

At two o'clock, Grayson received the call from Diane with the information on Phelan Tynan. Rather than listen to it over the phone, she decided to go to Diane. Grayson found Neala, who assured her everything was running smoothly; she'd still meet her in her office at four.

Grayson sat at Diane's desk leafing through the pages of information. She could feel Diane watching her. "So what happened to your face, Gray?"

Grayson explained briefly and Diane shook her head. "You certainly have had your share of injuries in the past couple of years. First Vic—" She stopped abruptly.

Grayson looked up and frowned deeply.

"I'm sorry, Gray."

Grayson then smiled slightly. "Don't be," she said. "Have you read any of this?"

"Some, yes. Doesn't appear to be anything out of the ordinary. Cian Enterprises founded in nineteen twenty. CEO and owner Phelan Tynan—"

Grayson read the first couple of pages. "Yeah, but nothing on Tynan. Where was he born? There's no date of birth. No record of his education if he had any. How does a guy own a company and not have any personal information?" Grayson impatiently flipped through the rest of the report. She stopped and looked at Diane.

"What?" Diane leaned forward.

"It says here that it was founded by Phelan Tynan."

"So? He's the owner."

"Phelan Tynan looks to be my age, perhaps a few years older. How can he start a company in the early twentieth century?"

Diane cocked her head. "That would make him—"

"Ancient," Grayson finished in a quiet voice. She looked up to see Diane's complexion change.

Diane swallowed and handed Grayson a manila envelope. "Th-these are photos that came along with the print-out. They're of Mr. Tynan."

Grayson took the envelope and opened it. The photos were all from newspaper articles. One photo was of two men shaking hands and smiling into the camera. Glancing at the top of the article, Grayson noticed it was from September 1938. The caption read: *England's Prime Minister Neville Chamberlain has an ally in Cian Enterprises.*

Grayson looked closer at the old picture and glanced up as Diane offered her the small magnifying glass. Grayson took it without a word and held it to the photo. It was him—Phelan Tynan. Oh, the hair was not long, it was cut in the fashion of the day, but the eyes were his; Grayson knew it.

She took out another photo from another article taken from 1953. There he was again with two other men, standing on the steps of a building. Grayson read the caption under the picture. *Professor Gilbert Murray, Phelan Tynan of Cian Enterprises, and Sir John Quigley of the Anthropological and Archaeological Society gather on the steps of the National Museum, Dublin, Ireland.*

Grayson slowly sat down. Her head was pounding. "Got any aspirin, Di?" she asked as she concentrated on the photos. She rubbed her forehead and closed her eyes.

Diane took out a bottle from her purse and handed Grayson the tablets and a glass of water. "Gray, you look horrible. What's going on?"

Grayson tossed back the tablets and drank the water. "I don't know, but this asshole is at the bottom of this, I know it." She looked at the photo once again and reread the caption. "Anthropology, archaeology, professors, and museums. He's connected to all of this, I can feel it."

"All of what?"

Grayson rubbed her temples, then traced her fingers against the stitches on her cheek. Disjointed visions flashed through her mind. She closed her eyes tight, trying to get a clear image. Visions of her mother, Sister Daniel, even Vicky flashed like a kaleidoscope in her mind, then they were gone. "I wish I knew."

Chapter 17

Grayson found Neala in the exhibit room. She was leafing through pages on a clipboard while a worker was taking the last box out of the room.

"Be careful," she pleaded as she watched them. She turned around to see Grayson standing there. "Well now, did you find out everything on Phelan?"

Grayson heard the edge to Neala's voice and took a deep breath. She really wasn't in the mood for banter. "I found out as much as I could, given the fact there is no record of his birth, education, family, colleagues," she said in a clipped voice. She then added sarcastically, "Oh, wait, there was a picture taken with Prime Minister Neville Chamberlain."

Neala blinked in confusion. "N-Neville Chamberlain was prime minister before Churchill. How can that be? You must be wrong."

Grayson leaned against the desk. "I have no idea. How much longer will you be?"

Neala ran her fingers through her hair. "Everything has been crated and tagged and will be held in the basement until the flight leaves tomorrow."

Grayson heard the anxiety in her voice. "What's the matter?"

"Nothing really. I just can't relax until I'm back in Ireland and the exhibit is back in the museum." She looked around the empty room. "However, my work is done for the day."

"Good. I have a few things to discuss, Dr. Rourke," Grayson said and noticed the raised eyebrow. "With you and my mother."

"Lieutenant Keller called you?" Grayson asked angrily and

tossed her jacket on the chair. Neala winced but said nothing. Grayson slipped out of the empty shoulder harness; it followed the jacket.

"Yes, he called because he cares." Maeve reached across and took Grayson's hand. "Did you have to quit, sweetie?"

"They gave me no choice," Grayson said, then took a deep breath. "That's not entirely true, but I—"

"You got your Irish up and you quit. Just like your father." She sighed and patted her hand. "Mike said he didn't blame you."

"He was following orders, Ma. I just couldn't have them bringing you into this, and if I agreed to their vacation, I felt as if I were giving credence to those fatheaded FBI agents."

Maeve and Neala exchanged glances, which Grayson saw. "Okay, what's going on?"

Maeve cleared her throat. "Well, as much I would never want to see you unhappy, sweetie, your quitting has made this easier."

Grayson sat back and gave her a wary look. "Made what easier?" She looked at Neala, who was fidgeting with a spoon. "Dr. Rourke?"

Maeve spoke first. "Grayson, there isn't very much time. We have to talk and we have to talk now."

"Okay," Grayson agreed. "You start, Ma." She again looked at Neala. "I have a feeling you'll be chiming in, as well." She knew she sounded as though she was accusing Neala, and by the angry glare from the redheaded doctor, Neala heard it, as well.

"Detective MacCarthaigh—"

"Dr. Rourke," Grayson replied with a smirk.

"All right, you two, we don't have time," Maeve said in motherly fashion. "Grayson, I need you to remember back when you were a child in Ireland—the monastery, the sisters, my friends. You need to remember."

"Ma, I remember. We used to sit around and you'd talk about—"

Her mother interrupted her. "Not just that. The rituals, the nights of Beltane and Samhain, the bonfires. You need to remember, sweetie."

Grayson frowned deeply and sat back once again. "I don't

remember." She looked at her mother. "Why is it important that I remember this, Ma? Why me?"

Their eyes locked and Grayson peered into her blue eyes. Visions flashed through her mind again: her mother and the other women, standing in a circle in the grassy field. The sun just setting behind the mountains. The bonfire rising to the heavens. She blinked and realized she was breathing heavily. "What does this all mean? It doesn't make sense."

"Must everything make sense?" Neala asked.

Grayson looked at Neala, her frown deepening. "Yes, it must." She saw the look on Neala's face, and as Neala watched her, Grayson thought she knew what she was thinking. Vicky— her dying made no sense. Their lives were planned; they were in love with a bright future together, starting a family. Then that one day, that one fucked-up day with that insane hostage-taker.

Neala touched Grayson's forearm. "Not everything makes sense, Grayson."

Maeve took a deep breath and sniffed. "Grayson—"

Grayson shook her head rapidly. "No, this isn't about Beltane and Samhain, the festivals of summer and winter solstice—"

"Samhain, Grayson, the—"

"I know what it is, Ma. The Celtic New Year and the Wiccan," Grayson said. "I remember when I first read the word and said *samhane*. You laughed and taught me my first Gaelic word, pronounced *sow-in*. I should have stuck with Latin." The three of them chuckled. "Samhain, actually it's almost that time of the year, isn't it?"

"Five days," Neala said absently.

Maeve watched Grayson. "And six hours," she said.

Grayson heard the solemn tone in her voice.

"Grayson, listen to me. We don't have much time. I'm going to explain what I believe is happening, and you're going to listen."

Grayson cocked her head to one side. It was not like her mother to be so serious. She nodded. "Okay, Ma. I'm listening," she said with equal seriousness.

"I'll make some tea," Neala said.

Grayson watched her mother as Neala was making the tea;

Maeve seemed to be collecting her thoughts.

Grayson waited patiently. Finally, Maeve spoke. "There is a belief that on the eve of when the Tuatha Dé Danann was to be defeated by the Milesians, the Druid hierarchy decided that all the magic, all the power of the gods and goddesses should not be in the possession of one entity. The essence of the magic was trapped inside the stone. For safety, they took 'invisibility' and minor magics to use with the elves and fairies, but their main powers were trapped in the stone and split in three equal parts, each piece given to the appointed guardian: the guardian of magic, healing, and invincibility. Supposedly, guardians were to keep their piece of the stone safe, until the time came when the magic was to be resurrected.

"The Tuatha Dé Danann entrusted the security of the stone to the hierarchy of the Druids, who chose a sorcerer, a healer, and an alchemist. Each was given their part of the stone, marked with the protected Ogham signs, and vowed to guard it through the generations until the chosen one of the Tuatha Dé Danann would be called upon to reunite the powers once again. The prophecy stated: *The stones would be united by the hand of the true descendant, and the powers would be at full strength and bring back the glory of the Tuatha Dé Danann in Ireland.*"

Grayson listened with her mouth gaping open. "Okay, for the sake of argument, who are these three keepers of the stone?" She closed her eyes as she rubbed the back of her neck.

"Through the centuries," her mother started, "one guardian did not know the whereabouts or the identity of the other two. This was the only way of keeping the magic and the power safe. I know only of the healer."

"You know? Why do you know this, Ma?" Grayson asked as Neala set the pot of tea on the table along with teacups.

Maeve looked at Neala, who shrugged as she poured the tea. "You're goin' have to tell her."

Grayson cautiously watched Neala and her mother. Neala sat down and poured the milk into her tea. Maeve glanced at Grayson and took a deep breath.

"We are the healers, Grayson," Maeve said softly and

winced.

Grayson blinked several times. "We?" she asked. "As in you and me, we?"

Maeve nodded and looked at Neala. "Me too," the redhead said as she sipped her tea.

Grayson shook her head. "Okay, I love a good Irish story as well as the next, but this is just a bit over the top, don't you think?"

Neala sighed deeply. "I knew you wouldn't believe it."

"How can I? Listen to yourselves: Druids, rituals, stones. Magical powers. Fairies and elves." She looked from one woman to the other. "It's too fantastic to believe."

Silence filled the small kitchen. Grayson watched as her mother drank her tea. She then glanced at Neala, who was staring at her teacup. This can't be happening, she thought. She remembered when she was a young girl back in Ireland. She did remember the Samhain rituals that took place on Halloween. She remembered watching her mother and her friends standing around the bonfire; the villagers would partake, as well, welcoming the Celtic and the Wiccan New Year. Grayson learned at a very young age that Samhain heralded the beginning of winter when the world starts to darken and the days grow shorter. It was the beginning of the dark half of the year and the end of the power of the sun.

"What are you thinking, sweetie?" her mother asked, breaking her from her reverie.

Grayson shrugged. "When I was a kid—Samhain with the bonfires and the villagers. I remember being cold and you hugging me as we stood by the fire," she said. "October thirty-first: it ushered in the dark half of the year."

"The bonfires kept us warm and reminded us that the sun would return," Maeve added. "We would all take an ember from that fire and light our fireplaces in hopes of a warm and safe winter."

"The bonfire also warded off the evil spirits," Neala said.

"I remember Sister Daniel saying on that night of the year the veil between the living and the dead is at its thinnest." Grayson looked at her mother. "She did say that, right?"

Maeve nodded. "Yes, she did. Pre-Christianity believed that the spirits roamed freely at Samhain. The Church tried to replace the pagan festival with All Saints Day. Or more accurately, All Hallows Day, then of course All Souls Day on November second."

"So the eve of All Souls Day became All Saints Eve or All Hallows Eve—Halloween. All Saints Day is said to be the day when souls walked the Earth," Neala added.

Grayson took a deep breath. "We all know how Halloween got started. Let's get back to the unbelievable. If all you say is true about the Druids, the gods, and the Tuatha, then what does this have to do with Jane Monahan's and Nan Quigley's death?" She stopped abruptly. "Nan Quigley…" she repeated.

Maeve leaned over and touched her arm. "What about Nan?"

"I don't know—something." Grayson rubbed her neck. "I dunno." She rapidly shook her head. "Okay, let's continue on with…whatever it is. Tell me more about this legend, or prophecy, Ma. How are we involved in this?"

"Grayson, we need to talk to someone who knows much more than I do. It'll be clearer to you then, sweetie."

Grayson raised an eyebrow. "Who?"

Maeve and Neala exchanged glances, which Grayson noticed. "Ma?"

"There's a man who's an expert in Irish mythology. He'll tell you all about it. We'll see him in a couple of days," her mother said.

"Good, where is he?" Grayson asked and lifted the teacup to her mouth.

"Ennis," Maeve mumbled into her teacup.

Grayson looked up so quickly the tea spilled out of her cup. She wiped her lap with a napkin. "Did you say Ennis, as in Ennis, County Clare? As In County Clare—"

Neala rolled her eyes. "Yes, Grayson, County Clare, Ireland."

Grayson knew her mouth was gaping once again. "We can't meet with this guy if he's in Ireland, and I'm not going to Ireland," she said seriously.

"Yes, you are. Your passport is in order, and I already got the tickets," Maeve said. "I get the window seat."

"Ma, this isn't funny," Grayson tried to point out. "We can't just fly off to Ireland."

"And why not?"

Grayson opened her mouth, then closed it. Her job was certainly not a reason now.

"Grayson, I have a bad feeling here. I-I would feel better if you and Maeve were with me," Neala said. Grayson shifted uncomfortably in her seat and looked at her mother.

"Sister Daniel said she'd love to see you again," Maeve enticed. When Grayson didn't respond, she went on, "And you can have the window seat."

Neala lowered her head, trying not to laugh. Grayson narrowed her eyes at her mother. "What's this guy's name?"

"Corky—"

"Corky?"

Maeve ignored the interruption. "Corky Kerrigan, he's—"

"I know." Grayson held up her hand. "An expert. We'll see."

"Then you'll go?" Neala asked. Grayson heard the excitement in her voice. She looked into her green eyes and smiled grudgingly.

"Well, you're still in protective custody," Grayson said, ignoring the fact that she was no longer a detective; protective custody was a moot point. "And well…"

Neala reached over and placed her hand on Grayson's forearm. "Thank you, Detective."

Grayson swallowed and felt the warm hand on her arm. "You're welcome, Doctor." She glanced over at her mother to see her grinning wildly. "And you can have the damned window seat."

They laughed for a moment, then fell silent. Grayson knew this trip back to her birthplace was not going to be a vacation. She wondered what would happen in the five days before the pagan festival of Samhain. To be honest, she wanted to know what her visions meant and why Vicky was in them. She wanted to meet this Corky fellow and hear just what Irish blarney he had to offer.

She suddenly felt that pulling sensation in the pit of her stomach and shivered. As if on cue, the image of someone, something flew through her mind. It was fast, but she saw the altar through the fog.

Instantly, her left palm itched, and she scratched at it. For some reason, the line from Macbeth flashed through her mind: *By the pricking of my thumbs—something wicked this way comes.*

Chapter 18

After a quiet dinner, Neala called for the fifth time to check on the exhibit. "Yes, I know I called before," she said into the phone. "You don't have to get snippy with me."

Grayson walked over to her and held out her hand. Neala, completely bewildered, obediently handed over the phone. "This is Detective MacCarthaigh of the Chicago Police Department. Dr. Rourke is concerned that the artifacts are returned to Ireland in one piece, safe and sound. I work very closely with the mayor's office, and if anything happens, I will hold you personally responsible. Is that clear?"

"Y-yes, Detective. Nothing is going to happen to it. I've got union workers all over the place here. It'll be put on the plane tomorrow safe and sound," the worried voice said.

"Good, thank you," Grayson said and hung up the phone. She looked at Neala. "Now, do not bother them again."

Neala turned bright red as Maeve laughed. Grayson even chuckled while she walked over to the fireplace and knelt down. "Mother, when was the last time you cleaned this thing?" She opened the flue. She placed wood in the grate and crumpled up newspaper for kindling.

"The last time you cleaned it, sweetie," she said absently as she leafed through the pages of the old book. "Grayson, do you have those pictures you wanted me to see?"

Grayson dusted off her hands as she got the fire going. "Yep. They're on the desk in that file along with information on Tynan."

Neala retrieved the manila folder and stood behind Maeve, who was sitting at the desk. She tilted the shade of the desk lamp to shine on the book. "All right now. I have the Ogham alphabet here, or at least some of it. So much has been lost, but I believe I have enough here to decipher this for you."

Grayson stood on the other side of her mother and picked up the folder. "Here are the forensic pictures of both victims." She took out the pictures and laid them on the desk side by side.

All three looked at the pictures in silence. Grayson had to admit, although they got a close-up of the markings, it was still gruesome.

Maeve took a deep breath and put on her reading glasses. "Well then, let's see if we can find out what this means."

Grayson watched as her mother leafed through the dusty old book. "Here." After a moment, she stopped and pointed. "Is this the same marking?"

Grayson and Neala leaned over Maeve. "I think so," Grayson said thoughtfully. "Look, there are two or three that are the same on both, but then there are these on top that are different. How do you read this alphabet, Ma?"

Maeve struck a thoughtful pose before explaining. "You read Ogham text beginning from the bottom left side, continuing upward, across the top and down the right side." She pointed to a picture of a large stone with Ogham printing on it. "In and around the sixth century, Ogham was carved or etched into flat stone. Inscriptions were written on stemlines cut into the face of the stone, instead of along its edge. These are known as scholastic. Ogham was occasionally used for notes in manuscripts, but not often, from what I understand."

"But in the case of Jane and Nan?" Neala asked.

"In this case, it appears that a set of the inscriptions means one word." Maeve continued leafing through the book. "And I will find it. I—ah, here it is."

Grayson leaned farther and saw that indeed her mother had found the same set of markings. "Does that say what I think it says?" Grayson asked quietly.

Maeve nodded and looked up at Grayson; she looked over her reading glasses. "Underworld."

Before Grayson gave herself time to think of the reason why

this word was carved in an ancient Irish alphabet, she asked, "What do the other marks mean?"

Maeve concentrated on the book once again. Grayson glanced at Neala, who looked very pale. "You okay?" Grayson asked.

Neala nodded. "This is a bit unsettling."

Grayson chuckled sarscastically. "Ya think?"

Maeve cleared her throat. "I found them. It's in Gaelic."

"What do they mean, Ma?"

"This is the mark on Nan," Maeve said and showed Grayson the book.

The old yellowed page was hard to read. "Alchemist," Grayson whispered.

"And this is Jane's marking," Maeve continued in a quiet voice.

Neala looked at the page then and gasped. "Healer." Maeve and Neala looked at each other. "I didn't know Jane was part of this."

"Neither did I," Maeve said.

"Part of what? Are we talking about the stone and its guardian again?" Grayson asked. "No, don't tell me. I know the answer."

Maeve slowly closed the book and ran her hand over the leather cover. Neala nearly collapsed into a nearby chair.

Grayson paced in front of the desk. "Okay, let me think. We've got three parts of a stone, a stone that is supposed to have so much magic and power that the Druid hierarchy decided to bust it in three and keep it safe until the time comes to resurrect it, am I right?"

Maeve watched Grayson as she paced back and forth. "Exactly." Grayson heard the hopeful tone in her voice. She saw Neala perk up, as well.

"Don't get nervous, ladies. I still say there's a logical explanation for these murders," Grayson assured them before she continued. "So we can assume that whoever killed Jane Monahan and Nan Quigley did so to get the part of the stone they were guarding."

Guarding... Grayson stopped and closed her eyes. She remembered what happened upstairs in the bathroom with the face in the mirror. She looked down at the palm of her hand and ran her fingers across the crescent-shaped scar that bisected her entire palm.

Garda.

She heard the voice in her head as she heard it the other night. Grayson looked at her mother, who was watching her intently. "Grayson, tell me…" she whispered.

"I-I had this vision the other night. I was looking in the mirror and suddenly a face was superimposed, and I heard someone whisper *garda*," she said and leaned against the desk. "I have no idea what it means."

"I think you do, sweetie," her mother said softly. "In the Gaelic, Grayson."

Grayson knew her mother was right. "Garda literally means guard."

"Irish police are called garda," Neala added.

"So what are you saying?" Grayson asked impatiently and looked at both women. "I'm supposed to be some sort of guardian? Well, I don't know where these stones are. I don't know any of this, so how can I guard or protect something I don't know exists?" Her voice rose with every sentence. She stopped and took a deep breath. "All I know is that there are two dead women brutally murdered and they're connected somehow to this legend or prophecy that somebody concocted out of their Irish imagination, and the only suspect I have is a man who may or may not be well over a hundred years old. How's that for logic?" She slumped against the edge of the desk. All at once, she was exhausted. "And I'm not even a cop anymore."

Maeve winced and heard the tone of sad resignation in her voice. Neala heard it, as well. She walked up to Grayson and stood in front of her. "It took a great deal of strength to do what you did this afternoon, Grayson MacCarthaigh," she said in a quiet but firm voice.

Grayson looked up into the green eyes but said nothing. Neala looked into Grayson's eyes. "I'm sorry for what's happened to you," she said and reached out and lightly touched the sutures on Grayson's cheek. For a moment, Grayson leaned into the soft touch of this woman she barely knew. A feeling of contentment swept through her that she had not felt in two years. Instinctively, Grayson knew Neala was not only talking about what happened to her and Stan.

Suddenly, the content feeling was gone, and in its place, an overwhelming sense of loss filled her. She felt tears sting her eyes and damned herself for her lack of control. She lowered her head in the hope that Neala would not see the tears.

Neala cupped Grayson's face and lifted Grayson's gaze to meet her own. "I loved her so much," Grayson whispered. She was shocked to see the compassion and tears welling in the green eyes.

"I know you did," Neala responded in kind. "And she knows it. She will always know it." She blinked, sending the tears streaming down her cheeks. "She will know it until the end of time."

Grayson closed her eyes and choked off the sob that stuck in her throat. Neala gently pulled her into her arms. Grayson wrapped her arms around Neala's waist and held on as she wept the tears that had been locked away for nearly two years.

Neala ran her fingers through Grayson's hair and murmured soothing words. Grayson felt so relieved that the heaviness she had been carrying in her heart seemed to lighten as she relaxed into Neala's comforting embrace. After a moment, she pulled back and wiped the tears from her cheeks. "Sorry."

"No need," Neala whispered and kissed her forehead.

Grayson sniffed and noticed her mother sitting there, smiling through her tears. Maeve stood and took off her glasses. "I think another pot of tea is in order before we all flood the room." She kissed Grayson on her head as she passed by.

"Neala," Grayson started, then stopped, not knowing quite what she was about to say. She then shrugged. "Thank you."

"You're welcome," Neala said with a warm smile.

"How do you know?" Grayson asked and looked into her eyes. Neala cocked her head in question. "That Vic will always know?"

Neala smiled and took Grayson's hand and turned her palm

upward. She ran her fingers over the scar. "We all have God-given powers, whether you want to believe it or not."

Grayson stared at the palm of her hand. For a moment, it looked as though the scar was larger… no—not larger, but what?

"Grayson?"

She looked up. Neala watched with a cautious eye. "What is it?"

Maeve came back rolling the old teacart. "I remember when I was a young woman, my mother used to have a teacart just like this and—" She stopped abruptly. "What's the matter?"

"I dunno." Grayson ran her fingers over the scar. "Look."

Maeve put on her reading glasses, took Grayson's hand in her own, and examined it. Neala watched in silence.

"It's different," Grayson said. "It feels different."

"It looks bigger or…" Maeve ran her fingers over the scar. "It's raised…"

Grayson studied the scar. "What the fuck is goin' on?" she asked, almost angrily. "No, don't tell me. Your guy in Ireland will have all the answers."

"Sit down and have some tea, sweetie," her mother said and pushed her toward the couch. On the way, Grayson swiped the folder from the desk and took it with her.

As she took a sip of her tea, she pulled a face. "This isn't your usual brand of tea, Ma."

Maeve looked up from her teacup. "You sound like a commercial. It's Neala's."

Grayson looked at the doctor, who smiled. "It's a mix of this and that. It'll help you sleep."

"Hmm, Dr. Neala Rourke, the healer?"

Neala grinned. "Yes, Grayson, the healer."

Grayson found she was smiling back and glanced at her mother's smug grin. She cleared her throat and opened the folder. "Nan Quigley," she said and drank her tea. "She's…wait a minute." She set her teacup down. She leafed through the articles and stopped. She grinned wildly and looked at both women.

"Oh, I know that grin. What have you found?" her mother asked and leaned in.

"Sir John Quigley." Grayson pointed to the man in the picture. "I need to know who this guy was."

"He must be related to Nan," Neala said.

Maeve stood and headed down the hall. "Let's find out."

Grayson studied the article. "There has to be a connection here. I—" She stopped abruptly as Maeve appeared with her laptop and set it on the coffee table.

"Let's Google him," Maeve said.

Neala laughed as she made room on the small table. Once she was ready, Maeve typed in the search. "We'll see if he's important or just a …" Her voice trailed off as she read.

"What is it, Ma?" Grayson sat on the arm of the couch next to her.

"He was knighted by the Queen of England in nineteen fifty-one. He was an anthropologist and worked with the Irish and English governments on archaeological expeditions. He taught at Cambridge and wrote several papers about Irish and English mythology…." She stopped and read further.

Grayson waited patiently as her knee bounced up and down. Maeve absently reached over and put her hand on her knee. She sat back then and let out a deep breath. "It appears he worked on a textbook for the university called *The Stone of Destiny: The Truth behind the Magic.*"

"And what is the truth?" Neala asked before Grayson could.

Maeve's fingers danced over the keyboard.

Grayson suddenly felt the room grow smaller. Her heart raced and she shivered violently. She vaguely heard her mother's voice as the buzzing in her ears started. Her palm itched and throbbed. The visions started again—disjointed and confusing. The robed figure; a woman lying on the stone altar wrapped in white linen; the crescent moon shining through the fog in a haze of moonlight. She heard someone chanting; she saw the stone on the altar; someone screamed. The visions abruptly stopped as if someone flipped a switch. She blinked several times and realized she was breathing like a bull.

As she ran her fingers through her hair, she realized she was soaked with perspiration. The rush she felt from the visions had exhausted her. She looked down to see her mother and Neala watching her.

"What did you see, Gray?" her mother asked softly.

Grayson took a deep breath and let it out slowly. She explained what she remembered of the vision.

"What else have you seen?" Maeve asked.

Grayson walked over to the fireplace and sat on the hearth, facing both women. She explained her dream of the altar and the wolf. She told them again of the apparition in the mirror the night of the explosion. Grayson retold all of this with slow deliberation, making sure she left out nothing. When she finished, she turned her gaze to the dancing flames and whispered, "Something wicked this way comes."

She looked back at the worried faces. "Something is going to happen in Ireland, isn't it?"

"Your fellow in Ireland better have some answers, Ma," Grayson said tiredly. She looked at Neala. "And what special 'this and that' was in that tea, Dr. Rourke?"

"Don't blame Neala. It was my idea," her mother said.

"Your idea to drug me?" Grayson felt her anger mounting.

"You weren't remembering fast enough."

"Remembering what? And fast enough for what?"

The irritated and exasperated tenor in Grayson's voice was unmistakable. Grayson looked at her mother, who suddenly looked old and worn beyond her years. "Ma, you have to level with me now. This is getting way out of hand, and I need to rein this all in."

Tears formed in her eyes, shocking Grayson, who was quickly kneeling in front of her. "Ma, goddamn it, please, tell me."

Maeve took Grayson's hands in her own and looked her in the eye. "Perhaps you were too young to remember back when you were a little girl in Ireland." She turned Grayson's palm upward. "This is not a scar, sweetie." She caressed the palm. "Haven't you ever wondered why this has grown as you have grown?"

Grayson frowned deeply and looked at her palm. It never dawned on her. Scars are dead tissue, they have no blood running through them; they do not develop and grow with the body. This "scar" covered the palm of her hand. She looked up at her mother. "What is this, Mother?"

Maeve blinked back the tears. "The stones would be united by the hand of the true descendant, and the powers would be at full strength and bring back the glory of the Tuatha Dé Danann in Ireland," she recited the prophecy in a whisper.

Grayson walked over to the fireplace still looking at her palm. Things were getting out of control, all logic was leaving her. She loathed her next sentence.

"When and where in Ireland do we meet with this Corky Kerrigan? And he had better have some answers."

"The exhibit is leaving tomorrow morning at eleven. Our flight leaves roughly the same time," Neala said as she watched Grayson. "You need to sleep now."

Maeve stood and stretched her back. "Yes, we could all use a good night's sleep. Gray, I already packed a bag for you. I have your passport, and I took care of everything today while you and Neala were at the precinct. We're all set. There's nothing to worry about."

"Let's not go too far, Ma," Grayson said and yawned. "I'll take the couch."

"No, I will," Neala argued.

Grayson shook her head. "No, the couch is fine."

"Grayson, I'll take the couch."

Maeve rolled her eyes and picked up the laptop. "I'm going to bed. You two settle your sleeping arrangements."

Neala said nothing as Maeve kissed Grayson, who was scowling. She then kissed Neala on the cheek. "Figure it out soon. You both need your sleep."

As she mounted the stairs, she said over her shoulder, "By the way, your bed is big enough for two, Grayson."

She disappeared without another word. Grayson raised an eyebrow and glanced at Neala, who was just staring at the empty staircase.

"Grayson, please don't be arguin'," Neala pleaded in a soft voice. "I just need to get my things from the bedroom."

She, too, walked upstairs. Grayson stood in the living room, not knowing what to do, which was not usual for her. She looked at the old lumpy couch and headed down the hallway, as well.

Neala gathered her suitcase and turned to see Grayson standing in the doorway. "I-I'll be out of the way in a moment."

Grayson reached over and gently took it out of her hands. She looked into her green eyes and said in a low voice, "Stay with me tonight, please."

Neala nearly gasped at the suggestion. "I...well, I don't really want to sleep on that couch."

Grayson smiled slightly. "No, I don't want you to, either. The bathroom is open."

Neala gathered what she needed and scooted past Grayson. "I'll just be a minute."

Grayson changed and slipped into bed. She let out a deep groan as Neala walked in.

"Are you all right?" Neala asked and sat on the edge of the bed.

"Yes, just unbelievably tired." Grayson closed her eyes. She felt Neala slip under the covers and settle beside her.

"Thank you," Neala whispered.

Grayson reached up and turned out the light. "You're welcome."

They lay in silence for a moment or two. "What's going to happen, Neala?"

"I don't know. There's so much I don't know. However, I think Corky can shed some light and explain the prophecy much better."

Grayson nodded and yawned. "My mother knows more than she's telling. I know her too well." Grayson could feel Neala hesitate.

"She loves you very much. I think she's hoping we're all wrong about this."

Grayson stared at the ceiling, then looked over at Neala, who turned her head toward Grayson. In the darkness, their eyes met and neither said a word. Grayson finally broke the silence.

"She's not wrong about any of it," Grayson whispered. She felt Neala's body shiver instantly. "Is she?"

In a quivering voice, Neala responded, "No, Maeve is not wrong, and I'm sorrier than I can say."

Grayson instinctively raised her arm, and Neala scooted over. Grayson draped her arm around the trembling shoulders and held her close.

As she drifted off to sleep, the visions started; they would visit and haunt Grayson throughout the night.

Chapter 19

Phelan looked out the small window as his private jet touched down at Shannon Airport. He saw the black limo with Ian standing next to it. Phelan smiled when he saw the lawyer straighten his tie and push his glasses up on his nose.

"Mr. Tynan," Ian called out as Phelan neared. "It's good to have you back, sir."

Phelan grinned sarcastically. "I'm sure you missed me, Ian. Open the door."

Ian swallowed and smiled weakly as he opened the limo door. Phelan slipped in and waited until Ian dashed around the limo and got in and sat across from him.

"I trust your trip was productive. I've—"

Phelan held up his hand. "Are they safe?"

Ian blinked several times and nodded. "Y-yes, sir, they are."

"Then fix me a drink and keep still."

Ian opened the small bar and poured the whiskey into the crystal tumbler. He handed it to Phelan with a trembling hand. Phelan grinned. "Don't be so nervous, Ian. You have nothing to fear," he said and accepted the drink. "Unless you disappoint me, dear boy."

Ian stretched his neck but said nothing. Phelan took a long sip and looked up. "You haven't disappointed me now, have you?"

"No," Ian said and cleared his throat. "No, Mr. Tynan. Everything is as you requested."

"Good. Now stop sweating like some barnyard animal. You're beginning to annoy me." He finished his drink. He looked from the empty glass to his trembling lawyer. He impatiently shook the glass.

"Oh, yes, sir." Ian prepared another whiskey.

"Now tell me. What have you found out about Maeve MacCarthaigh? And it had better be good news," he said in a dark threatening voice, which he knew would have Ian Hennessy pissing himself. He smiled happily as he sipped his whiskey.

Ian opened his briefcase and took out the manila folder. He cleared his throat before starting. "Maeve Grayson, born County Roscommon in—"

"Get on with it," Phelan said tiredly.

"Yes, well… She studies Wicca. She's a professor of Irish mythology and history. She is also a Druidess, Mr. Tynan."

Phelan cocked his head to one side and smiled. "Is she now? And is she associated at all with Mother Abbess?" he asked, already knowing the answer.

The young lawyer grinned and nodded. "From what I have obtained, she is a very close friend to Sister Daniel."

"The Abbess," Phelan whispered as he stared at his glass.

"Sir?" Ian asked and leaned forward.

"Go on," Phelan directed him with a wave of his hand.

"Maeve Grayson married Dermott MacCarthaigh—"

"He's unimportant. Tell me about the Druidess and the abbess—the pagan and the Christian," he said with utter distain; he swallowed the rest of his whiskey and held his glass out to Ian, who replenished it. "They and their ancestors have annoyed me throughout the centuries. I will be annoyed no longer."

Ian blinked, then concentrated on his findings. "Well, it appears that the Church is somewhat disenchanted with Sister Daniel. She has been associated with paganism since she joined the order when she was eighteen. She never condemned it as the Church wanted her to. Evidently, the Church can't do much with her. The villagers love her. I believe there would be too much of an uproar if the Church took any action against the old abbess. It's quite amazing actually—to be loved so much."

Phelan glared at his lawyer, then took a deep breath. "It's Brigid all over again," he said with disgust and shook his head.

"Beg your pardon, sir?"

"Do you know your Irish history, Ian?"

"Well, if you mean St. Brigid, who doesn't? Next to St. Patrick, she's the most revered person in Ireland and beyond. Some say even more so than St. Patrick."

"And why do you suppose that is, dear boy?" Phelan asked with a hint of sarcasm. He was so sick of hearing about this woman. Now this abbess…

Ian thought for a moment and shrugged. "I suppose it was because she was so well loved."

Phelan snorted. "Being well loved," he mimicked, "does not get one canonized by the Catholic Church."

"Miracles?" Ian offered hopefully.

Phelan closed his eyes in disgust and sighed. "Ian, you are an idiot. I don't know why I keep you in my charge." He stopped and struck a thoughtful pose. "Well, that's not entirely true. You are unscrupulous, that's a monumental point in your favor—don't ever forget that. No, it was not through her miracles that she became a saint, though the Church will tell you that. They had no idea what to do with the pagan goddess."

Ian now sported a confused look. "Sir, there's no proof that Brigid was a goddess. There's speculation true, but—"

Phelan looked out the window and laughed heartily. "Yes, there is speculation. Was Brigid a mythical triple goddess who took human form? Or a human who became a saint?"

"If you believe what's written, she was a real person. The rest is mythology, Mr. Tynan, like the gods and goddesses."

Phelan offered a smug grin as the limo pulled into the circular gravel driveway. "You don't believe in the gods, goddesses, or in the Druid and Druidess?"

"Well, not really," Ian said slowly. "D-do you?"

Phelan leaned forward and grinned. Ian leaned back against the seat. Phelan gently sniffed the air; he could smell Ian's fear. "Get out and open my door."

Phelan never saw anyone move so fast as Ian Hennessy.

Ian assisted the limo driver with Phelan's luggage. Phelan was leafing through his mail when Ian walked into the library. "It's damp. Light a fire," Phelan said absently as he continued.

When Ian had the fire roaring, Phelan tossed the mail on the desk and sat in a huge leather chair by the fire. "Another whiskey, Ian."

He gazed into the flames until Ian handed him the drink. "Make one for yourself."

"No, thank you, sir, I—" He stopped abruptly when Phelan shot him a challenging glare. "Yes, thank you." He made a strong drink and stood there, seemingly awaiting his orders.

Phelan grinned and motioned to the chair opposite him. Ian sank into the deep cushion and tried to get comfortable. Phelan reveled in his discomfort. "Continue…"

Ian took a deep breath and ran his fingers through his thick black hair, then pushed the glasses up on his nose. "Well, as I see it, St. Brigid was—"

"Not her, you idiot," Phelan said. "Maeve Grayson. Tell me of her being a Druidess."

"Oh, yes. From what I could gather, her mother and grandmother were heavily into Wicca, and I'm told that several farmers would come to their homes to procure the potions for their harvest. The old villagers remember old Mrs. Grayson and young Maeve mixing the potions in the kitchen. One old woman in particular." Ian stopped as he reached in his breast pocket for his notebook. "Yes, here, a Mrs. Donnelly remembers Maeve's mother telling her that somewhere Maeve was going to do something great. She was destined for it."

Phelan rolled the glass, staring at the amber liquid. "Did she now? And how did old Mrs. Grayson know this about her daughter?"

Ian shrugged. "I don't know. The old woman just repeated what she heard."

"Destined, eh?" Phelan repeated and intently stared at the fire. He then blinked and looked at Ian, who was staring at him; he swallowed his drink. "Have you found out anything of her lineage?"

Ian grinned. Phelan was sure the young lawyer was happy he did his research. "Yes, indeed, sir. It appears that Maeve Grayson comes from a long line of paganism. As I said, her mother and grandmother practiced the magic. They also were very revered by the villagers for this. And they were the prime movers when it came to the pagan festivals. Um, two in particular. Let me see...." He flipped through the pages of his notebook.

Phelan stared into the fire and answered for him. "Imbolc and Samhain."

Ian looked up from his notes. "Y-yes, exactly so. I wonder why only those two..."

"Let me enlighten you to pagans, dear boy." Phelan sipped his whiskey. "Imbolc was a very important time to the ancient Irish. Did you know that at the burial mounds throughout Ireland, such as the Mounds of the Hostages in Tara, the inner chamber of the passage tombs are perfectly aligned with the rising sun of Imbolc and Samhain?" he asked.

Ian shook his head. "No, sir, I've never heard of it."

Phelan smiled thinly. "No, I don't suppose you would. Not many have. Have you heard of Newgrange? A similar phenomenon takes place there. The rising Imbolc sun shines down the long passageway and illuminates the inner chamber of the tomb." He finished and stared at the fire. Ian watched and said nothing as he, too, drank. Phelan glanced at his confused look and chuckled.

"You're wondering what all this means, aren't you?"

"Quite frankly, yes. However, I just gather the information you require."

Phelan nodded in agreement, then gazed into the fire. "Imbolc and Samhain. The beginning and the end, hope and despair."

"Imbolc is the first of the four seasonal festivals," Ian said and continued, "It says here that it is either held in February, which is also the feast day of St. Brigid—"

"There's that name again," Phelan interrupted in an exasperated voice and drank his whiskey. "Or the first sign of spring. Yes, yes. However, dear boy, it is Samhain where all the fun begins. That is truly my favorite time in the Irish calendar. The approach of the dark half of the year, when on one night, the dead become part of the living under the dark of the new moon. But it is the waning days after the new moon. The residual effect of that moon holds more magic than you could ever imagine."

"The waning days, sir?"

Phelan nodded and smiled. "Yes. The astronomers call it the waning moon or the crescent moon. But what do they know? Idiotic mortals." He let out a deep sigh. "The waning days of the residual moon."

"Residual moon? I-I never heard of that, sir."

"And why should you? The old Druid knew what he was doing. The hierarchy tried to stop him," he said, completely unaware of his young lawyer. "They tried to keep it all to themselves. Squander all that power, all the magic." He looked out of the big window and stared out into the twilight sky. "Soon, so very soon."

Phelan blinked then and looked at Ian. "You've done a good job, Ian, very good."

He saw the relief spread across Ian's face.

"Thank you, Mr. Tynan," he said as he put the glass to his lips.

"Leave…now."

Ian rose and put the glass on the bar. He picked up his briefcase. "Good day, Mr. Tynan."

Phelan stared once again at the fire. He waved his hand in dismissal and heard the door quietly close.

He had waited so long, spent centuries destroying anything in his path in his quest to fulfill his destiny. The time was at hand; he could feel it deep within him. Ian Hennessy had assisted him, as his father and his father before. The Hennesseys were good toadies, he thought with an amused chuckle. How willingly they prostituted themselves for money. Perhaps that was their destiny. He stared into the fire—we all have a destiny. Just as it was the Graysons' destiny to annoy him now.

His breathing became deep and his nostrils flared. Maeve Grayson, he thought. Throughout the centuries, he had waited. Could she be the one? He was so close, so close to procuring the power that the old Druids denied him and his father. He stared angrily at the roaring fire and watched the flames grow in the confines of the large fireplace. The intense heat filled the library as the fire hissed and burned, taking on a life of its own.

He heard it then, the chanting in the ancient tongue—voices

low and rhythmic, chanting, beckoning him. He felt the pulling sensation deep in his being. As he stared into the flames, he saw it: the face of his father staring back at him, challenging him.

Our time is at hand, my son—four days hence. The true descendant must be destroyed.

Never blinking, Phelan nodded his agreement. The image of his father faded, and in its place another face—Maeve Grayson—appeared through the dancing flames, taunting him. Phelan's eye twitched. He closed his eyes and clenched his fists, breaking the glass in his hand.

The flames now licked outside the fireplace walls, fueled by Phelan's deep breaths. Visions flashed through his mind's eye: the altar, the waning crescent moonlight through the fog. The time was close at hand.

As Phelan breathed heavily, the flames grew with intensity. The roar of the fire mingled with the low chanting voices as he suddenly opened his eyes and watched the flames. Grinning, he took a deep breath and blew a steady stream toward the fireplace. In an instant, with a whining almost animalistic cry, the flames shot up through the flue on Phelan's command and were extinguished.

Phelan stared at the empty fireplace, then looked out at the silence of the evening twilight. "So very soon."

Chapter 20

"I lied to you," Maeve said over her shoulder as they walked onto the plane.

Grayson grunted as she adjusted the carryon backpack. "What the hell did you pack in this thing?" Maeve heard Neala chuckle behind them. "What did you lie about?"

"I'm not giving you the window seat," she said and slipped into the seat.

Grayson groaned as she lifted the backpack into the overhead storage. "I didn't expect the window seat, Ma." She stepped aside to allow Neala, who was still chuckling, to sit in the middle.

Grayson eased into the aisle seat and buckled her seat belt. She winced and flexed her shoulder.

"Still a bit sore?" Neala asked. Grayson shook her head and Neala raised an eyebrow. "Would you like to try that again?"

Grayson shot her a look, then smiled slightly. "It's a little sore," she mumbled.

Maeve smiled as she listened to their conversation. "I love takeoff," she said and fastened her seat belt.

Grayson groaned and put her head back as Neala laughed. "I'm happy for you, Maeve."

Grayson yawned. "I don't know why I'm so tired. I slept like a baby." She stopped and glanced at Neala, who was hiding her grin in her magazine.

Maeve raised an eyebrow as she remembered late the night before when she poked her head into her daughter's bedroom. Neala was missing from the couch. She found her in her daughter's bed, wrapped around Grayson like a second skin. Later that morning, when it was way past time for either woman, she knocked at the door. When she heard no signs of life, she once again poked her head in. She smiled affectionately when she saw Grayson spooned behind the good doctor, her arm encircling her waist. It was the most peaceful Grayson had looked in her sleep since Vic died.

Neala leaned over to Maeve and whispered, "I like the takeoff myself." She smiled as the plane taxied down the runway. Maeve grinned at the childlike tone.

"So, Ma, you haven't said where we'll be staying."

"Oh, I didn't?" she asked. "Hmm. Well, we're staying at our house."

Grayson lifted her head and looked past Neala. "Our house? I thought you and Da sold it."

Maeve smiled affectionately and shook her head, her blue eyes tearing. "Nope. I couldn't do it. Your father understood but didn't like it. He wanted to sell, but it wasn't his birthright, it was mine and I couldn't do it. My mother and grandmother were born in that cottage."

"Good for you," Neala said and patted her arm.

"Who's been taking care of it all these years?" Grayson asked. "Shit, Ma, it's been a while."

"Sister Daniel sees that a woman comes in monthly to clean, and the villagers keep an eye out."

"That's wonderful, Maeve. I'm glad you still have your home. I can't wait to see it."

The plane lifted off the runway, and Maeve held Neala's hand as they looked out the window. In a moment, the plane leveled off and both women sighed. "Well, settle back, ladies. It's a long flight to Shannon," Neala said.

Grayson once again put her head back as Maeve pulled out her book. "I can put a good dent in this book." She adjusted her reading glasses.

They sat in silence for a time—Maeve reading her book, Neala leafing through a magazine, and Grayson staring off into space. Maeve glanced at her daughter, who was now absently running her finger over the sutures across her brow and cheek. Maeve hoped with everything in her being she was wrong, that the prophecy was wrong, that it was all a bad dream and Grayson would not be called upon to fulfill her destiny.

When Grayson was born and Maeve noticed the crescent-shaped scar on her tiny palm, she thought nothing of it. It wasn't until Grayson was nearly two that she brought it to Sister Daniel's attention. She remembered her friend's reaction.

Sister Daniel held Grayson on her lap; the eighteen-month-old happily played with the rosary beads as the nun examined her tiny palm. She then looked up at Maeve, who was biting her bottom lip. "Well? It could be just a birthmark, right?"

Sister Daniel took a deep breath and let it out. "It could be just a birthmark," she agreed with a grin as she watched Grayson. "But I fear it is her birthright, Maeve, and so do you, or you wouldn't have shown this to me." She continued to smile and laugh as she tickled little Grayson, who squealed with delight.

Maeve sank into the kitchen chair next to her friend. "How can we be sure?"

"We can't, not now," the nun said. Grayson started squirming in her lap when she saw her mother.

Maeve laughed and reached for her daughter. "So what do we do, Sister?"

"We wait for the signs and see. Perhaps we're both wrong. Perhaps it's nothing." She reached over and ran her fingers through the mass of black curls. Grayson giggled once again. Sister Daniel said wistfully, "Perhaps God did nothing more than kiss her palm when she was born."

Maeve nodded as she watched her daughter play with the rosary; she was chewing on the crucifix. "I hope you didn't get those from the pope," Maeve said with a hint of sarcasm.

Sister Daniel laughed outright. "I'm not in his favor, I'm sure. Or the bishop's." She ruffled Grayson's hair. "I'm sure our Lord understands teething."

They sat in silence for a time, both watching Grayson's fascination with the large beads. Maeve knew what her old friend was talking about: Wicca, the festivals, the pagan beliefs that so many Irish still held onto. Though she was a nun in the Catholic Church, Sister Daniel understood the pagan ways, and many a night, she had stood next to Maeve and watched the bonfires of Beltane and Samhain and hoped and prayed for the coming season.

Once the bishop got wind of that tidbit, Sister Daniel was called to his office in Dublin. Maeve met with her old friend after that. "Well, he's none too pleased with me. If I were a priest, I would not be gettin' my own parish anytime soon. As it is, I'm a mere woman, and we know how they view that."

Maeve nodded and slipped her arm through Sister Daniel's as they walked down the cobblestone street. "Yes, it was so much easier in the ancient times when women were revered," Maeve said.

"Well, perhaps one day, your daughter will be called upon to rekindle those days."

Maeve now watched Grayson as she put her head back, let out a deep sigh, and tried to get comfortable. Neala took the small pillow and touched Grayson's arm. "You'll be getting a stiff neck."

Maeve watched the look on her daughter's face and nearly cried. Grayson's blue eyes searched Neala's and Maeve saw myriad emotions flash across her battered face. Although Maeve knew her daughter wanted to say more, Grayson opted for a quiet, "Thanks," before allowing Neala to place the pillow behind her head. Grayson settled in and closed her eyes.

Grayson could not deny the childlike feeling of anticipation as the plane touched down at Shannon Airport. It had been quite a few years since she was home. She chuckled inwardly as the plane taxied to the terminal. Home… How long had it been since she referred to Ireland as home?

Her mother broke her reverie. "I'm excited to see Sister Daniel again."

Grayson smiled then. "Me too. I just realized how much I missed this. I haven't been back…" Her voice trailed off as the heartache started. She remembered back to the time she and Vic tried to plan their vacation and go to Ireland. Time and again, something always got in the way, whether it was Grayson's job or Vicky's. They usually settled for long weekends here and there.

Then two years earlier…

As they finished dinner, Grayson sat back and drank her wine. "Man, what you can to do a roast. Ten more years of you cooking like this, and I'll be as big as a house. Baby, that was wonderful. Ma will be jealous."

Vic laughed as she drank her ice water. "I don't think Maeve has anything to worry about, honey. Now," she said and wiped the corner of her mouth with the napkin.

Grayson refilled her wineglass and looked up. She couldn't help herself; she grinned at the happy smiling face across from her and waited.

"I think we need to start saving and try to get to Ireland," Vic said.

"Okay, if we can finally get our times together," Grayson said and drank her wine. Then she looked at Vic. "Hey, you want a glass? You usually have wine with dinner."

Vic grinned and shook her head. "No, thanks, honey. Now I want to get to Ireland before the end of the year, say in October." She thought for a moment. "Early October."

Grayson chuckled. "I know you're quitting the force, baby, about which I'm extremely glad. I don't like you negotiating hostage situations anymore, but why the timeline? Do you have to put in for vacation?"

Vic, still grinning, shook her head. "Nope."

Grayson gave her a curious look. "Then why October?"

Vic sat back and sported such a serene look that it melted Grayson's heart. "I want our baby to be born in Ireland."

"Oh, is that…what?" she exclaimed and jumped up, knocking over the glass of wine. Vic laughed and shook her head as Grayson dashed over and knelt in front of her. "Did you say our baby? It worked? The first time? You're pregnant?"

Vic nodded. "Yes, yes, yes, and yes!" She ran her fingers through Grayson's hair and pulled her in for a long loving kiss. "We did it," she whispered against her lips.

Grayson groaned as she felt the fingers in her hair and pulled back. "Boy or girl? No, don't tell. I don't wanna know," she said quickly. "Do you know? 'Cause if you know, then I want to know, but if you don't..."

Vic placed her fingertips against her lips. "You dope, relax. We have about seven months. Don't get crazy on me yet, Detective MacCarthaigh."

Grayson felt the color rush to her face. "I love you," she said and laid her head against Vic's stomach. "I love you, too, baby whoever."

Vic laughed and held Grayson's head close to her. "In a few months, we won't get to hold each other this close."

Grayson laughed and held on tight. She felt Vic's soft kiss against her hair. "I love you, Grayson. And if it's a girl, we name her Maeve."

Grayson closed her eyes and swallowed the tears of joy; she could only nod.

So long ago, Grayson thought. It seemed like a lifetime away. The next week, Grayson got the call for the hostage situation; Vic was the negotiator. When Vic jumped in front of that gunman, it was the end of Grayson's life, as well. Three lives ruined... Threes, Grayson thought angrily. Everything happens in threes; it was the Druid way of teaching.

"Grayson?"

She heard Neala calling her name, bringing her back to the present. She looked around to see the passengers gathering their belongings. "Oh, sure," Grayson said as she got up.

As they walked out of the airport, Grayson look around at the green countryside. "Ah, this is what I miss."

Maeve and Neala agreed. "I need to call the museum," Neala said as she pulled out her cell phone and walked away.

Maeve and Grayson looked up as they heard a horn blare. A small old van pulled up and stopped. "What the hell is that?" Grayson set down the luggage.

With that, a young woman poked her head over the hood of the van. "Hello. Mother Abbess described you all perfectly. I'm Therese Mahoney. I volunteered to bring you to the monastery."

She dashed around and opened the back hatch. "Sorry, this clunker will have to do. We don't have too much use for a fancy ride."

"Fancy?" Grayson repeated and got an elbow to the ribs from her mother.

Therese swiped the windblown hair away from her face and chuckled. "I see your point. You must be Grayson. Mother Abbess said you'd be tall and raven-haired." She stuck out her hand, which Grayson took.

She turned to Maeve. "I can't tell you how nice it tis to finally meet you, Mrs. MacCarthaigh. Mother Abbess talks of you often. I feel as though I know both of you." She shook Maeve's hand, then picked up her suitcase.

Neala walked back to them. "Well, all's well. The stone is safely in the museum." She slipped the phone into her purse.

"You must be Dr. Rourke," Therese said and shook Neala's hand.

Grayson noticed Therese was an attractive woman; you'd have to be blind not to see it. She was a little shorter than Neala, but she had a very fit figure. She looked as if she spent her day doing physical labor. Her brown field jacket was worn at the elbow and collar, which was pulled up around her neck. Grayson suddenly realized how chilly it was. She had forgotten the unpredictable Irish weather. As she looked up into the late afternoon sky, the rain clouds swirled and a light breeze started. It was then she noticed it—a hawk lazily circling overhead.

Therese looked up, as well. "Now that's something you don't see often. Hawks aren't as plentiful as they used to be. Well, we'd best be goin' before the downpour starts," she said as she and Grayson loaded the van.

Grayson gave her surroundings a cautious glance as everyone piled into the old van. She shivered as she looked once again up at the cloudy sky and the hawk, still circling. Then inexplicably, she glanced back at the terminal. A man stood by the glass doors. Grayson thought he was waiting for a cab. He was tall with dark windblown hair. Impeccably dressed, he absently pushed his glasses up on the bridge of his nose. He was watching them; Grayson was sure of it. How was she sure? At first, she thought perhaps it was her years of police work. However, in the past week, Grayson's logic was dissipating and now she just "felt" this guy was watching them.

She slipped into the front seat of the van and looked back. He had vanished as if he had never been there.

"Mother Abbess will be so thrilled to see you," Therese said as she shifted the grinding gears.

Sitting next to her, Grayson winced and grimaced as the woman shifted again and the engine groaned painfully.

"I would think Sister Daniel would have some pull with the bishop to at least get a good car."

Therese snorted rudely as she watched the road. "Bureaucrats. They've all but forgotten her."

Maeve leaned forward from the backseat. "What do you mean?"

She looked in the rearview mirror and hesitated. Grayson watched carefully as Therese drove the winding narrow road. "Why have they forgotten Sister Daniel?" Grayson asked pointedly.

Therese thought for another moment. "I'll let her tell you. But if you ask me—"

"Which we did," Grayson interjected.

"The Church has turned its back on Mother Abbess and the monastery. There are only a handful of nuns and novitiates, and even we have been told we must leave for another convent. It's a shame. We love Mother Abbess."

Maeve let out a sad sigh and sat back. Grayson looked forward and watched the Irish landscape whiz by as their driver raced down the small road. There was little else said until they reached the monastery.

Grayson watched the familiar road that wound and wound up to the monastery. It was set back in a small grove of oak trees that seemed to welcome them as they passed. The late afternoon sun filtered through the strong old trees, and a sudden gust of wind swept across the road. Therese struggled to control the old van.

"Well, where did that come from?" she asked breathlessly and held tight to the steering wheel.

Grayson absently scratched her palm but said nothing as she

watched the trees swaying in the wind. She glanced in her side mirror and noticed the trees were perfectly still behind them, yet ahead the Irish wind blew, shaking the leaves from their trees.

Therese looked up. "Odd sky."

"That is a strange sky," Neala agreed as she peered out the back window.

Grayson rolled down her window and looked at the dark clouds mixed with the billowy white clouds as they swirled together. Lightning flashed off in the distance. It was chilly and damp but no rain. She glanced back at her mother, who was silently looking up at the sky, as well.

All at once, there was a loud clap of thunder; the lightning streaked across the sky in front of them. "Good Lord!" Therese exclaimed as she shifted gears once again.

Grayson heard her mother and Neala cry out, as well, then laugh nervously. "That gave me a fright," Neala said as she let out her breath.

Then the rain started. Therese turned on the wipers as it pelted the windshield. Grayson turned in her seat. She was about to say something to Neala when she looked out the back window.

Behind them, the late afternoon sun shone brightly in the cloudless sky; there was no rain, no thunder, no lightning. Only dead calm.

As they turned onto the small road that led to the monastery, the rain and wind suddenly stopped. The dark clouds broke, and the sun shone brightly on the green fields.

No one spoke as the monastery came into view.

Chapter 21

Grayson got the anxious feeling in the pit of her stomach as Therese drove up to the monastery. It was as Grayson remembered: a lone gray stone building set back in a grove of oak trees. She remembered the open field to the left of the monastery was filled with grazing sheep; the short stone walls that were so prevalent throughout Ireland separated sections of the field, making them appear to have some purpose. However, as anyone who visited Ireland knows, these stone walls have no rhyme or reason. It's just part of the "Irishness" of the country.

As Therese pulled up the circular drive, Sister Daniel walked out to greet them. Grayson grinned when she saw her. She was older now, but her smiling face was still the same. She wore a brown tweed skirt and blazer. Her short white hair lay in waves, delicately framing her face. If it was not for the ornate Celtic cross hanging from a long chain around her neck, one would never think this little woman was a nun.

She waved wildly as she stood on the steps. Grayson was grinning like a kid as she watched the old nun. "I think she's happy to see us," she said with a laugh.

Therese pulled up, and Maeve was out of the car in a shot. Sister Daniel rushed around to meet her. "Maeve, my old friend," she exclaimed and opened her arms.

Maeve laughed. "I must be in heaven."

Both women hugged and kissed each other. Grayson was still smiling as she and Neala waited for the two old friends to get reacquainted.

Sister Daniel pulled back first, her eyes filled with tears. "My God, how I've missed you, Maeve."

"So have I, Sister. Or should I say Mother Abbess now?" Maeve asked as she wiped away the tears.

Sister Daniel waved her off. "Don't go on about that. It was a formality from the bishop. His Grace didn't know what else to do with me."

Both women laughed as Sister Daniel turned toward Grayson. Her eyes rimmed with tears as she let out a sigh. "Grayson MacCarthaigh, I haven't seen you in so long. You were a scrawny thing when you left," she said affectionately and shook her head. "And look at you now." She opened her arms.

In two long strides, Grayson was in her arms, amazed at the contented feeling that spread through her. "I've missed you, girl," the old nun whispered.

Grayson held on tight and whispered in kind, "Me too, Sister. I just realized how much."

"You've come home, Gray," she said and pulled back. "And I'm sorry for the reason."

Grayson frowned deeply and said nothing. The old nun took her hand and turned her palm up. Grayson looked, as well, at the crescent-shaped scar that bisected her palm. It was then they heard the hawk screeching overhead.

All of them looked up into the late afternoon sky. The dark clouds came once again, as the hawk lazily soared above them.

Sister Daniel patted Grayson on the cheek, then smiled at Neala. "Neala, it's so good to see you again."

Neala grinned as she walked over and hugged her. "It's so good to see you, too, Mother Abbess."

"Is it safe, child?" Sister Daniel asked. Grayson heard the worried tone.

"Yes, it is. I called from the airport. I'll see about driving to the museum tomorrow, perhaps."

Sister Daniel nodded in agreement. "Well, let's get you inside. The autumn air is a bit brisk this afternoon. I have a fire goin'."

Grayson assisted Therese with the luggage as Therese struggled with the one bag. Grayson heard her grunt and turned as they walked up the steps. "I have no idea what my mother packed in that thing."

Therese laughed as they entered the small foyer. Grayson noticed her mother smiling fondly as she followed Sister Daniel down the hall and into the kitchen.

"It still smells the same." Maeve sighed happily and took a deep breath.

A peat fire was glowing in the small fireplace across the room. Grayson felt the same. The distinct heady and earthy aroma of the burning peat bricks filled the kitchen.

"You can't mistake that smell," Grayson said.

They turned around when two young women walked into the kitchen. Sister Daniel made the introductions. Grayson saw the look of awe on their faces as she and Maeve were introduced. "Would you take the bags to the rooms, ladies?" Sister Daniel asked.

"You'll stay here for tonight, Maeve. I know you want to get back to your home, but it's getting dark. I'd rather not have you out," Sister Daniel said, and Maeve agreed.

"That'll be fine, Sister. I, for one, am exhausted." She sat at the kitchen table and fondly ran her hand over the old wood.

Everyone else sat down. Therese excused herself. "Well, I have chores to finish before it gets too dark."

"Come back for dinner, Therese," Sister Daniel said. "Sister Rose is going to do wonderful things with a leg of lamb."

"How I remember sitting at this very table just before you were born, Gray," Maeve said.

Grayson reached across and took her hand. "I remember sitting right here. I was maybe twelve, thirteen." She stopped as more visions flashed through her mind. "The others..." She looked up and Sister Daniel smiled.

"What others, Grayson?" she asked as she rose to get the whistling kettle. Neala put her hand on the nun's arm and shook her head. Sister Daniel smiled her thanks and turned back to Grayson.

Grayson lost the image and let out a dejected sigh. "I don't know." She started feeling restless; a wave of anxiety rippled through her.

Neala placed the teapot in the middle of the table along with the cups. She placed her hand on Grayson's shoulder and gave it a reassuring caress before she sat down.

"Do you believe, Grayson?" the old nun asked as she poured the milk in her tea.

Grayson frowned deeper and looked at her palm. "I don't know. I suppose I must. It just defies every ounce of reason and logic."

Maeve groaned and put her hand to her forehead. "If your father was alive, I'd slap him right now."

Sister Daniel threw her head back and laughed openly. Neala joined her. Grayson scowled and drank her tea. Sister Daniel cleared her throat. "Grayson, I know this is hard for you to comprehend, and perhaps we should have explained more when you were younger, not just familiarized you with the pagan beliefs."

"Why me?" Grayson asked seriously as she looked at her palm.

Maeve let out a dejected sigh. "I have no idea, sweetie."

Grayson glanced at Sister Daniel, who was concentrating on her tea. "Sister? I've been a cop for many years, and right now, you look a tiny bit guilty. Is there something on your mind?"

Sister Daniel raised her eyebrows and looked at Maeve, who sported an exasperated look. "You now see what I'm up against, Sister." She shook her head.

Grayson ignored her mother and Neala's soft laugh. "How about it, Sister?"

The old nun struck a thoughtful pose for a moment, then drank her tea. "Tomorrow, we'll take a ride to Clare and meet with Timothy Kerrigan. But for now, let's get you settled in your rooms, then supper."

"You're not telling me something," Grayson said, her brow furrowed in a deep frown.

The old nun reached across and held her hand. "Comes from dealing with the bishop all these years."

Dinner was heavenly. Grayson never tasted a better prepared leg of lamb. She took the last piece of homemade bread and lavished it with butter, then popped it into her mouth. Neala watched her with a raised eyebrow. Grayson swallowed, then grinned. "What? It was homemade bread."

"If you eat like that all the time, Detective, I'm surprised you're as fit as you are," she said and drank her coffee.

Grayson chuckled and wiped her mouth with the napkin. "Vic used to tell me that all the time." She stopped laughing and stared at her plate. "I have no idea why that came to my mind."

Maeve and Sister Daniel said nothing as they watched Neala lightly touch Grayson's arm. "You're healing, Grayson. The more you heal, the easier it will be to talk of Vicky."

"I suppose you're right," Grayson said thoughtfully.

"And the memories won't seem so sad."

Grayson shot a curious look at her. "How do you know the memories are sad?"

"I don't know. Perhaps it's the sadness in your voice or the melancholic look on your face. Whichever it is, I don't blame you in the least."

Grayson nodded and damned the tears that welled in her eyes. The truth was, she had been thinking about Vic constantly. Her face kept flashing through her mind—her soulful brown eyes, the subtle scent of her perfume, the way her voice sounded when she laughed.

Grayson's heart felt so heavy right then; a horrible feeling of loneliness tore through her being. "I used to smell her perfume everywhere," she whispered as she stared at nothing in particular. "Now I can't even picture her face." She looked up when she heard her mother sniff loudly. She smiled then. "None of that now, Ma."

Sister Daniel rose and let out a small groan. "Come, Grayson. Walk with me."

They strolled down the path that Grayson remembered from her youth. Though it was pitch dark, Grayson knew her way as Sister Daniel slipped an arm into hers.

"We used to have nice walks, you and I," she said wistfully. She looked up into the cool night. "It's a new moon."

Grayson looked up, as well, and nodded. "The festival of Samhain." She stopped, as did Sister Daniel. "I have no idea why I said that."

"Don't you?" Sister Daniel questioned softly; she then continued down the rugged path. When Grayson didn't respond, she went on. "When you were six years old, you witnessed your first festival. The villagers made a grand bonfire to usher in the Celtic New Year on All Hallows Eve. I remember you standing there with your mother. You gazed into the flames of the bonfire and—"

"And scared the daylights out of myself. Now I do remember," Grayson said with a laugh. Sister Daniel laughed along.

"That you did, but it was because you were young and didn't understand the vision."

Grayson frowned again as she tried to remember. She felt the old nun's hand tighten around her bicep. "Don't think so hard, Grayson Fianna. Let it come back to you."

Grayson nodded as Sister Daniel stopped and leaned against the short stone wall. Grayson faced her and looked into the starry sky. "I had a vision then that I had a week or so ago. Well, a dream actually."

"Tell me."

Grayson thought for a moment before speaking. "In the dream, as in the vision when I was a kid, there was fog everywhere. I felt like everything was hidden and I was scared. I thought something was going to jump out at me. I stood there, and through the fog, I saw an altar and a woman lying on it, she was wrapped in white linen. Then I heard a man's voice, a deep voice. He was talking in Gaelic, I think, but I can't remember. Then I heard a wolf howling, and out of the fog, I saw …"

She stopped and Sister Daniel asked, "What did you see, child?"

Grayson heard the soft determination in the nun's voice. "I saw a man walking out of the fog, yet it wasn't a man. It, he—" She stopped and absently ran her fingers over the heavy sutures on her cheek. Sister Daniel said nothing as Grayson looked into her eyes. "It was a wolf that ran out of the fog and lunged toward the stone altar." She took a deep breath and realized she was sweating; she wiped her thumb across her brow.

"That's when my dream and the vision stopped. I wish to shit I knew what it meant." She blushed horribly when she realized what she had said. "Sorry, Sister."

She laughed and slipped her arm through Grayson's as they walked back up the path to the monastery. "No apologies, child. I'm afraid it will get much worse—"

A mournful howl stopped her and Grayson. They stood still as it continued far off in the distance. The low baying went on as Grayson took a firm grip on the nun's arm. "I don't know what's going on, Sister, but I don't like you being out here like this. C'mon."

They quickly walked back to the monastery, all the while Grayson tried to ignore the feeling they were being watched.

A nervous Maeve and Neala met them at the door. "Did you hear that?" Maeve asked as she stepped back into the foyer.

Grayson nodded and shut the door. "It's a wolf, Ma, or some other animal."

"There are no wolves in Ireland, Grayson. Perhaps one in the Dublin Zoo, but they were killed off well over a hundred years ago," Neala said.

Grayson saw her hands shaking and grinned. "Well, St. Patrick took care of the snakes. Maybe he took care of the wolves, as well."

Neala glared playfully. "Ha, ha."

"Well, I think that's enough fright for your first night back. Off to bed with all of you," Sister Daniel ordered. "Now we've only two rooms to spare. I'll let you draw straws to see who doubles up with whom. It's grand to have you back home, all of you. Good night and God bless you."

She kissed each woman and walked down the long hall to her room. Maeve watched her, then turned to Grayson and Neala. "To heck with the straws. I get my own room." She kissed Grayson and Neala, then headed down the hall, laughing quietly all the way.

That left Grayson glancing at Neala. "It appears we're destined to share a bed, Dr. Rourke."

Neala turned as red as her hair and grinned. "It does indeed, Detective MacCarthaigh." She turned and walked down the hall.

Grayson chuckled and followed her.

They lay in the darkness, both listening to the autumn wind whistling through the window. Grayson could see the stars in the cloudless sky. New moon, she thought. In a few days, it would be the beginning of the Celtic New Year. She wondered what would happen; she then looked at her palm. When she felt Neala's warm comforting hand on hers, she looked at her through the darkness.

"I don't know what's happening, but I want you to know, I'll be here for you if you need me." She chuckled softly. "I know we didn't get off to a very good start at the exhibit in Chicago."

Grayson held onto her hand; the scar seemed not to itch as much. "We're fine now."

"Yes, we are."

They lay in comfortable silence, holding hands. "I wish I knew what to expect," Neala said, her voice on the edge of sleep.

Grayson yawned. "Well, your Corky fella better have some answers."

Neala then turned on her side to face Grayson. She reached over and lightly traced the stitches on her cheek. "Does it hurt much?"

"Not the way you're touching me, no," Grayson said honestly. She felt comforted by this woman. "You have a nice touch. Thank you."

She closed her eyes as Neala caressed her forehand and lightly ran her fingers through her hair.

"I am so sorry for all your pain," Neala said. She leaned over and lightly kissed her forehead.

Grayson felt the tears once again catch in her throat. After a moment, she whispered, "Vic was pregnant. We were gonna start a family. It was her last week as a hostage negotiator. She was gonna teach."

She heard the soft exclamation of surprise from Neala, who gently pulled her into her arms. Grayson lay her head against

Neala's breast and felt the tears cascading down her cheeks. She hadn't said those words to anyone since the day Vic died.

Neala wrapped her arms around her and held her close. "Sleep, Grayson, please," she pleaded and kissed the top of her head.

Grayson let out a deep tired breath and relaxed and fell sound asleep in the arms of the healer.

Chapter 22

"I don't like leaving Ma and Sister Daniel alone. I have a bad feeling," Grayson said as she gazed out the window.

Neala drove the old van toward Dublin and the museum. "They need time to get reacquainted. I'm sure they're on a second pot of tea already."

Grayson had to smile at the truth in that statement. She glanced at her watch. "Well, we started out early enough. Thank God, this is a small country, and it won't take that long to get to Dublin. We can make sure the stone is safe, then head back, grab Ma and Sister Daniel, and go see this Corky."

It took the better part of the early morning to get to Dublin. As Neala entered the town, Grayson felt a pulling sensation in the pit of her stomach; she shifted anxiously in her seat. "Oh, um, thanks for last night," she said in a hesitant voice.

Neala smiled and nodded. "Not at all," she said kindly. "So here we are."

She pulled into the parking spot that had her name on it. Grayson raised an eyebrow. "Your own spot, eh, Dr. Rourke?"

"Indeed, Detective MacCarthaigh," she said in a haughty voice that had Grayson laughing as she got out of the van.

They walked up the steps to the National Museum. A security guard met them at the door and raised his hand. Both stopped and Neala flashed her ID. "This is Detective Grayson MacCarthaigh. She's a visitor from Chicago."

The guard grinned. "Chicago, is it? Is that near Boston?" Grayson heard the hopeful tone in his voice.

Neala hid her grin as Grayson glared at the guard. "No, but we get the northerly breezes every now and then." Neala cleared her throat and dragged Grayson along.

"Near Boston," Grayson repeated as Neala laughed.

They made their way to Neala's office. Grayson looked around at the cozy décor. A huge mahogany desk with an overstuffed chair was situated under the large window. The walls were lined with bookcases. Grayson looked around the office and noticed several diplomas on the walls.

"Properly impressed?" Neala asked as she sat at her desk and leafed through her mail.

Grayson nodded as she sat on the other side of the desk in an unbelievably comfortable chair. As Neala picked up the phone, someone knocked at her door. "Come in."

Grayson turned around to see a very confused looking young man and woman enter the office. Neala offered the introductions; handshakes were exchanged. "What's wrong, Michael?" she asked.

"Dr. Rourke, why did you place Phelan Tynan in charge until you returned?"

Grayson and Neala exchanged glances, and Neala walked up to Michael. "What are you talking about? I did no such thing."

The young woman swallowed convulsively. "He told us you were coming back, but until then, he was to make sure the stone was safe, which I assured him it was. He said he was going to take the stone to a safe place. He said there were rumors that someone wanted to steal the stone. He's down there now, planning to—"

Grayson bolted toward the door. "Neala, lock down this museum." When Neala stood there for a moment completely confused, Grayson walked back to her.

"Grayson, you can't think that Phelan would take the stone. Why?"

"Trust me on this. Lock this museum down. Now."

Neala nodded and picked up the phone. As she dialed, she glanced at her associates. "Go with Detective MacCarthaigh, Michael. Take her to the exhibit."

As Grayson ran out the door, she heard Neala's commanding voice. "This is Dr. Rourke, get security down to exhibit room 231. Do not let anyone near that stone, even Phelan Tynan."

Grayson followed the young man as he ran toward the elevator. Michael pushed the button and waited. Grayson waited impatiently, then hit the elevator door with her hand. "Where's the room?"

"Uh, down one flight and to the right," Michael said.

Grayson was already flying down the stairs not waiting for the young man running after her. As they got to the room, several security guards met them. "It's all right. She's with Dr. Rourke."

"Let her in," Neala called out as she ran up to them.

They opened the double doors. There were several glass exhibits placed on pedestals around the large room. Neala ran over to the glass case and stopped dead in her tracks. Grayson was right behind her and looked at the empty case.

"Mother of God," Neala whispered.

Grayson swore under her breath and turned to the security guards. "Check every door, every room of this museum. Now!"

The guards looked at Neala, who nodded. "Do as she says."

They scurried, transmitting Grayson's instructions into their walkie-talkies as they ran out of the room.

"Michael, how long ago was Phelan here?"

"It couldn't have been more than five minutes before you arrived, Doctor. He didn't have enough time to take it…"

Grayson looked around the old room and nodded. "He had time." She ran her fingers through her hair. "Was he alone?"

"Yes."

"No one else was in this room?" Grayson continued. Michael swallowed and nodded.

"I'm sorry, Doctor. It's my fault," Michael said in a dejected voice. "We couldn't understand why you would put him in charge, so when we got word that you were in the building, we came right to you and left Mr. Tynan alone. I-I swear I never thought he would take the stone knowing you arrived."

"It's not your fault, Michael. Mr. Tynan has given a great deal of money and time to this. I-I can't imagine why he would take the stone."

With that, the security guards came back. "We're checking every room in the museum, Doctor. Thank God it's early and there are no visitors yet. Shall I call the garda?"

"No, no police as yet. If Mr. Tynan took the stone, there has to be a good reason. Let's wait until I talk to him. Keep the museum locked down, however, until all the rooms are searched," Neala said with a heavy sigh.

"There's nothing more we can do here. He took the stone," Grayson said.

"Grayson, why? Why would he take it?" Neala asked, seemingly stumped. "I don't understand."

"I'm sure Timothy Kerrigan will. Let's go."

They drove back to the monastery. Grayson was in constant contact with her mother; she called her every twenty minutes until they pulled down the small road. Grayson jumped out and ran up the steps. Her mother and Sister Daniel met her.

"Are you all right?" Grayson asked and put her hands on her mother's shoulders.

"Yes, we're fine, sweetie," Maeve assured her. "Is it true about the stone?"

"Yes, it's true," Grayson replied angrily. "I'm tired of being in the dark about whatever is going on here. I want answers from this Kerrigan fellow. I don't care if he thinks there's a pot of gold at the end of the fricking rainbow as long as he has proof."

They said little on the drive to Timothy Kerrigan's until Neala spoke. "I've talked with Corky on many occasions about what is Irish history and what is myth. You can imagine what he thinks. I've never seen a man more obsessed with legends and myths. He's bound and determined to prove them."

From the backseat, Sister Daniel and Maeve agreed. "I remember Timothy and me discussing St. Brigid. He truly believes she was a goddess and not human. She took human form when the Milesians defeated the Tuatha Dé Danann and sent most underground."

"Most?" Grayson asked from the front seat. She was listening and looking out the window at the gray day. There was a fine rain falling; she was lulled by the slow cadence of the windshield wipers. Her mother answered her.

"Yes, some believe that not all were defeated during that battle. Some believe that certain Druids, gods, and goddesses stayed behind."

"That's where Timothy gets the idea that St. Brigid was a triple goddess and not human. She became so popular with the Irish, the Church had no idea what to do with her but make her a saint in the eyes of the Irish people and the Church," Sister Daniel said. "But make no mistake, she was a beautiful soul, whether saint or goddess."

"How can she be a goddess? There's history there. Her father was a chieftain. He was real," Grayson argued.

"So was Jesus," Sister Daniel said.

Grayson quickly turned in her seat. As she opened her mouth, Sister Daniel put up her hand. "I'm just preparing you for Timothy Kerrigan and his beliefs."

Grayson glanced at her mother, who offered a weak smile. "Wonderful," Grayson muttered.

"This is his road," Neala said. Grayson looked at her surroundings. They had driven east heading toward County Clare and the Atlantic. The landscape turned decidedly desolate, mostly rocky hills—a stark contrast to the lush patchwork green fields they had been driving through. There were no signs of life now, only white thatched cottages here and there, set back well off the narrow road. There was not one telephone pole to be seen.

This was the area of County Clare that many visitors wanted to see—the Burren. There were ancient tombs built out of slabs of limestone. Nothing grew in the Burren except delicate wildflowers that sprang up through the cracks of limestone. There were no trees, not enough water in the soil—nothing but rocks and ancient history.

"Don't tell me this guy lives in the Burren," Grayson said.

Neala chuckled, as did the others. "No, well, not quite that isolated, but Corky does like his privacy."

"Why would someone want to live in a place like this?" Grayson looked around the gloomy landscape. "It's not logical to me."

"That's an understatement," Maeve said sarcastically from the backseat.

Grayson turned her head. "What, Ma?"

Maeve leaned forward. "I said that's understandable, sweetie."

Neala turned down yet another narrow road. Grayson didn't even see it coming it was that narrow. To Grayson, it appeared to lead nowhere. After a good five minutes of slow driving and no change in the landscape or signs of life, Grayson was about to make a comment when a small white thatched cottage came into view. The cottage definitely needed a good white washing, but the thatching was in excellent shape. It looked like every other Irish cottage.

As they pulled up to the cottage, three enormous Irish wolfhounds came bounding out from the back. Their deep resonating bark was unmistakable.

"They're good guard dogs," Neala said.

"Against what? Who could find this place?" Grayson asked.

As she opened her door, she heard all three women exclaim, "No, wait!" but Grayson had already gotten out of the van. The wolfhounds dashed up to her and stopped barking. "Some guard dogs you are."

She allowed all three to sniff and get acquainted. She then looked to see all three women standing there, gaping at her. "What?"

"Grayson, we usually have to wait until Corky comes out. Those dogs are trained to guard the property and let no one approach his cottage. I-I don't believe this," Neala said. Grayson heard the amazement in her voice as she crouched down to pet the dogs.

The noble dogs sat as Grayson scratched their ears. "You guys are huge," she said as they walked to the small door of the cottage.

The green door opened and a young man stood there, wide green eyes staring at Sister Daniel in surprise. Grayson took in his appearance: wavy thick rust-colored hair looked as if he had just woken up. Green almond-shaped eyes sparkled and stood out against the white freckled face. He wore an oversized Irish sweater that had seen better days, and blue jeans. His wire-rimmed glasses were on top of his rusty red mop.

He looked at all four women and nodded. "Mother Abbess. I've been expecting you," he said in a solemn voice.

She gave him a curious look. "You have?"

He nodded, then motioned to the sky. Grayson looked up to see several hawks lazily circling overhead. "The messengers. They've been gatherin' for a couple of days now just as it's written. I knew the time was at hand." He stopped and took a deep breath and looked at Neala. "Neala, I knew you would be here," he said kindly, then looked at Maeve. His eyes grew wide. "But, Maeve, what are you doing here?"

"Well, Corky," Maeve said and glanced at Grayson. "This is my daughter, Grayson."

Corky looked at Grayson and swallowed with difficulty. Grayson swore she heard the gulp. "Are...?" He started, then stopped and tried again. "Are you the one?"

Grayson raised an eyebrow and offered her left hand, palm up. "I have no idea, pal. You tell me."

Corky looked down at the crescent-shaped marking and blinked several times. He started swaying. "The prophecy?" His voice came out in a high squeak. "Mother of God."

His eyes rolled back in his head, and he fell into Grayson's arms in a dead faint. Grayson held the slumping figure and shook her head.

"This is encouraging," she said with a grunt as she hoisted the listless redhead over her uninjured shoulder. She looked at her mother. "Lead on, MacCarthaigh."

Maeve chuckled as she led the way into the small cottage. As she followed, Grayson gave one last look at Timothy Kerrigan's desolate property. It looked as though they were in another world or at least another time. There were no other cottages or dwellings for miles along the stony landscape. No signs of life—Grayson didn't know if that was a blessing or not. She looked up and watched the hawks circling overhead, and once again, had the unsettling feeling they were being watched.

The little cottage was dark with the peat fire dimly illuminating the living room. Grayson found a couch under a huge picture window and gently deposited the groaning historian. When Neala came out of the kitchen with a cool cloth and sat on the edge of the couch, Grayson stepped back to survey her surroundings. It was a typical Irish cottage, not unlike the one she grew up in. The low beam ceiling seemed to give the dwelling a cozy atmosphere. The windows on either side of the fireplace were small, but the window over the couch was large and airy. Off in the corner was an enormous desk, enormous but messy. With books and papers piled all over it, Grayson wondered if there was a desk there at all.

Sister Daniel had gone down the hall, and hearing the pots rattle, Grayson figured she must be in the kitchen. Maeve walked over and turned on the small desk lamp, adding more light to the living room. She watched Neala tend to poor Corky.

"Corky, for heavens' sake, man," she whispered and tapped his cheek. When he groaned, Neala tapped his cheek again, a little harder this time. Grayson winced and Corky's green eyes flew open. He sat up, completely disoriented.

"What happened?" He ran his fingers through his thick hair.

"You fainted," Neala said with a smirk.

"No, I didn't," Corky said, slightly amazed, then chuckled. "I suppose I did." He then looked at Grayson, who said nothing. She had her hands in her pockets as she sat on the arm of the couch. Corky reached out. "Let me see again."

"Not if you're gonna faint," Grayson said and cautiously offered her left hand.

"No, it was a fright, that's all."

Corky reverently traced the outline of the raised mark on Grayson's palm with his fingertips. "*As written on the moon and stars—Their power veiled North, South, and East—*" He stopped and looked up at Grayson before continuing, "*While in the West a noble birth—A crescent locks its destiny.*"

Complete silence filled the room. Grayson was vaguely aware of two things: the quiet hissing of the peat logs in the fireplace and a low annoying buzzing in her ears.

Suddenly, a vision flashed through her mind. She was getting so tired of these little snippets of her memory—or was it her memory? She locked eyes with Corky.

"Are these my memories?" She didn't know why this odd young man would know, but she did.

He shook his head. "I don't believe so." He stopped and walked over to his desk. "I've been reading and rereading this for years now, as my father and his father before."

Sister Daniel came back juggling a tray heavy with the teapot and cups. Maeve offered her help. "What's happened?" the old nun asked.

"Corky's about to rock Grayson's logical world," Maeve said.

"High time, if you ask me."

Grayson ignored the old friends' banter and stood by Corky. The others followed.

He impatiently pushed papers out of his way, seemingly clearing a path. Grayson and Neala assisted him, and when asked where to put them, he waved them off. "Anywhere you like."

Neala shook her head and took the papers from Grayson, who smiled at her irritated posture. She remembered how immaculate the doctor's office was. Neala neatly stacked the papers on the small table by the fireplace.

At the bottom of the papers was a huge, thick old leather-bound book. Corky looked at Grayson and winked. "This is it," he said and with great care, leafed through the old timeworn pages. Grayson leaned in and noticed the pages were more like parchment as Corky mumbled absently.

"Right then, let me see. We have shape-shifters…" he said happily and wiggled his eyebrows at Grayson while he flipped the pages.

Grayson raised an eyebrow as she watched. *This guy is a nut.*

"Witches and warlocks, we don't want that…" he continued thoughtfully. "Vampires and—"

Grayson stopped him there by putting her hand on his sleeve. Visions of that young man in the warehouse with Stan flashed through her mind. He had the Ogham marking on his forearm and the puncture wounds on his wrists.

"Vampires?" she asked and cursed the curious tone in her voice.

Corky nodded happily, as he waved her off. "We can talk vampires another time. You have no idea how ancient Ireland truly is," he said and continued with the book. "There are also things happening in London right now that would curl your toes. There's a buzz in their community, something's going on in the catacombs under Guys Hospital. Someone named Sebastian has..." He stopped and shook his head. "Let's not get distracted."

"Yeah, let's," Grayson agreed. "So what is this, Corky? 'The How To Book of Wizardry'?"

Corky glanced up, looked at the other women, and grinned. "I love a disbeliever," he said in a thick brogue. "So much fun to watch them turn."

He looked into Grayson eyes and smiled, and Grayson thought she saw a flash of sadness in that smile. "And you will believe. You're the true descendant. You must believe."

Chapter 23

As Phelan walked into his library, he turned to Ian, who was walking behind him.

"Well, sir, they went directly to the monastery from Shannon. Is there anything more I can—?"

"No." Phelan shut the door on his last words.

"I'll just let myself out then," Ian's muffled voice called out.

Phelan walked over to the desk and gently set the stone, wrapped in heavy burlap, down on the desk. He opened the wall safe and took out the two other triangular-shaped stones. Taking a deep calming breath, he placed the stones together, and as in a jigsaw puzzle, the three pieces of the stone fit perfectly together. All three aligned with the ancient Celtic alphabet describing the ritual intact. Phelan was so close to having it all—the power, the magic, the knowledge of the ancient ones. As he stared at the large stone, which was perhaps twelve inches in diameter, he remembered the original ceremony as if it were yesterday, though he was only a child and it was centuries ago.

His father, majestic in flowing black robes, extended his staff into the moonlit night calling on those who dwell in the darkness to come forth. He stood before the altar covered with the blood of the sacrifices and summoned the forces in the primeval tongue of his ancestors.

Phelan could feel the wind from the sea, surrounded by the circle of stones. In the darkness, he saw the silhouetted figures of the Druids in attendance, as still as the stones that bordered the ceremony. Phelan could feel the air thicken. As the moon seemed to become brighter, his father's voice merged with the wind. The triangular stone on the altar seemed to pulse with life, and to the small boy's amazement, the markings became deeper and seemed to move with each word his father uttered.

Suddenly, there was a flash, bright and blue with energy. A voice boomed from the darkness and called his father by name, "Figol."

The force of this voice silenced his father and the chanting of the celebrants. Young Phelan could feel the fear in the air as he glanced around the open glen.

The voice continued, "This cannot be. You have the blood of innocents on your hands, the royal blood of your wife, and the faith that has been placed in you. You have gone too far. This cannot be."

Phelan turned to his father, astonished that anyone dare intrude on the ceremony. His father was furious and stepped closer to the altar.

"You are too late, Old One, I have prepared the stone for this, sacrificed all for this, and you are not strong enough to prevail. You are not equal to the battle you will find here."

Another voice spoke, "That may be true if he were alone, Figol, but he is not alone. We stand together against the terror you summon here tonight. He speaks the truth—this cannot be."

Phelan was terrified. He recognized the voices from the Druid hierarchy and could not mistake their meaning. He froze as he saw the three imposing figures approach out of the darkness and fog. Instinctively, he moved closer to his father. At the sight of the clerics looming toward the altar, the frightened participants ran into the darkness to escape their wrath. Only Phelan and his father remained.

"You were given the responsibility to protect that stone, to remain faithful to the desires of the elders, to defend this world from the very forces you beckon," the Druid reminded him in a dark angry voice. He took a step toward the altar. "I will stop you," he continued and crashed his staff into the ground before him.

"You may stop me, but my son will prevail. He will reassemble the stones, he will bring back the magic you fear and abandon. He will be more powerful than even you can imagine. He will survive

the generations. He will outwit the keepers and triumph in the end." His voice had the strength Phelan heard earlier.

Figol placed his son between him and the altar. He grabbed both Phelan's wrists and placed his open hands on the stone. The effect was devastating. Phelan could feel the stone move beneath his palms. The energy seemed to come from the very ground on which he stood; it radiated up through the stone altar and into the boy's body.

For a moment, he thought the sun was rising; the light around him was so bright. He heard a growl, deafening and savage, and definitely wolf. Then he realized it was he who was growling—he was the wolf. He felt the dominance, the power, and the force that was now his essence. He looked up into the fearful faces of the clerics. In one lupine movement, he was over the altar and upon them, snapping their necks one by one.

He turned to look to his father; they both understood: the final sacrifice. The ceremony was complete. As Figol walked over to his son, Phelan observed that his father's long flowing hair was now completely white. He was not surprised, very little would surprise him for the rest of his existence.

Figol put his hands on his son's shoulders. "This is only the beginning, my son. We have but one fragment of the total stone. You need all three. However, you have time and the power. Remember this: You are the child of the Tuatha Dé Danann and of a great Druid sorcerer. What we have done here tonight has given you immortality, but it is what you do from this day forward that will make you more powerful than any who have come before. To find the stones, you must find the guardians."

He then handed young Phelan the bloody athame, which his son took in both hands. "Destroy them with this dagger. Mark them, my son, so that I may know them. This is your legacy...this is your destiny."

The vision of that night, the beginning of it all, faded as Phelan opened his eyes. He remembered his father's voice: Destroy the true descendant. He remembered seeing Maeve MacCarthaigh's face as he stared into the fire's light.

To have the power that was locked for centuries in this stone,

Phelan knew he must fulfill this part of his destiny. He wished his father had imparted that little bit of information to him all those centuries ago. Perhaps, Figol, the Druid sorcerer, did not know who the true descendant was.

Phelan had been on his own since then. It took him all this time looking, waiting, using everything in his power to find the other stones. As he looked down, he chuckled openly. To look at them, they looked like ordinary ancient Celtic stones found at any one of a hundred archaeological sites in Ireland. To the average scientist, like Dr. Rourke, they were more proof that ancient Ireland was teeming with intelligence, not the barefoot barbarians that the world thought. *Most people assumed Ireland's existence truly started when the fool, Pádraig, oh excuse me,* Saint *Patrick, set foot on this island in the third century.*

Phelan had to admit it was ingenious of the saint to use the Druid way to spread Christianity throughout Ireland. Using the shamrock to explain his Trinity of Christianity was inspirational, if not plagiarized from the Druid and pagan way of teaching: All things were taught in a trilogy. Their beliefs: wisdom, creativity, and love, all living within and respecting nature and the earth, the stars and moon.

Phelan rolled his eyes as he poured himself a drink. "A Druid or a Druidess—they both bore me." He sighed and took a long drink. "Self-righteous bunch, all of them. Deciding wars, advising kings."

"Presumptuous lot," he continued. He sat down and kicked off his shoes. "I like Caesar's idea when he invaded Britain: To be successful, we must first kill all the Druids," he said happily and stretched his long legs out in front of him. He sipped his drink once more. "Being the son of an ancient sorcerer is much more profitable. I do enjoy being a wizard."

He remembered his travels through the centuries trying to find the ancient stones. He had to admit the alchemist did a splendid job of keeping his portion of the stone safe throughout the centuries. It wasn't until he was associated with Neville Chamberlain in 1938 that he found Sir John Quigley. Years later, Phelan would meet the young Irish archaeologist and would discover he was indeed the descendant of the alchemist. Fifty years later, his great-niece Nan Quigley would have the stone safe in her possession.

He laughed again, thinking it was very resourceful of this young librarian to keep such power, such magic on the mantel of her fireplace among the other pagan artifacts she accumulated. At first, Phelan thought her to be a colossal fool.

"Well now, you were the one who couldn't find it for nearly two thousand years. So who's the fool, Phelan?" he asked with a chuckle as he sipped his drink. However, it was a pity that he had to kill those two other women.

He shook his head. "I thought for sure they knew something," he said thoughtfully, then shrugged. "I hope father was not disturbed by the unnecessary offering."

He should have known when he felt nothing as he killed those women decades earlier. There was not the surge of power he felt through his body as when he sent Nan Quigley to the otherworld. He felt the same with Jane Monahan, the healer. She was instrumental. She was the guardian of the last stone that Dr. Rourke, et al, dug up. She also knew who possessed the ancient text, which foretold the ritual, the beginning, and the prophecy of the stone and its power and magic.

He felt the anger welling deep inside at the thought of not finding the text, even though he took great pleasure in sending Jane Monahan to the otherworld. Even using all the wizardry he possessed, she would not divulge the keeper of the text.

Staring at the segments of stone, he said simply, "It matters little. I was there for the beginning. I know of the prophecy—the true descendant who will try, unsuccessfully, I might add, when I destroy her and send her with the others."

He would fulfill his destiny with the ritual and all the power, all the glory of ancient Ireland would be his and his alone.

Chapter 24

Grayson rubbed her temple. "Okay, so what were you just saying about the North and South and East…?"

Neala interrupted her and handed her a cup of tea to which Grayson raised an eyebrow. "Is it safe?"

Neala grinned and nodded. "It tis."

Corky took the mug of tea and took a healthy drink. "Right then. The prophecy."

Neala pulled up a chair for Maeve and Sister Daniel, who now sat by the glowing peat fire. Corky situated himself, as if preparing for a good story. Grayson watched and waited.

"Shall I tell you from the beginning?" he asked and looked around the room. All nodded. "Right then. Maeve, you know some, as does Mother Abbess. Before I read the prophecy, I'll tell you what happened to bring all this about.

"The Tuatha Dé Danann, as we know, were the people of the goddess Danu. They lived a marvelous, magical life for centuries. Most thought this was all mythology—"

"Some still do, Corky," Neala said.

He gave her a stern look. "Who's tellin' this?"

Neala smiled. "I apologize."

"Now as I was saying, most thought this was all mythology, but for generations, the gods and goddesses roamed ancient Ireland with the mortals, the Druids, and the teachers." He looked at Maeve, who narrowed her eyes. "And the Druidesses," he amended.

"The Tuatha possessed great power and magic and bestowed some of this on the mortals, but not often. Take Niamh of the Golden Hair. She lived in Tir-nan-Og, the Land of Ever Young.

185

She's in the prophecy, as well, though I haven't figured out why…" he said thoughtfully and looked out the window.

Grayson waited a moment or two, then glanced at Neala, who rolled her eyes. "Corky!"

He jumped and looked around. "Oh, right then. Niamh was the daughter of Mannanan, the Celtic god of the sea. She took a lover, Oisin, who was a mortal. She took him to Tir-nan-Og where they lived for three hundred years. In any event, it's a famous mythological story," he said. "There are many other stories, hundreds of them. The Tuatha defeated Balor and the Formorians, and all was well until the Milesians came. The battle ensued, and the Tuatha were defeated. The compromise: The Tuatha ruled the otherworld and the Milesians ruled the mortal world. However…" he said with a grin.

Grayson gave him a cautious look. "However?"

"Our troubles begin on the eve of the Tuatha's defeat," he told his audience, who seemed enthralled. "The Tuatha knew they would be defeated. The battle of Teltown would be fought with iron weapons. It was the only thing that could defeat them. So they devised a plan to save the power and magic and not lose it to the Milesians. They would surrender minor magic and mystical powers to the mortals, but the bulk of the magic would be stored in a sacred stone, and on that stone was written in the ancient Ogham alphabet the ritual that would be performed at an exact moment in time. The stone was then broken in three pieces, each piece given to its guardian: the sorcerer, the alchemist, and the healer. When everything aligned in the universe, the true descendant would be revealed and stones would be reunited and the power of the Tuatha would once again give glory back to Ireland."

He stopped and took a deep breath. Grayson listened but said nothing. She drank her now cold tea and grimaced as she set the mug down. She glanced at her mother, who was staring into the fire. Sister Daniel was toying with the Celtic cross that hung around her neck. Neala was watching Grayson.

"What does St. Brigid have to do with this?" Grayson asked.

"It is my belief that Brigid was the healer," Corky said. "One section of the stone was handed down to her and kept near the monastery. She entrusted her nuns to guard it at all costs and secure it through the generations until the time was at hand.

"It was under the fortification of Brigid's Sisterhood that their part of the quest was taken from the ground and placed in the monastery in Ireland. Upon her death in 525 AD, Darlughdach, her successor, made sure the commitment continued and has to this day." Corky ran his fingers through his hair before he continued.

He leaned in and said, "You see, the myth is that the strength of Brigid came from the pre-Christian Brighid who was a triple goddess and represented the spiritual fires of poetry, healing, and smith craft. The last archaeology dig was a variety of stone, silver, and copper artifacts related to those associated with Brigid's most famous foundation at Kildare. The artifacts included the third stone."

"So was Brigid a goddess or a saint?" Neala asked.

"Perhaps she was both," Sister Daniel said.

Grayson scratched her head. "Okay, let's skip Brigid for now and get onto the prophecy. I want to know what's going on with this and why I'm part of it."

"Right then." Corky turned back to the ancient text. "If you don't mind, I'll read it and explain what I know, or what I surmise, as I go."

When the women all nodded in agreement, he started:

The glory that was Erin's joy
Under Danu and her clan
Conquerors of the Formorians
Dwelt victorious in Balor's land.

Teltown iron spears wound deep
Danu backed to the sea
A choice is made, a plot conceived—
Retreat but not fatality.

The morning sun portends defeat
This night the rock is severed three
All secrets are secured in oaks
Omnipotents reduced to ghosts.

"The first two stanzas, I have already explained," he said. "Now, this next one. On the night before the defeat, they put all the magic in the stone, split it, and gave it to the Druids, who were also called 'oaks.' They chose to retain the fairies magic and invisibility, hence the ghosts."

Grayson nodded in understanding and Corky went on:
As written on the moon and stars
Their power veiled North South and East
While in the West a noble birth
A crescent locks its destiny.

"This is where you come in, Grayson, I'm sure of it now," Corky said with assurance. "North, South, and East, I believe they mean the three sections of the stone—Noble birth in the West. The crescent moon birthmark—this is you, Grayson. The crescent locks its destiny."

Neala leaned forward. "It has to be correct. What other explanation could there be, Grayson?"

Grayson nodded reluctantly. She was so hoping for a different prophecy—one that did not include her or anyone else in the room. "Go on, Corky," she said and glanced at her mother, who winked and smiled.

"Right then," Corky agreed and cleared his throat:
In Tir-nan-Og the Golden Hair
Gives birth to she who Danu sealed
Whose moon will sway the set of scales
When moon's true meaning is revealed.

"This took some time to figure out, but I think I have it. See, you remember I told you about Niamh and her being a goddess and living in Tir-nan-Og—the Land of Ever Young. She takes Oisin as a lover and lives for three hundred years. He wants to go home and realizes he will die if he does, but still leaves, and dies. This is a very popular story in Irish mythology. Even Yeats wrote about him in *The Wanderings of Oisin*." He stopped and scratched his head.

Grayson watched him. "What's wrong?"

"Well, according to this prophecy, Niamh has a child—a daughter. I've never read that anywhere else in all my research. And I'm thinking, from reading this passage of the prophecy, that Danu, the mother goddess of us all, chose Niamh's daughter to be the forbearer of the true descendant." He stopped and looked at Grayson. "Wh-which is you, you see."

Grayson blinked several times, trying to comprehend this insanity. Neala sat forward. "Are you saying that Grayson and Maeve are related to a goddess?"

Corky shrugged in agreement and adjusted his glasses.

Maeve laughed quietly. "Corky, I am flattered, dear, but I'm not related to a goddess. I think my mother or grandmother would have told me. Don't you?"

Grayson walked over to the fire and stared into the flames. A vision flashed through her mind. An old beautiful woman with white hair and flowing robes, holding a long staff, wearing an ornate medallion hung around her neck.

Garda…

Her back stiffened as she clearly heard the voice in her head. She turned back and looked at Sister Daniel, who was staring into the flames, as well. The old nun looked up, and their eyes met in knowing.

Never taking her eyes off Sister Daniel, Grayson spoke. "Not if you were all better off not knowing, Ma. Not if you were being protected—guarded by the healers, the keepers of their section of this stone. Am I right, Sister?"

Sister Daniel nodded and smiled. "You're getting good at this, Grayson." She turned to Maeve. "She is exactly correct. It has been handed down through the centuries. We not only guard the stone, but the ancestors of the true descendant. The less you knew, the safer you were. This is part of the prophecy. Niamh did have a child, both mortal and goddess. Danu chose this child. She would come before all of you. This is your bloodline, Maeve." She looked at Grayson. "And yours, my child."

Maeve was astounded. "I can't believe this. All these years and you knew?" Grayson saw the flash of wonderment and anger in her mother's eyes.

"It makes perfect sense, Ma," Grayson said, then chuckled. "If any of this makes sense. It was better you didn't know."

"I am sorry, Maeve," Sister Daniel said in a tired voice. Maeve looked at her and smiled. She then reached over and held her hand.

"I understand, Sister."

Grayson looked at Corky, who was sitting there completely amazed.

"Are you tellin' me, I was right?" Grayson heard the amazement in his voice.

"Well, it makes sense, and it fits the prophecy," Neala said.

He then grinned. "Right then, let's continue."

Century score and cardinal prime
The skies ally and nature bows
The Knowing manifests in time
Void with voices confirm old vows.

"This is my favorite part. It took me quite a while to figure out the first sentence," he said proudly. "Now century score—"

"A hundred years and twenty?" Neala said happily.

Corky's mouth dropped. Neala looked around the room. "I- Isn't a score twenty years?" she asked.

He now narrowed his green eyes at the doctor, and Grayson hid her grin but said nothing.

"As I was saying," Corky went on, still glaring at Neala. "Century score means, one hundred times twenty. And the cardinal prime…" He stopped and looked at Neala, who shook her head. He gave her a smug grin and continued. "Seven is a cardinal and prime number. So what do you have?"

Grayson thought for a moment. "One hundred times twenty is two thousand and the prime…" She stopped, then nodded her approval. "Very good, Corky. It's a date—two thousand seven."

"This year," Maeve said in amazement.

Corky winked and nodded. "Exactly so." He concentrated on the text once again. "Now the last part of this has to do with the Knowing. In another text…" He stopped and leafed through the pages. "Here it tis."

He turned the book and handed it to Grayson. On the page was a picture of a cave or some type of rock dwelling. Standing in front of the cave was a figure dressed in a long robe, looking up to the heavens with arms outstretched.

"It is said that at this place, the true descendant will gather the Knowing."

Grayson looked up. "The Knowing?" she asked cautiously. She absently handed the book to her mother, who shared the page with Sister Daniel.

"Yes, Grayson," the old nun replied. "The Knowing will take place here. You must stay in this place—"

Grayson shot her an incredulous look. "For how long?"

"Sister, may I?" Corky offered and gently took the text from her. He read the bottom of the page. "One passage of the moon." He looked at Grayson, who was still incredulous. "Th-that would be o-one night," he explained.

Grayson glared at him. "I get it."

"Oh, right then."

"What Knowing am I supposed to gather?"

Corky offered a weak smile. "I don't know. I suppose we'll find out."

Grayson took a deep calming breath. Maeve chimed in, "Corky, sweetie, continue before Grayson spontaneously combusts."

Corky went on, "Well, the last of the prophecy I've yet to decipher. However, when you read it, it seems simple enough, though there are certain references that I cannot understand that is truly annoying me."

A bright star falling left to right
The wolf behind her in the night
The Connacht queen now knows the prize
The star must fall—the moon must rise.

Great gifts are given and received
The gift of life and life again
A sacrifice unique to She
Her triumph masked in sorrow's rain.

The lupine son erect as man
Above the altar set with stone
Bold from blood of innocents
Calls down the darkness for his own.

The power of the ancients rise
The clash of old—the dark, the light
Embodied in their champions
The Warrior Moon, the Lord of Night.

Combat waged on sacred ground
Supremacy the victor's pawn
To wolfen howl the moon responds
And Erin's fate awaits the dawn.

When Corky finished, he leaned back and took off his glasses. "Well, that's it. There seems to be a concern here with a wolf. Perhaps it's symbolic. I'm not sure," He rubbed his eyes. "And I'm not sure about the Connacht queen, but it appears there will be a confrontation between you and this Lord of Night. Perhaps there was something in history about the Connacht queen that will make this clearer for you. I've researched but can't find anything that has happened that fits this prophecy or can assist you. It's been frustrating. I-I don't know."

"Well, I can see the wolf part," Grayson said evenly.

Corky shot her a curious look. "Can you? How?"

Grayson explained her dream and her visions to Corky, whose mouth dropped as he listened. She told him of the howling wolf in the warehouse in Chicago and of the howling she and Sister Daniel heard the night before. "I heard the howling, I saw the visions. So that's about the only thing I'm sure of."

"With all three sections of stones missing, I'm sure we'll find out soon enough," Neala said in a dejected tone.

"What?" Corky asked in disbelief. "You don't have the stone?"

Grayson shook her head and explained. "So we think Phelan

took the stone to keep it safe." She didn't even try to hide the fact that she did not believe what she just said.

Corky let out a loud groan. "I knew you should never have taken it out of Ireland. I was close to stopping you."

Neala snorted sarcastically. "The garda was kneeling on your chest, Corky. You didn't even get ten feet."

Corky ignored her. "Why would this man take it if it were perfectly safe at the museum?"

Grayson agreed completely. "That's exactly what I think."

"Phelan has donated nearly a million dollars toward this, Grayson. I can't believe he'd sabotage—"

"Phelan? His name is Phelan?" Corky swallowed with difficulty.

"Yes, why?" Grayson asked.

"Phelan in Gaelic means little wolf."

Chapter 25

"Little wolf." Grayson groaned.

"Perhaps it's a coincidence," Neala said.

Grayson chuckled. "That would be nice, but I'm afraid it's the only thing so far that's making any sense. I had a bad feeling about that guy when I first met him in Chicago." She looked at Neala. "No matter how much money he's donated to the cause."

"I'd have to agree with Grayson on this one, Neala," Corky said. "It's too much of a coincidence, and at this point, I'd trust Grayson's instincts." He looked at Grayson. "Good thing you were the garda," he said and grinned. "In your previous life."

Grayson raised an eyebrow. "Well, in that life, being a police officer was very tame compared to this."

Maeve reached for the text. "Let me give this a try. I work crossword puzzles."

"The lupine son erect as man, above the altar set with stone. Bold from blood of innocents—calls down the darkness for his own," she recited and looked at Grayson. "Well, if you think it's Phelan Tynan and he somehow manages to change from man to wolf, then it appears that he is the Lord of Night in the next stanza. Apparently, he will call upon the ancients, and he thinks because he has the complete stone, he has it all."

"But he can't because Grayson is the true descendant. Could it be that he doesn't know this?" Neala asked.

"If he has the complete stone, how is he going to get the power or whatever the hell is in that stone? I mean, if I'm the true descendant, and I can't believe I'm saying that out loud, then what do I have that he doesn't? It doesn't make sense, and damn it, something has to start making sense here," Grayson said angrily.

Sister Daniel had been quiet up to this point. She cleared her throat. "Timothy, find the picture of the stone. You must have it in that book."

Corky took the book and leafed through the pages. Once he found it, he grinned. "I love this." He pointed to the page.

Maeve, Grayson, and Neala all leaned over the book. It was a drawing of an oval-shaped stone. Markings and etchings bordered the stone, but it was the center that caught Grayson's attention. In its center was a small crescent shape etched into the stone.

Grayson looked at her palm and ran her fingers over the raised crescent-shaped scar.

"Do you want to know what I think?" Corky asked in an excited voice.

"No," Grayson said dryly.

Corky laughed but continued. "I believe that you, and only you, bring all the power, the magic back. Because you're the true descendant, placing your hand on the sections of the stone will accomplish this. You see, in the prophecy, it's to happen in this year at the time of the waning new moon—the crescent moon. It's been written that this is the most powerful time of the year. On that one night, the veil between the living and the dead is at its thinnest. One can move between our world and the otherworld freely. This moon has been called residual because it has the lingering effects of the new moon."

"Now that you've mentioned it, Corky, I've read that, as well," Neala said. "The residual moon."

Corky looked at Grayson. "The Lord of Night, or the Dark Lord, as he is also known, is Phelan Tynan, and you are the warrior of the residual moon. That's what I believe."

Grayson took a deep breath and let it out slowly. "So how many days do we have until this residual moon?"

Corky looked at the text and read for a moment, then recited in a lyrical voice, "Twice the moon must pass the earth, and in that time—"

Grayson closed her eyes and growled in frustration.

"Two days," Corky amended quickly and closed the book.

Maeve rose and stretched her back. "Well, I can't think

anymore." She grabbed her sweater. "I need a whiff of my pristine Irish air." She slipped into her sweater and looked over to see Sister Daniel standing by the door. "Go for a walk, Sister?"

The old nun shook her head. "No, Maeve," she said and kissed her cheek. "Walk with God, my friend."

Maeve pulled back and chuckled. "Is that God with a capital G?"

"Ya heathen," Sister Daniel said as Maeve headed outside.

"Well, we still haven't figured out the other stanzas about the bright star falling left to right, the Connacht queen, and the sacrifice that is unique to her," Neala said pensively as she read the text. "Connacht queen," she whispered thoughtfully, then walked over to the big window.

"What are you thinking, Neala?" Grayson asked as she watched her look out into the darkness.

Neala looked back at Grayson. Corky leaned forward in his chair. "You have an odd look there, Neala. What is it?"

"Corky, you said you looked through the history books to find a connection between the Connacht queen and the prophecy. Well, I remember ancient history, and I don't know anything about Queen Maeve other than she bedded quite a few men in her time. She—"

"Queen Maeve?" Grayson asked as she jumped up and startled Neala.

"Y-yes, she was known as the Connacht queen," Neala explained.

With that, they saw a flash of light scream across the night sky. All three of them dashed to the window to see the fleeting star blaze through the sky.

"The falling star from left to right," Corky whispered. "The wolf behind her in the night."

They stood in deafening silence. Suddenly, Grayson's stomach knotted as she looked around the room. "It's not history. It's not Queen Maeve," Grayson said frantically. She looked down at the text. Things started tumbling into place. "It's my mother."

Corky looked as though he might faint. "Oh, my God, of course—Maeve."

Without another word, Grayson ran out of the cottage. Corky pulled a flashlight out of one of the desk drawers as the rest of them followed Grayson.

Maeve pulled her sweater around her as she took a deep breath in the cool autumn night. She looked up at the unbelievably bright starry sky and started down the rugged path. Her mind wandered as she walked away from the cottage and continued down the path, not worrying how far she walked. She loved the night, and she loved Ireland. This was her home, and she just realized how much she missed it.

As she walked, she tried to decipher the prophecy. The Connacht queen, she thought. "Okay, use Grayson's logic. Who was the Connacht queen?" Then it leapt into her mind. "Good grief, how could you not think of this?" She shook her head. "Maeve was the Queen of Ireland, but what does she have to do with…" She stopped and let out a frustrated groan and looked up into the starry night.

"Okay, Lord, give me a sign. Something to go on here," she said pensively.

With that, a shooting star streaked across the sky from the south to the north—left to right. Her eyes widened as she remembered the prophecy.

A bright star falling left to right
The wolf behind her in the night
The Connacht queen now knows the prize
The star must fall—the moon must rise.

She shivered and pulled her sweater close to her. "It's me," she whispered in amazement. When she recited the second part of her prophecy, she knew.

Great gifts are given and received
The gift of life and life again
A sacrifice unique to She
Her triumph masked in sorrow's rain.

Maeve's smile spread across her face when she realized her

part of the prophecy. "The gift of life—I brought you into this world, Grayson Fianna, and I will do my part to keep you safe, sweetie," she said as tears rimmed her eyes. "A sacrifice unique to me. Thank you, Lord." She closed her eyes and allowed the tears to fall—sorrow's rain.

Behind her she heard it, as she now expected. The low growl was unmistakable.

"Druid…"

Saying a small prayer to God and the gods and goddesses, Maeve took a deep breath and turned.

There stood Phelan, his long black hair blowing in the autumn wind; it was no longer pulled back as she remembered in Chicago. In the dark of the starry night, Maeve could see his dark eyes watching her. "Do you have any idea how long I have waited for this moment, Druid?"

Maeve tried to summon every ounce of courage, then she heard Sister Daniel's voice in her head—*Walk with God, Maeve.*

"That's Druidess, but no, I have no idea, Mr. Wizard, or Phelan, if that's your name," Maeve said, surprised at the calm albeit sarcastic, tenor in her voice. Knowing she was saving Grayson gave her strength she never knew she possessed.

Phelan glared at her, then chuckled. "I am a wizard, this is true. My name is as ancient as I am, Druid. Your time is all but finished. You are the true descendant, but I will have the power. I have waited for nearly two thousand years. I will wait no longer."

True descendant? Maeve thought and laughed inwardly. *What a colossal idiot!* She understood everything now. *The star must fall—the moon must rise.*

"You haven't been keeping up with the prophecy, Wizard. You won't prevail," Maeve said with a smile. She saw the angry dark look as if he couldn't believe her boldness. Quite honestly, she could not believe it, either.

"I have prevailed for over a thousand years, Druid. I am the son of Figol, the sorcerer, and the original guardian of the stone. He was wise and knew the Druid hierarchy was foolish to squander the power of the ancient ones. Now I will have the power and glory. But enough of this, you bore me, as all you Druids have from the beginning of time."

He took a step toward her and Maeve held her ground, even though she was petrified beyond belief.

"Before I destroy you, I believe you should bow to me," he said with a thin grin. "Bow to me, Druid!"

Images of Grayson as a child, as a young girl and woman, flashed through her mind. Looking through her tears, Maeve smiled.

"As you wish," she said. "I bow to the Wizard of Nothing." She stopped and looked into his dark furious eyes before she made a dramatic sweeping bow.

"Ma!" Grayson cried out as she ran down the old path. She stumbled and ran as fast as she could. They all stopped abruptly when they heard the howling off in the distance.

"God, please no," Grayson pleaded. She turned and grabbed the flashlight from Corky's shaking hand and headed down the rugged path away from the cottage.

She stopped dead in her tracks when she saw her mother lying in the middle of path. "Ma!" she cried out and ran up to her. She knelt down and handed Corky the flashlight; he knelt, as well. Neala exclaimed as she and Sister Daniel caught up to them.

Grayson gently took her mother into her arms, desperately trying not to cry. There was blood all over her. Through the flashlight's beam, Grayson saw the blood covering her neck.

Maeve's eyes fluttered open as she recognized Grayson. "Ma, don't talk. We'll get you back to the house," she said.

Maeve reached up, held onto Grayson's shirt, and shook her head. "Ma, please," Grayson pleaded.

Her mother smiled as blood seeped from her mouth. Grayson could see she was trying to speak but knew she couldn't. "Was it Phelan?"

Maeve nodded. She mouthed something, and Grayson bent down and put her ear to her lips.

"My destiny," she whispered. "Your destiny."

And for the second time in her life, Grayson lost a woman she loved. Maeve was still smiling as her life slipped away.

Neala sobbed and knelt down behind Grayson while Sister Daniel gently pushed the stunned Corky out of the way. Grayson took a deep quivering breath as she rocked her mother.

Sister Daniel whispered her blessing in Gaelic as she touched Maeve's forehead. "So it was written, so shall it be." She then leaned in and kissed Maeve on the cheek. "Godspeed, my old friend."

Grayson watched her as she slumped forward and sobbed. She looked up into the starry night as she held her mother, trying to quell the rage that was welling from deep inside her.

My destiny; your destiny.

"I will fulfill my destiny if for no other reason than to avenge my mother's death," Grayson said, her voice void of any emotion. "Now tell me about the Knowing."

Chapter 26

Grayson stood outside the small chapel at the monastery where the young sisters were waiting. They had taken Maeve's body back there upon Sister Daniel's request. Grayson was numb and acquiesced.

The sun had yet to rise and the cold damp autumn wind whipped around her feet. Neala stood next to her, close but not touching. It was only when Grayson leaned into her that Neala reached over and held her hand. Corky stood on her other side, and Grayson glanced at him and put her arm around his shoulders. He was desperately trying not to cry.

The old rugged door opened and Sister Daniel appeared. "She's ready, Grayson."

The three of them walked into the small chapel. Grayson's body shook when she saw her mother's body lying on the small altar; she was wrapped in white linen. It was then Grayson realized this was the vision she had seen.

She walked up, knelt by her head, and pulled back the linen. She ran her fingers over her cool forehead. Her mother looked so peaceful, for a split second Grayson thought she might just be sleeping. She smiled sadly at the impossible idea.

"You were Christian and pagan, mother and friend," she whispered, then placed a kiss on her brow. "You were the best of everything God created. I will fulfill my destiny, Ma." She tried not to cry, but the tears came streaming down her cheeks. Her body shook, and when she felt as though she might not be able to stop, she felt a hand on her shoulder. She took a deep breath and wiped her tears away.

It was Sister Daniel standing beside her. "Grayson, you must continue before the sun rises."

Grayson sniffed and took another calming breath. "Okay, let's get on with this." She turned to see Neala and Corky standing there, both of them crying. She walked up to Neala and placed a hand on her cheek. "Thank you." She kissed her cheek. She turned to Corky, who smiled as his bottom lip quivered.

Grayson placed her hand on his shoulder. "Tell me what's next."

Corky ran his sleeve across his face and stood tall. "Right then."

The rock dwelling looked uninviting. Grayson and Neala exchanged glances. Neala leaned in. "I'm glad it's not me that has to go in there."

"Thank you," Grayson said. "Corky, are you sure this is right?"

"Yes, this is it," Sister Daniel said.

Corky appeared with a flashlight. "You must be in there at sunrise."

"Just what is in there?" Grayson asked. "And what's going to happen?"

"I don't know and I have no idea," Corky said. Grayson heard the excitement in his voice.

"Grayson," Sister Daniel called to her. "You will see all those who came before you. They will guide you. All will become clear. You must have faith."

Grayson looked down at the little woman. "How do you know this?"

Sister Daniel smiled. "All will be revealed."

Corky flashed the light over the rock mound that stood about six feet high. "I don't see an opening," he called out. He and Neala walked around the mound.

"I don't, either," Neala said.

"Fine, now what?" Grayson asked and looked at Sister Daniel.

She looked to the horizon; the sun was just beginning to rise over the hill. "Grayson, step aside."

Grayson stepped back and the four of them watched the sun as it started to rise. "Look, child." Sister Daniel pointed to the rock dwelling.

The sunbeam shone on the front of the dwelling but still they could see no doorway or opening. "Place your left hand on the rocks, Grayson."

In somewhat of a daze, Grayson walked over and did as the nun bid. She placed her hand on the warm rock. Suddenly, her hand moved into the rock as if it were made of thin air.

She looked back at Sister Daniel, who nodded. "It can truly move mountains." She smiled.

Neala and Corky watched in awe as Grayson pushed her hand through the rock up to her wrist. She pushed forward up to her elbow. She watched in wonder as her arm disappeared into the rocks.

"Go quickly, Grayson," Sister Daniel urged from behind.

"Shit," Grayson mumbled. "I feel like what's his name in *Field of Dreams*." She took one last look over her shoulder. "I'm gonna feel very stupid if this doesn't work," Grayson angrily called out. She closed her eyes, and with a deep breath, she passed through the rocks.

She stood in total darkness. "I can't see a fucking thing," she said, her voice echoing in the darkness. *Of course, Corky has the flashlight*, she thought. She tentatively put her hand out in front of her to feel her way. "Okay, MacCarthaigh, this thing is about six feet in diameter. Walk forward until you feel the other side."

She started walking. Four steps, eight steps, twelve steps. *I should be at the other end by now*, she thought. She continued walking in the darkness. "I think I've walked about a hundred feet by now. What gives?" She turned and tried another direction with the same results.

There are no boundaries, mortal.

She stopped dead in her tracks and instinctively reached for her weapon, which of course, was not there. Her mouth went dry and her heart pounded in her chest. The voice was neither masculine nor feminine, but it was familiar to her somehow; she knew this voice.

"Who are you?" she asked.

Hold out your hand.

Cautiously, she did and turned her palm up. She was shocked when a bright light flashed from her palm; it was like a beacon in the darkness. "Fuck me," she whispered and tried to swallow.

We have been watching your journey. You have been given a great gift.

"What gift? What am I supposed to do with this?" she asked angrily.

Look up into the light, mortal.

Grayson looked up. She watched the light and suddenly saw an open field with cloaked figures standing in a circle around an altar. Fog swirled around their feet. One figure in white robes lifted a staff and held it to the heavens. Grayson winced as a bright flash of light came down on the altar. It looked as if a hand grenade had gone off. There was an explosion that engulfed the altar. The smoke and fog had cleared and the figure in the white robe held up three sections of the stone.

"This is the ritual for that stone, right? You guys put all the power in there to keep it safe, then blasted it in three sections. Well, that's just fine," Grayson called out to the voice. "But Phelan, the asshole, has all three sections. How the fuck did that happen?"

She should have felt extremely asinine talking to the darkness, but with all that had happened, it now seemed perfectly natural. "Fine, this is my life from now on," she mumbled, then looked into the darkness. "Did you hear me?"

Watch.

"Shit." She looked into the beam of light.

Another field, this time it was dark. Torches lit up the night. Again there were cloaked figures standing around an altar, looking like the one before. Only this time, one figure was covered in blood; he held a dagger. Grayson watched as a young boy stepped up to him.

Figol.

"Who?" Grayson asked stupidly as she watched. The one covered in blood held up a section of the stone and presented it to the young boy. The others looked as if they were arguing with him.

There was another flash of light. Grayson's mouth dropped when she saw the young boy turn into a wolf. "Fuck." She watched as the wolf tore into the others.

"Okay. Phelan is the boy and the wolf. He kills the others and keeps the stone. I get that. I—"

She stopped when the images changed. She saw it all: Phelan killing Nan Quigley and Jane Monahan. He was there when that bomb went off in the warehouse. She saw images of Phelan at different times throughout the centuries. Grayson remembered the pictures of him. "So he's been looking for the other two stones and has finally found them. Now he has all three, and it's up to me to get them back."

The true descendant.

"So I've heard. What exactly does that mean? And will you please show your face?" she asked angrily. "Who the hell am I talking to?" She turned her palm away and the beam of light faded.

All will be revealed.

Grayson took a deep angry breath and ran her fingers over the sutures on her brow. Standing in the darkness, she lost all concepts of time and space. Her mind wandered. Flashes of her past streaked in front of her—her childhood here in Ireland; her grandmother laughing while Grayson, as a child, sat on her lap. Coming to America when she was a young girl. Going to the academy, becoming a detective... Meeting Vic.

Her heart grew very heavy, and all at once, she was exhausted. She sat down on the cold earth and pulled her knees up to her chest and wrapped her arms around them. "I don't want this. I don't want to be the true fucking descendant. I want my mother back. I want my life back."

Grayson.

She looked up when she heard her voice. It was then she felt her presence. "Vic?" she whispered in the darkness.

A light illuminated the dwelling, and Grayson blinked as her eyes tried to adjust. She looked around her and now saw the rocks. Out of the corner of her eye, she saw it—a willowy figure now stood in front of her.

"Oh, my God." She jumped to her feet.

Vic stood before her; the vision was clear. "Vic."

Grayson, you must continue on, honey.

Tears leapt to her eyes so fast she had to wipe them away with both hands. "Vic. I miss you so much," Grayson said and stepped closer to the vision.

I'm at peace, Grayson, but you must go on. Phelan has great power. He'll destroy anything he can. You were born for this, honey. Remember, you always said you believed something great was going to happen.

"It did…you." Grayson looked down at the wedding ring on her finger that she had yet to take off. "And the baby."

We're all at peace, honey—your mother and little Maeve.

Grayson looked at the willowy vision. She saw Vic's smiling face. "I wish I could hold you just one more time."

I do, too, honey, but we both know that can't happen. Maeve is here, Grayson.

Grayson said nothing as the image of her mother appeared in a mist of fog. She stood next to Vic.

Gray, the prophecy is real. It's all true, sweetie. You must go on. There's great danger if you don't. He's more powerful than you think.

"Ma, I'm so sorry I didn't figure out the prophecy in time to save you," Grayson said, on the verge of tears.

Oh, sweetie, it was my destiny.

As it was mine, Gray.

When Grayson heard Vic's soft affirmation, her heart broke. "I didn't want either of you to die for me. I miss you both so much." She lowered her head and hid her face in her hands, trying to stop the tears.

Grayson, look at your hand, sweetie.

Grayson brought her hand up and felt the heaviness on her ring finger. She looked down to see three rings on her finger now. As she examined them, she realized it was Vic's wedding ring, as well as her mother's. She let out a mournful sob.

This is your strength, Grayson. You are my daughter and the true descendant. Our lineage is clear, sweetie. Look…

Grayson stood close to the spirits of Vic and Maeve as they looked around the stone dwelling.

We're all here, sweetie, from the beginning, every woman who ever lived and fulfilled their destiny to bring you to this moment.

Grayson looked around in awe at the images of the women, all from their own time throughout the centuries. She looked up; they were all around her etched in the stone walls. Grayson never felt so much energy as she felt then. She turned around in a circle, looking at the women, some of them smiling, some of them somber. All of them…knowing.

Close your eyes, honey, and listen to them.

Vic's voice was so soft, just like she used to talk to Grayson to lull her to sleep long ago. She closed her eyes and listened to the whispers of the ages, listened to the Knowing.

They whispered in the ancient language, a dialect she had never heard, yet now completely understood. Grayson's mind was reeling as they spoke of all that had gone on before her… and all that was yet to be.

The whispering stopped and the sense of loss was palpable. Grayson opened her eyes. She looked around the dimly lit dwelling as the images of her ancestors faded.

"Wait!" Grayson called out. She looked at Vic and her mother. "Will I see them again?"

The image of her mother laughed softly.

Yes, sweetie, we're all here. You'll see us every now and then. Just look at the rings. We're always here.

Till the end of time, honey.

Grayson smiled when she heard Vic's voice.

Go now, mortal, your time is at hand.

This was the familiar voice from the beginning. Grayson noticed the images against the stone walls had vanished. She looked at the willowy images of Vic and her mother. They were smiling as they, too, faded into the fog.

She was alone once again, but she did not feel the sense of loss she expected when the visions of Vic and her mother faded away. She took a deep breath and looked around the pitch darkness. "I hope to shit I can get out of here the same way I got in."

Chapter 27

A stupefied Neala and a near faint Corky greeted Grayson on the other side. Sister Daniel was smiling as she spoke. "Nice entrance. Good to see you, Grayson."

"It's good to be seen, Sister," she said seriously. "What a rush." Her body was still tingling from the journey. She felt lightheaded and at the same time exhilarated.

"Y-you look different, Grayson," Neala finally said. Corky nodded in wonderment.

"That's all you have to say?" Grayson asked. "I mean, I walked through a stone wall, for chrissakes. Don't you want to know what happened? Aren't you the least bit curious as…?" She stopped. "I look different?"

Corky scratched his head. "Are you taller?"

Neala gave him an exasperated look. "She's not taller, you fool." She then looked back at Grayson and let out a small screech. "Your face!"

Grayson backed up as they both approached. Corky put on his glasses and examined her face as if she were a lab specimen. "What's the matter with my face?" All at once, she felt like Jeff Goldblum in *The Fly* when he stepped out of that chamber.

"Children, we have more important—"

Neala interrupted Sister Daniel as she dashed to the van to retrieve her purse; she took out a small mirror.

Grayson took the mirror from Neala's shaking hand and looked at her reflection. "I'll be damned." Her face was unblemished by any scar. There was no evidence of any wounds.

Neala reached out and gently caressed her cheek and brow. "Are you all right then?" she asked in a soft voice. "You had us worried."

Grayson smiled and reached up to hold her hand. "I'm just fine, Neala."

"You were gone more than twenty-four hours," Corky advised her as he looked at his watch. "I can't believe how you just disappeared into those rocks. We are astounded. Now tell us, who did you see? What did it feel like? What do we do next? Did you see any—?"

Grayson raised her hand to quiet him, and Neala gently took it. She examined the three rings on her ring finger. She gave Grayson an amazed look. "What is this?"

She held her left hand out. "My mother's wedding ring and Vic's wedding ring."

"Who's Vic?" Corky asked and looked back and forth from both women.

"You were visited by your mother and Vic?" Neala asked and smiled fondly. Grayson nodded.

"Who is Vic?" Corky asked again.

"My partner, my wife. She died two years ago," Grayson said. "Saving my life."

"B-but," Corky started and pointed to the rings. "Those are real. Maeve and your wife, God rest them, are spirits. They cannot touch the physical world. It defies—"

"Logic?" Grayson asked, then reminded him, "Corky, I walked through a stone wall."

"Grayson, we haven't much time," Sister Daniel said.

"Yes," Corky agreed. "What did you find out?"

Grayson thought for a moment. In her mind, she heard all the whisperings, all the knowing. "The sorcerer who the Tuatha had entrusted a section of the stone turned out to be a greedy wizard. He devised a ritual. He wanted all the power. The hierarchy of the Druids intervened and he killed them. Well, he had his wolfen son kill them—Phelan."

"It's all true?" Corky asked in amazement.

Grayson nodded. "Every bit of it. It also appears that Phelan, too, is a wizard. He has roamed for nearly two millennia in search of the other two sections. He killed Nan and Jane and those two women who were innocent and had nothing to do with this. He also planted that bomb in the warehouse. He was planning something, I'm not sure what, but when that kid contacted us, I think he was gonna spill everything. Phelan knew it and thought he'd get all three of us." She stopped as the images of Stan lying there and the poor kid dead because of this asshole flashed through her mind.

"He shook hands with every dignitary and every slime ball in the world, and he has more money than you can imagine. And that money buys him power," Grayson said. "But not this kind of power."

She looked up into the late afternoon morning sky. "I was in there a whole day? It seemed like minutes."

"What else happened?" Neala asked.

"I cannot even begin to describe," she said. "It's the Knowing, that's all I can say. However, I know now where Phelan is, and I know where he plans to reunite the stones. He has the ritual handed down from his father."

"Where, Gray?" Neala asked. Grayson looked into her green eyes when she heard her name. Neala cocked her head to one side in question. "What?"

"Nothing…" Grayson said. For a moment or two, they looked into each other's eyes. It was Neala who blinked and turned bright red. "He plans on reuniting the stones in Lissiviggeen, in County Kerry."

"The stone circle at Lissiviggeen?" Corky asked.

"It's part of the Killarney National Park and protected by the government," Neala explained. "We wanted to do some research there last year, but the government said it was purchased and…"

Grayson nodded. "Purchased by someone who had unlimited wealth, who promised in writing to financially assist in protecting the ancient ceremonial site. No one will ask why the philanthropist who donated millions to ensure its safety is there late at night. It's a perfect place to have a ritual."

She looked at Sister Daniel, who nodded in agreement. Corky looked deflated.

"What's the matter, Cork?" Grayson asked.

He shrugged. "I just thought you'd be...I don't know, different."

Grayson placed her hand on his shoulder. She felt a slight buzzing in her ears and a tingling sensation shot up her arm. A vision, which she was now coming to accept, flashed through her mind: a young redheaded boy holding a violin. The vision faded when she took her hand away.

"You'll have to play the violin for us someday," she said as she walked away.

Corky's green eyes nearly popped out of his head. He ran to catch up with her as she winked at Sister Daniel. "How...?" he asked and pulled at her arm. "You read my mind?"

Grayson thought for a moment and looked at her left hand and the crescent-shaped birthmark. "No, I don't think so. A picture just flashed through my head. This is all new to me."

He grabbed her hand and placed it on his shoulder and said eagerly, "Do it again."

Sister Daniel gently nudged the young historian. "Enough play for now, Timothy. We have to prepare for the ritual tonight."

Grayson held Sister Daniel back as they headed to the van. "You know more than you let on, Sister. I get nothing when I touch you, as I did with Corky. What's happening and what do you know?"

Sister Daniel looked up into Grayson's eyes. "You will need to clear your mind, Grayson. I will tell you this: I believe the stone was conceived to harness the Tuatha's power and magic for all time. No one person was to have it. However, Figol, you're right, was very greedy and forced the ancient ones' hand. They could not stop the one they trusted and the prophecy was born. Phelan must be stopped. He is as his father was."

"How can I stop him, Sister?" Grayson asked. "He's an immortal."

Sister Daniel continued to look into her eyes. "Do you believe in all this? Do you see how dangerous Phelan is to Ireland—to the world?"

"Yes, I do," she said and looked down at her palm. "I need to find a way to get to those stones." She held out her palm to the old nun. "This is the key, isn't it? This birthmark."

Sister Daniel nodded. "You must reunite them." She looked up into early evening sky. "We have but a few hours to prepare. Phelan believes that in killing your mother, he has destroyed the true descendant. He won't be expecting you. This is your advantage."

Grayson nodded, then offered a smug grin. "And just how did you know Phelan thought my mother was the true descendant?"

Sister Daniel smiled as she nodded. "You are getting good at this, my child."

Once they returned to the monastery, they sat in subdued silence at the kitchen table. One of the young nuns placed the teapot on the table. Grayson looked up. "Thank you."

The novitiate nodded; she looked as though she wanted to say something. Grayson placed her hand on the young woman's forearm, and the tingling sensation started. "Thank you for taking care of my mother," Grayson said softly.

"It was my honor. We were chosen, as well, by Mother Abbess. She told us many stories of your mother and her mother before. I am sorry for your loss, but she is blessed in her sacrifice." She looked down at Grayson's palm. "When Mother Abbess told us of the prophecy, I didn't quite believe her or understand."

"I don't blame you at all," Grayson said seriously. "Even with all that has happened, I still have a hard time believing it."

Grayson sat in silence looking at her hand as the nun walked away.

"I can't imagine what's going through your mind, Gray," Neala said quietly.

"Nor can I," Corky agreed as he drank his tea. "I could use something stronger."

Grayson laughed and looked around the table. "Seems kinda lonely without Ma here."

"Yes, it does," Neala said, then lightly touched the rings on Grayson's finger. "This is an unusual wedding ring," she said, motioning to the middle ring.

It was a platinum band, broader than Vic and Grayson's more traditional gold bands. It also had symbols and etchings around it. "My mother said she wanted a wedding band that had everything she believed on it: Christian, pagan, and Celtic. She said my father grudgingly agreed to this," Grayson said with a fond smile. "She told me Dad never understood her beliefs, but she never doubted his love for her."

Grayson made a fist and chuckled. "I could do some damage if I hit someone with these rings like this."

"And you say they just appeared on your finger?" Neala asked in amazement.

"Which I still find hard to believe," Corky threw in.

"Well, as hard as it seems—yes, I looked and there they were. Don't ask me how," Grayson said with a wry chuckle. "All logic seems to be failing me now."

Neala laughed along. "After what's happened since we met, I can see how."

They sat in silence for a moment, all seemingly lost in their own thoughts. Grayson spoke first. "Look, I don't know what's going to happen tonight," she started, "but I want you both to know I'm very grateful for all you've done to help figure this mess out." She stopped and ran her fingers over her brow, still amazed to find no stitches, no wound there. "I hope I'm up to the task. My mother's sacrifice will not be in vain."

Corky leaned in. "Well, if we remember the last lines of the prophecy: The power of the ancients rise; the clash of old—the dark, the light. Embodied in their champions—the Warrior Moon, the Lord of Night."

"What does that mean?" Neala asked.

"It means Phelan is going to summon some help tonight. I hope I get some, as well," Grayson said.

"The power of the ancients rise," Corky repeated. "The dark, the light."

"Good and evil," Grayson said.

Once again, silence filled the kitchen.

Corky looked at the clock. "I wonder what Phelan is doin' right now."

"He's preparing for battle," Sister Daniel's voice called out from the doorway. "Which is what you must do, Grayson. And do it quickly. The residual moon has risen."

Chapter 28

Ian struggled with the heavy pack following Phelan as he walked through the woods of the park. "Mr. Tynan," he said with a groan, "do you think it's wise to be skulking around government property at nearly midnight? I—"

His next words came out in a strangled cry as Phelan whirled around and grabbed him by the throat. "I am the government or soon shall be. Now do not say another word."

He roughly let go of Ian, who staggered back and let out a hacking cough as he continued to follow.

"Did you set the altar as I told you?"

"Yes, sir. A cutting from an oak tree placed on the stones. It looks as you describe," Ian said. "You know, it's amazing how all I had to do was mention your name, and the guard let me right into the park. I—"

"Did you procure everything else?" Phelan asked over his shoulder. He looked up into the autumn sky. The crescent moon was not yet over the tree line.

"Yes, sir," Ian said in a coarse voice. "Though it was hard to find mistletoe at this time of the year. Usually, we have it at Christmas—"

He stopped and backed up as Phelan turned around. "Christmas? Have you any idea what mistletoe really is, Ian, or can you be that stupid?"

Ian blinked as if not knowing how to answer the question; he said nothing.

Phelan let out a dejected sigh. "I suppose you can be that stupid. Mistletoe, dear ignorant Ian, is considered the soul of an oak tree, it grows on the oak, but it is not part of the tree." He saw

215

the blank look as his young minion pushed the glasses up on the bridge of his nose. "Why do I bother?"

He continued down the path until he came to the stone circle. He closed his eyes as he ran his fingers over the ceremonial stone. The large stones, or boulders, were situated in a circle. As instructed, the primitive altar was erected in the middle of the circle.

"This is it?" Ian asked and nervously looked around.

"Do not speak again," Phelan said and took the backpack. "And stand still."

He opened the bag, and in the light of the waning moon that just rose over the tree line, he prepared for the ritual. The thought of possessing all the power and all the magic was intoxicating to him.

His blood raced through his veins as he placed all the elements needed for the ritual: the large hammered copper bowl, the mistletoe, and the bark from the oak tree. The athame, which Figol gave him over a thousand years before; the ancient blood on its hilt mingled with the blood of Phelan's victims.

Everything was in place on the altar. He closed his eyes and unbuttoned his shirt. Stripping to the waist, he raised his head to the sky. He looked down at his torso, covered with the glyphs and ancient tattoos up and down his left arm. He was especially proud of the ancient Celtic glyph etched around his left bicep. The lupine figure wrapped around his arm. It moved now, shifting in a circular motion. The wolf's head slithered upward toward Phelan's shoulder. He watched, and in the next moment, the etching was still, as if it had never moved at all.

Phelan pulled his long black hair back and tied it with a leather strap, then started. He burned the mistletoe and oak bark in the copper bowl; the incense rose from the bowl, filling the stone circle with a light fog. Phelan held the athame in his right hand and closed his left hand around the blade, then pulled it downward.

Blood dripped down the blade of the dagger onto the hilt. He held the dripping athame and cast a circle around the copper bowl as he recited the ancient ritual.

"I stand between the light and dark, strong and powerful. The old one's force I circle out with earth and air. With fire and blood, I call upon the ancients of the dark moon—the circle is cast."

Suddenly, the smoke of the incense rose in a stream up to the sky. The wind ceased; the trees stilled. With outstretched arms, Phelan looked to the residual moon.

Ian, completely intrigued, stepped toward the circle and placed his hand on the large stone. A bolt of pure energy sent Ian flying backward through the air, and he landed on his back. Phelan shot him a venomous glare.

"I told you to stand still and say nothing," Phelan growled. "It is bad enough that mortals have trounced around this ancient site for centuries as if it were their playground. You will not defile this sacred place by entering its circle…you moron."

Ian's eyes grew wide, and he backed up as Phelan moved toward him. "Leave now."

Hearing the low growl, Ian backed up even farther. "Y-yes, Mr. Tynan." He got to his feet and started down the dark path.

"Oh, and, Ian? If you breathe one word of this to anyone, I will rip your throat out."

"N-no, no, I would never," Ian said as he stumbled down the path and out of sight.

Phelan sported a feral grin as he watched his whimpering minion run down the path. "That felt good. I may rip his throat out anyway. Now where was I?"

He closed his eyes and continued. "I stand before you as ordained by my father, in this most sacred place in the last light of the new moon." He set the athame on the altar and continued with outstretched arms.

"I draw down the power of the ancient ones to be one with the essence of all that have gone before me. You, who embrace the dark moon and exist in the black skies of eternal night, grant me now, in the shadow of this residual moon, the secrets of all knowledge past, present, and to come."

Phelan then took the three sections of the stones out of the bag and placed them on the altar, close but not touching. "The time is at hand."

They stood on the edge of the clearing. Grayson turned to her three companions. "I have to go on alone. Stay here out of sight." She looked at Sister Daniel. "You'll know when to come."

"We'll be ready."

Grayson took a deep breath and turned to Neala and Corky. "Cork, stay alert. Phelan doesn't have anyone with him, I just sensed his little yes-man scurrying away."

Corky nodded and stuck out his hand. "Be quick about it."

Grayson smiled and took his hand. "I'll see what I can do." She then turned to Neala, who was smiling through teary eyes.

"I'll come back," Grayson said in a sure confident voice.

Neala nodded, afraid to speak. Grayson put her hands on Neala's shoulder. "I will come back," she said again.

Neala threw her arms around her neck. "I know you will. Please be careful." She pulled back and looked down at the ground.

Grayson lifted her face to meet her gaze. "Neala, I—"

Neala placed her fingertips against her lips. "Come back safe, Grayson. That will be enough for now."

Grayson smiled slightly and nodded. Sister Daniel gently pulled at Grayson. She reached up, and Grayson lowered her head as Sister Daniel placed her hands on Grayson's head and offered her blessing.

Grayson then stood tall and Sister Daniel smiled. "I guess if they could make Brigid a bishop, I can give you my blessing."

She pulled Grayson down in a fierce embrace. "They are all with you, my child—always."

Grayson pulled back and nodded. "Thank you, Sister."

She turned, and without another word, she walked alone to face her destiny.

Grayson sensed him before she actually saw him. She made her way through the dense woods and came up to it. There he stood arms outstretched and bare-chested. She knew he was calling down the darkness, pleading for help.

It was time. She looked up into the clear starry night and saw the crescent moon. As her ancestors instructed, she lifted her hand

and presented her birthright to the heavens. Then she waited for the Knowing. As the whisperings promised, a flash of lightning streaked across the cloudless sky.

Suddenly, she felt lightheaded, as she did when she left the rock dwelling. The blood pulsated through her veins. Her heartbeat quickened, and the rush of adrenaline was palpable. It was time.

She slowly walked up to the stone circle undetected by Phelan, who was concentrating on calling down the dark forces.

"I draw you down to grant me what is foretold to be mine, to share your wisdom, that I may know victory over those who would oppose me, to accept my offerings that I may defeat my enemies. Reveal all as it had been predestined by the blood of my mother spilled at the hands of my father, by the blood of those who thought to impede my destiny that I have drained and offered up for your glory, and the blood of any who will attempt to usurp me now. I have been exact to the directives of my father all these many years, hear me now, and it shall be done.

"I beseech you bestow that power that only you can discharge. I call upon you, Oh Lord of Shadows, attend to me now in this circle I have prepared in the ways of my fathers. Aid and protect me, I invoke you to seal my fate thus."

He then placed his hands on the stones. Grayson felt the ground shudder beneath her. She saw the large copper bowl shaking, as well. She knew now the stones were together as one. Her time was at hand.

"Grant me supremacy over the Mother Danu, that she shall know my sovereignty, Over Manannan, who holds the keys to the otherworld. My time has come. I have destroyed the true descendant as my father, Figol, the great sorcerer has instructed. Hear me, Oh—"

"Oh, shut up," Grayson called out as she walked to the outer edge of the stone circle.

Phelan's eyes flew open as he looked, stunned, with his hands still covering the stone.

"Good grief, you're longwinded," Grayson exclaimed as she walked up to the stones.

"Leave before I destroy you," Phelan growled and leaned on

the makeshift altar.

"I was just going to say that to you."

"Do you have any idea who I am, Detective?" Phelan asked with a feral grin.

Grayson rested her elbow on the large stone, glad to see the shocked look on Phelan's ugly face when nothing happened to her as it did to his minion.

"Yes, I do," Grayson said in a dead calm voice. "You've murdered innocent people throughout your existence. You nearly killed my partner and the poor lost kid," she said and stopped when she saw the startled look. She grinned then.

"The Knowing," Phelan hissed angrily.

"Yes, you asshole, the Knowing. I don't know—yet—just what you were up to in Chicago with that kid. You had your mark on him, but he had another mark, one you didn't put there. He was ready to blab, wasn't he? So you thought you'd get all of us at once." She folded her arms across her chest and leaned against the stones. "So, yeah, you crazy fucker, I know who you are. You are the Wizard of Nothing."

Phelan's nostrils flared with anger as he watched her.

"Nice tats, though."

"I will destroy you as I destroyed your mother, the true descendant."

Grayson calmed the rage that tore through her at the mention of her mother. "Yeah, well, we need to discuss that, Wizard." Grayson raised her left hand. "Pretty careless. You knew about the prophecy. Didn't you get this part: While in the west a noble birth—the crescent locks its destiny?" She shook her hand and wiggled her fingers.

Phelan glared at her. "Your mother died at my bidding."

"No," Grayson said evenly. "My mother died at her own bidding. She gave up her life in a noble, unselfish gesture: saving her daughter, the true descendant."

She easily walked inside the circle and caught her breath. Phelan smiled. "You have no idea how to handle the power inside this circle." He held his hand over the copper bowl. As he raised it, the heavy bowl floated upward and hovered over the altar.

Grayson smiled. "You'll have to do better than that. I walked through a stone wall," she bragged and jabbed her finger at her chest.

With a flick of his wrist, the copper bowl flew as if shot out of a cannon, hitting Grayson square in the face. The force sent her flying backward as she crashed into a large stone. She let out a cry of pain as she fell to the ground.

"Mortal," Phelan spat out and walked around the altar holding the dagger.

Grayson, stunned, shook her head. Phelan grabbed her by the back of her head and hauled her to her feet. He held the athame to her neck. "So you are the true descendant, eh?" he whispered in her ear.

"Yeah, you fucker," she grunted, and with all her might, she pushed backward, slamming Phelan into the ancient stone.

The dagger flew out of Phelan's hand and landed on the wooden altar. Grayson and Phelan dove for it. It was then Grayson saw the stone. Phelan progressed so far as to unite them.

Phelan let out an unearthly growl as he reached for the dagger. Grayson had to make a choice. She desperately needed to place her left hand on the stone, but in doing that, Phelan would easily have the dagger. Her logical mind said get the dagger and kill Phelan, then fulfill her destiny.

She looked up at the moon; it was positioned perfectly. There was no time for logic. She let go of the dagger and scrambled to get her left hand on the stone. Behind her, Phelan let out a triumphant howl and Grayson felt the dagger sink deep into her back. She let out a cry of pain as she slackened away from the stone.

"Ma…" she whimpered as she desperately grabbed for the stone.

She could feel Phelan's hot feral breath on her back as he growled and twisted the dagger. She looked at the rings on her finger and in one swift movement, she swung backward and backhanded Phelan with all the strength she had; the heavy rings slammed into his nose. She heard the bones break as he let out an animalistic scream and staggered back.

It was just enough time for Grayson to lunge for the stone. She placed her hand perfectly in place but was unprepared for what happened next.

Lightning streaked across the sky in every direction. The ground beneath shook so severely it felt as if the earth itself was shifting. The heavy ancient stones vibrated as a flash of lightning bolted out of the sky and struck the stone on the altar. The light was so bright and the force so great, Grayson cried out as she felt the jolt through her entire body. It took every ounce of her being to keep her hand firmly attached to the stone.

She could smell the electricity in the air as the force blew her completely out of the circle, past the stones, and into the clearing, nearly thirty feet away. When she could stand, she looked at the altar, which was a smoldering pyre. It was then she saw it—a wolf, an enormous wolf, stalking her. Phelan…

"Fuck you," she hissed, and as the wolf started for her, something—someone whisked by her in a blur. Grayson stumbled out of the way; she looked up to see the wolf whimpering and whining as it vanished into the woods.

Grayson saw the willowy figure in black and ran to the smoldering altar. She frantically searched the rubble.

"What are you looking for, Grayson?" a voice asked.

"The stone, damn it, I lost it. I tried to hold it and—"

"It's not there. It's gone."

"It can't be."

"It's not needed any longer."

"But the power the—"

"It's all in you. You are the power, you are the magic."

Grayson slowly stood and took a deep breath. She then remembered she was stabbed.

"You have no wounds."

Grayson looked at the figure shrouded by the black robes. "So now what?"

"So now you live, you learn, and you protect, just as you did in your previous life as a detective. Only now you have more power."

"I don't feel different."

"Not now, but you will. You will learn. You will do what you have never done before. You will see things. You have the Knowing. You were chosen long ago. You are both human and goddess, mortal and immortal."

"What about Phelan? I can't find the dagger. He got away," Grayson said, suddenly feeling familiar with this apparition. Her voice…

"Yes, I'm afraid that's true. You see he, too, is both human and god, mortal and immortal. He still has his power. You must always guard the power they entrusted you with. This is your destiny."

Grayson merely nodded. "I understand." She searched the darkness once again. "Who are you? You sound familiar somehow."

The figure walked out of the shadows and slipped the cloaked hood from her face. Her blonde hair shimmered in the moonlight, as it did not so long ago.

"Vic," Grayson whispered desperately and took a step toward her. Vic put her hand up to stop her. They stood close to each other.

"Please, can I just feel you one more time?"

"Close your eyes, honey."

Grayson closed her eyes and gasped as she felt Vic's arms around her; she smelled her perfume, felt her warm sweet breath on her cheek. "You said long ago you wanted to serve and be a part of something special. It's why you became a police officer, not because of your father. You knew all along, deep in your soul, this was your destiny. This is your chance, honey."

"God, Vic, I miss you."

"I'll be around, honey. Have a good life. Do this for me."

She felt the comfort of Vic's embrace leave her as she opened her eyes and was alone in the fading moonlight. She felt different. She looked down at her hand and noticed the crescent-shaped scar was still there but not as pronounced as it had been. The three rings that broke Phelan's ugly nose were still on her finger. She knew she would never take them off. She didn't understand the change in her body, but she expected there would be many things she would learn to understand.

She looked up at the waning moon that had drifted across the starry night and was now ready to yield to the morning sun. A smile spread across her face.

"Goodbye, Vic," she whispered as the moon descended behind the rolling green hills.

Epilogue

Grayson met them in the clearing. She stopped when she saw Neala running to her. Corky was right behind her. Sister Daniel followed slowly.

Neala stopped short of her, completely breathless. "Are you all right?" she asked, tears rimming her green eyes.

"Yeah, I'm fine. Phelan got away, though."

Corky couldn't help himself. He flung himself into her arms. "I can't believe you did this." He pushed himself away and frowned. "You did do this, didn't you?"

"Yep," Grayson said. "I'm an immortal."

Neala's mouth dropped. "You're joking."

"No. She isn't," Sister Daniel said from behind them. She did not come any closer. "You are human and goddess, mortal and immortal."

Something flashed through Grayson's mind: a woman, elegant in white robes with gold lining. Her white hair pulled back in golden combs. "Who are you, Sister Daniel?"

Neala and Corky exchanged glances and stepped aside. "Grayson is a goddess?" Corky whispered; Neala nudged him in the ribs.

Grayson and Sister Daniel faced each other. "You have pleased us more than you know, my child. You have done more than Brigid herself and all those who came before her and since. It is right that you are the keeper of this power for my people."

"Your people?" Grayson asked. Then it dawned on her. "Sister Daniel—Danu."

Before their eyes, Sister Daniel transformed into a vision of elegance, dressed in white robes, her long white hair pulled back in golden combs. Around her neck was a necklace made of heavy gold and silver roping, shining so bright in the morning sun Grayson nearly had to look away. Her blue eyes sparkled with mirth. "You are getting good at this."

Danu held out her hand, and Grayson held it in her own. The goddess turned her palm up and placed her other hand over it. "Believe in the gods and goddesses, and your God, as well, Grayson. We are all one."

Grayson nodded, unable to speak as she felt the transference of power flow through her body.

Danu smiled in knowing, and as her image faded into the mist of the morning sun, she whispered, "So it was written, so shall it be."

Grayson looked over at the stunned Neala, who was…stunned. They both looked at Corky, who had passed out and lay sprawled on the wet grass. As they both knelt by Corky, he groaned and lifted his head. "What happened?"

Grayson and Neala helped him to his feet. "If you keep fainting, Corky, you're going to miss quite a bit, I'm thinkin'," Neala said.

The three comrades headed back to the old van. "Well, what now?" Corky asked.

"I have to see to my mother's funeral," Grayson said in a pensive voice.

Neala and Corky walked on either side of her. "We'll help you anyway we can," Neala said softly as they headed up the wooded path.

"Sure we will," Corky agreed.

"Thank you, both of you," Grayson said. "After that, I'm not sure what happens next."

"Perhaps there's something in that book of yours, Corky," Neala said.

Grayson suddenly thought of the lost soul in Chicago who was blown up by Phelan's hand. Detective Carey Spaulding flashed through her mind, as well. "I can't believe I'm about to ask this, but what about the catacombs at Guys Hospital in London?"

Corky grinned wildly and winked. "Right then…vampires,"

he said with relish. "I've been working on this text for someone in London. It seems back in ancient times, as the legend goes…"

Grayson listened as Corky went on with his myths and his legends, but in the back of her mind, she realized there was more truth there than myth. Nothing was the same anymore. Maeve and Vic had given their lives for her. Her life as she knew it was over. And now, a new beginning, a new life was formed. She had no idea what was going to happen next.

She looked down at her palm and lightly ran her fingers over the crescent-shaped birthmark. All at once, her body tingled; she felt her entire being expand and her senses seemed to heighten.

As they headed up the wooded path, Grayson glanced at a hill far off in the distance. It did not surprise her that the hill was clearly too far for the average eye to see—the human eye.

A wolf stood on the top of that distant hill, and as it turned, Phelan raised his hand, then faded out of sight.

-The End-

About the author

Kate Sweeney was the 2007 recipient of the Golden Crown Literary Society award for Debut Author for *She Waits*, the first in the *Kate Ryan Mystery* series, which was also nominated for the Lambda Literary Society award for Lesbian Mystery.

Her novel *Away from the Dawn* was released in August 2007. She is also a contributing author for the anthology *Wild Nights: (Mostly) True Stories of Women Loving Women*, published by Bella Books.

Born in Chicago, Kate resides in Villa Park, Illinois, where she works as an office manager—no glamour here, folks; it pays the bills. Humor is deeply embedded in Kate's DNA. She sincerely hopes you will see this when you read her novels, short stories, and other works by visiting her Web site at www.katesweeneyonline. com. E-mail Kate at ksweeney22@aol.com.

You can purchase other Intaglio
Publications books online at
www.bellabooks.com, www.scp-inc.biz, or at
your local book store.

Published by
Intaglio Publications
Walker, LA

Visit us on the web
www.intagliopub.com